D1553210

Can't Fight the Moonlight

Whisper Lake #3

BARBARA FREETHY

BARBARA
FREETHY
—BOOKS—

Fog City Publishing

PRAISE FOR BARBARA FREETHY

"I love the Callaways! Heartwarming romance, intriguing suspense and sexy alpha heroes. What more could you want?" — *NYT Bestselling Author Bella Andre*

"I adore the Callaways, a family we'd all love to have. Each new book is a deft combination of emotion, suspense and family dynamics." — *Bestselling Author Barbara O'Neal*

"Once I start reading a Callaway novel, I can't put it down. Fast-paced action, a poignant love story and a tantalizing mystery in every book!" — *USA Today Bestselling Author Christie Ridgway*

"A fabulous, page-turning combination of romance and intrigue. Fans of Nora Roberts and Elizabeth Lowell will love this book." — *NYT Bestselling Author Kristin Hannah on Golden Lies*

"Powerful and absorbing...sheer hold-your-breath suspense." — *NYT Bestselling Author Karen Robards on Don't Say A Word*

"Freethy is at the top of her form. Fans of Nora Roberts will find a similar tone here, framed in Freethy's own spare, elegant style." — *Contra Costa Times on Summer Secrets*

"Freethy hits the ground running as she kicks off another winning romantic suspense series...Freethy is at her prime with a superb combo of engaging characters and gripping plot." — *Publishers' Weekly on Silent Run*

PRAISE FOR BARBARA FREETHY

"PERILOUS TRUST is a non-stop thriller that seamlessly melds jaw-dropping suspense with sizzling romance, and I was riveted from the first page to the last...Readers will be breathless in anticipation as this fast-paced and enthralling love story evolves and goes in unforeseeable directions." — *USA Today HEA Blog*

"Barbara Freethy is a master storyteller with a gift for spinning tales about ordinary people in extraordinary situations and drawing readers into their lives." — *Romance Reviews Today*

"Freethy (Silent Fall) has a gift for creating complex, appealing characters and emotionally involving, often suspenseful, sometimes magical stories." — *Library Journal on Suddenly One Summer*

Freethy hits the ground running as she kicks off another winning romantic suspense series...Freethy is at her prime with a superb combo of engaging characters and gripping plot." — *Publishers' Weekly on Silent Run*

"If you love nail-biting suspense and heartbreaking emotion, Silent Run belongs on the top of your to-be-bought list. I could not turn the pages fast enough." — *NYT Bestselling Author Mariah Stewart*

"Hooked me from the start and kept me turning pages throughout all the twists and turns. Silent Run is powerful romantic intrigue at its best." — *NYT Bestselling Author JoAnn Ross*

'

CAN'T FIGHT THE MOONLIGHT - BLURB

Justin Blackwood can't remember a time when he believed in the magic of anything, least of all love. A cynical businessman, who grew up in a broken home, he guards his heart with every breath he takes. His job has taken him all over the world and roots are the last thing he wants...until he meets a beautiful innkeeper in Whisper Lake.

Warm-hearted, free-spirited Lizzie Cole wants it all—the dream job of running her own inn and a man who wants to settle down. Despite a previous romantic setback, she still believes in happily ever after and her perfect soulmate. She just has to find him. While the dark-haired man with the shockingly blue eyes makes her heart beat faster, Justin Blackwood is the last man who should leave her breathless. He's her complete opposite and they don't want the same things.

But when a lunar eclipse throws Whisper Lake into darkness, Lizzie and Justin find themselves struggling to fight the moonlight and a love that could change their lives—if they're willing to take the risk.

CAN'T FIGHT THE MOONLIGHT

CHAPTER ONE

THE COLORADO MOUNTAINS were majestic and inspiring, and Justin Blackwood knew he should be appreciating the long, winding road through the pine trees. He should be taking deep breaths, clearing his mind, finding a way to relax and appreciate the unexpected break, but he couldn't. He had a big deal on the line, and this was probably the worst possible time to take days off. He'd also been trying to get his partner and oldest friend, Eric Stark, on the phone for the past hour, but the farther he got away from Denver, the fewer bars he had on his phone.

This was one reason why he didn't appreciate nature. He didn't want to disconnect with the world. His life was his job, and that job required him to be on the phone and at his computer, to be able to communicate with people on the far side of the globe at any time of the day. He needed to move fast. He didn't know how to do slow.

His phone buzzed, and relief ran through him. He quickly answered the call, putting the phone on speaker as he set it on the console. "Eric, it's about time. I've left you a dozen messages."

"Sorry, I just got back into the office," Eric replied, with his usual slow drawl. "My plane from Cabo was delayed six hours.

It was not the way I wanted to end my honeymoon, but we had enough time to drink a few more margaritas."

"You always find the silver lining."

"I do," he said with a laugh. "What's going on?"

"Too much." He'd thought he'd covered himself when he'd agreed to this trip, but that had all changed in the last few hours. "I need your help."

"What? Say that again. I can barely hear you. Where are you? It sounds like you're on Mars."

"I'm on my way to Whisper Lake."

"Where the hell is Whisper Lake? I thought you were going to London today."

"I had a change of plans. Whisper Lake is in the Colorado mountains, and it's where my grandparents are going to renew their wedding vows this Saturday. It's their fifty-seventh wedding anniversary. I told them I could not come about a dozen times, that I had too much going on, including the biggest deal of my life."

Eric gave a knowing laugh. "And yet you're driving to Whisper Lake. You can't say no to Marie. It's impossible."

"It is. My grandmother's voice choked up like she was going to cry. I had to agree."

"She played her ace."

"She did."

"Well, fifty-seven years is impressive. It's something to celebrate. Are your parents going?"

"No. I made sure of that. Anyway, I have another problem, Eric. I had Jessica set up to handle the meeting in London, but her mom broke her hip, and Jessica is now on her way to the hospital."

"I just heard something about that. I hope you are not going to ask me to take the meeting in London."

"I know you just got back from your honeymoon."

"Which took me six months to work into our schedule."

"But you got it in, and Teresa must be happy. I'm sure she won't miss you for a few days."

"I'm sure she would. I'm a very good husband," Eric joked. "But that's not the real problem, and you know it. I'm the tech guy. I talk to engineers. I don't do sales meetings. People in suits and ties make me sweat. You're the closer. You're the person investors want to give their money to."

Everything Eric was saying was true, and his stomach churned at the realization that his deal could very well fall apart.

"Why don't you push the meeting back a week?" Eric suggested.

"I can't. I have Tokyo next week and Australia after that."

"You are living a crazy schedule, Justin. When's the last time you saw your apartment?"

"I honestly can't remember."

"But that's the way you like it."

"Business is good. What can I say?"

"If you can't push the meeting back, you'll have to bail on your grandparents. I'm sure they'll understand."

"They won't understand, and they're the only two people in the world who I really can't let down. My grandparents were there for me when no one else was. You can do this, Eric." He could hear the mix of desperation and doubt in his voice. While he respected Eric's incredible intelligence and innovation, he was much better at a computer than in a boardroom. But they were running out of options.

"Even you don't believe that," Eric said. "What about Anthony?"

"He's too green. He's only been with us nine months."

"He's better than me. You have to give him a chance. I've been telling you for a year that we need more help. It took you five years to believe in Jessica, but we don't have that kind of time anymore. Things are moving fast."

"I know, but it's difficult to trust anyone to do it right."

"I get it. But you don't have a choice."

"Is Anthony in the office now?"

"What? I can't hear you."

"Is Anthony there? If he's going to London, we need to get him on a plane as soon as possible."

"I'll find him."

"Good. I need to set up a call with him."

"What? You're breaking up."

He blew out a breath of frustration. He'd known this trip was a bad idea from the start. He never should have said yes. "Tell Anthony what's going on and I'll call you back as soon as I get to town." His gaze caught on an upcoming sign for Whisper Lake. "I'm about five miles away. Once I get to the inn, we can do a call."

"I didn't get that. Call me when you have better reception," Eric said.

Before he could say he would, the call disconnected. He pressed down on the gas. He needed to get to town quickly. Anthony was a smart guy. He'd graduated from UCLA with a degree in economics and had spent the last three years working in sales. But he didn't have a lot of experience with the company. Anthony was also only twenty-seven years old, and while Justin wasn't a lot older at thirty-two, he'd been living and breathing his business for the past ten years. But Eric was right. He didn't have a choice. He was going to have to trust Anthony. Or…

As his doubts began to grow, he wondered if he should try to make some wild attempt to get to London for the meeting on Thursday and then back to Whisper Lake before Saturday. Then he remembered the emotion in his grandmother's voice when she'd told him how important it was to her to have him there for the week. He hadn't seen her or his grandfather in over a year. He couldn't bail on them now.

He took the exit for Whisper Lake, driving along a tree-lined two-lane highway, past several small farms and a riding stable.

On either side of the road, the mountains loomed. It was April and the higher slopes were still covered with snow. He had no doubt the spring skiing would be good. Not that he had time for skiing. Every minute that he wasn't spending with his grandparents, he would be working.

His grandparents wouldn't be happy to see him focusing on business. They were always on him to take time off, to stop and smell the roses, as his grandmother liked to say. But he didn't have time for roses; he had a global business to run, and that business was his life. There would be time for roses later. Maybe…if he could ever figure out a way to slow down. He had been moving full speed ahead for a very long time. He preferred a fast pace, a changing landscape. Too much time to think or stew was never good for him.

Impatient to get to the inn, he sped up, then had to slow down as he went around a curve and ended up behind an old truck that was laboring down the road, laden with trees and plants and barrels of fruit, probably from one of the farms. "Dammit," he swore, frustrated once more by a pace that was not to his liking.

He drew closer to the truck, hoping it might pull over if the driver saw him right on his tail. But then a deer darted across the road, and the truck slammed on the brakes, sending a barrel-full of lemons onto the road in front of him.

He swore as he hit the brakes hard and swerved to avoid hitting the truck. His car skidded to the side of the road, losing traction in the rolling lemons. He couldn't stop. He pushed the pedal to the floor, but there wasn't enough time to avoid smashing head-on into a fence. The windshield shattered as the front end of his rental car crumpled, and the airbag hit him in the chest.

It took him a few breathless seconds to realize he was still in one piece, although the car was not. He forced open the door and stumbled out onto the side of the road as a woman jumped out of the truck and came running toward him.

"Oh my God, are you all right?" she asked, fear and concern racing through a pair of spectacularly pretty light-green eyes.

He couldn't believe she was the driver of the truck. She appeared to be in her late twenties and was dressed in tight-fitting ripped-at-the-knee jeans that showed off some very nice curves. Her brown boots were scuffed as if she did actual work in them, and her long-sleeve cream-colored top had a streak of dirt running down the front of it. Her light-brown hair was pulled back in a ponytail, with loose, messy layers falling around her face.

"You're not talking," she said. "I'm going to call an ambulance." She patted her pocket, then swore. "Damn. My phone is in the truck. I'll get it."

"Wait," he said, finally managing to speak. "I don't need an ambulance. I'm fine."

"Are you sure?"

"I just need a minute." He looked around him in bemusement. He was surrounded by bright- yellow lemons. They seemed to be everywhere. And then he remembered the deer, the squealing brakes, and the fact that he'd been following way too close—not that he was going to tell her that.

"I'm really sorry about this," she said. "But you were right on my tail."

"I was in a hurry."

"Well, I was going as fast as I could in that old truck. I had a heavy load." She groaned. "And half of it is now on the road." She drew in a breath, squared her shoulders, and forced what had appeared to be a teary look out of her gaze. "But I didn't lose everything. This is going to be fine."

"Fine?" he echoed in disbelief. "Have you looked at my car?"

"Cars can be fixed. People can't. The important thing is you're not injured. We should exchange information. I'll get my bag and my phone. You may not need an ambulance, but you will need a tow truck."

He would definitely need that. As she ran back to the truck, he returned to the car. Pushing the airbag out of the way, he looked for his phone, but it was no longer on the console. And that's when he realized he had an even bigger problem. He'd taken out his laptop when he'd stopped for gas and it had flown off the front seat and was now crushed by the collapsed dashboard. He had a feeling his phone was in the same place.

This was bad—really bad. He needed his phone and his computer. He had work to do today, in the next hour, in fact. He didn't have time to hunt down replacements, and he had a feeling the notes he'd made this morning had not made their way into the cloud. Anger ran through him. This trip was turning out to be a disaster.

"I called Tom's Towing," the woman said, coming back down the road with her phone in her hand. "He's on another call. He can't get out here for about an hour."

"That's not acceptable. I'll get someone else."

"The other service is on the west shore of the lake. It will take them just as long to get here, and they're more expensive."

"Your insurance will have to pay; I need a car."

"My insurance? This was your fault. You were following too close. That's on you. And I only braked fast because of the deer."

She made a good point, which he found annoying as hell. "So, you're not responsible at all?"

"I'm not, but if you want me to call the police, we can do that. My brother is working today. I'm sure he'll come out."

"Your brother is a cop in Whisper Lake? Great." He knew exactly how that accident report would go down.

"Fine, I won't call my brother; I'll call 911 and whoever comes will come."

"And report back to your brother."

"That you were tailgating and ended up driving into the

fence?" she snapped. "Yes, I'm sure that's exactly what they'll say."

"I hate small towns," he muttered.

She frowned. "Now you want to blame the town for your accident? Look, you're upset. I get that. Why don't I give you a ride to wherever you were going, and we'll take it from there? If you were just planning to drive through Whisper Lake on the way to somewhere else, there's a rental car service in town; I can drop you there. I'm sure you can get a replacement vehicle. It's all going to be okay."

"You have no idea how *not* okay it already is. My computer and phone are smashed. I'm going to need to replace both as quickly as possible."

"Well, our small town does sell phones and computers," she said dryly. "Can I give you a ride?"

Considering he hadn't seen a car since he'd crashed, he wasn't going to say no. And he actually wasn't all that interested in filing a police report because he had a feeling it would go down exactly the way she'd said it would. "Yes," he said.

"You're welcome," she replied.

He tipped his head. "Thank you." He walked to the back of his car and managed to pop the trunk. He took his overnight bag out of the vehicle and then made one last attempt to retrieve his phone and computer, but they were trapped somewhere in the mangled mess that was the front end of the car.

"We'll work this out," she said, as she gathered armfuls of lemons and put them back in the barrel from which they'd come. Then she carried the barrel to the truck.

"Are you a gardener?" he asked, as he put his bag into the truck next to the barrel, hoping it wouldn't end up on the road the next time she stopped.

"Today I am. I wear a lot of hats." She got behind the wheel as he slid into the passenger seat. The cab of the truck smelled like manure, and there were a bunch of empty food wrappers on the floor.

"You like tacos, huh?"

She followed his gaze. "Ramon likes tacos and burgers and anything else that comes fast and hot. This is his truck. My gardener sprained his ankle and couldn't make the pickup, so I had to do it." She paused. "Where can I take you?"

He thought about that. He needed a car, but the first thing he needed to do was call his office. "That depends. Can I borrow your phone?"

"Sure." She handed him her phone. "But I still have to drive you somewhere."

"If I can make a call, then I don't need to get a car just yet. I'd rather go to the inn. Maybe they'll have a computer I can use until I can get a new one."

Her face paled as she stared back at him. "The inn?"

"The Firefly Inn. Do you know it?"

"Yes. I'm Lizzie Cole, the owner. Who are you?"

"Justin Blackwood. My grandparents made the booking. They're coming in tonight."

"Actually, they won't be here until tomorrow. I got a call a half hour ago that their flight was canceled and the next flight they can get is tomorrow."

Of course their flight was canceled, he thought cynically. So far, the trip was a complete bust.

"All right then," Lizzie said, as she started the truck. "I'll take you to the inn and we'll get your vacation going in the right direction."

"It's not a vacation," he said automatically. "I don't take vacations."

"Then what would you call it?"

"An obligation. My grandparents want me at their vow renewal."

"I know. They told me how excited they were that you were

coming. It's going to be a lovely ceremony," she added, as she pulled back onto the road. "In fact, this whole week will be packed with fun. It's a busy time in Whisper Lake. We have our usual Wednesday night happy hour tomorrow, the lunar eclipse beach picnic on Friday, and the ceremony Saturday night will be in the garden, with candles and music. It's going to be very special—magical, really. I want your grandparents to have a day they'll remember. And I want your visit to be memorable, too. I know it's not starting off on the best note, but it will get better."

He gave her a doubtful look. "Is being an optimistic cheerleader part of your duties at the inn?"

"Sometimes. But I'm just a positive person. Problems are challenges. Most can be fixed."

Despite her words, there was a tension beneath them that suggested she didn't quite believe her own hype. "I don't think my rental car, computer or phone can be fixed. Not unless you have a magic wand to go with that idealism."

"No wand, but…" She smiled as she turned her warm gaze on him.

"What?" he asked, curious about the gleam in her eyes.

"I have lemons, and I know exactly what I'm going to do with them."

"Make lemonade," he said, as a reluctant smile crossed his lips.

"Exactly. It's what I do. I make lemonade out of lemons. You're going to love it. It's delicious."

He didn't want to love her lemonade. He didn't want to like her happy, determinedly cheerful spirit, but he had a feeling he was going to lose on both counts.

"You know what else I'm going to do?" she asked.

"I'm afraid to ask."

"I'm going to turn your obligation into a vacation."

"That's impossible."

"Challenge accepted."

He shook his head. "You will fail."

"I don't think so." Her eyes sparkled with confidence. "You're going to have the time of your life, Justin Blackwood. Just wait and see."

There was a very small part of him that wanted to believe her, but he'd lost his faith in the impossible a long time ago.

CHAPTER TWO

LIZZIE DREW several deep breaths as she drove Justin to the inn. Despite her confident words, she was not feeling that sure of herself, but that's the way she rolled. She believed in faking it until she could make it. She'd spent most of her life finding ways to cover up her deficiencies and look like the success story she believed she would one day be. But even her positive attitude was starting to sag under the weight of one problem after another. And this latest problem…well, her heart was still beating way too fast, and it wasn't just because of the crash she might have inadvertently played a role in; it was also because of Justin.

When Marie and Benjamin Blackwood had said they were booking a room for their grandson, she'd had no idea he would be the epitome of tall, dark and handsome. Justin's dark-blue eyes were the color of the sea, his brown hair was filled with thick waves, and the scruff on his cheeks only made him sexier. But the man was also wound super tight. And his obsession with his work, his phone, and his computer made it clear he was all about his job.

Not that she minded a man with a passion; she certainly had

passion for her work. But she tried to keep at least a little balance in her life. She wondered if Justin had any balance. It didn't appear that way. He'd called his vacation an obligation, which seemed strange, because his grandparents were two of the nicest people she'd ever met, and they were fun. They had energy and charm. They liked to dance and eat and talk to people. Coming to their wedding should not have been a chore for him.

"Why aren't you excited about your grandparents' vow renewal?" she asked, the question slipping past her lips before she could stop herself from butting into his life. On the other hand, being a good innkeeper meant understanding her guests—knowing what they needed and trying to meet that need.

"It's not coming at a good time for me. I was supposed to be in London on Friday," he answered.

"For work?"

"Yes. I'm about to close a big deal. The person I had hoped to send in my place is now unavailable, so I have to hand off a very important presentation to someone who probably isn't qualified to do the best job. That's why I need my electronics. I have to help him with the pitch, make sure he can get through the presentation without looking like an idiot."

"What kind of deal is it? What do you do?"

"I own a robotics company."

"Robots?" she echoed, flinging him a surprised look. "How did you get into that? Are you a geek?"

He smiled, bringing warmth into his eyes for the first time, and damn if it didn't make him more attractive. "Maybe. I got into robotics a long time ago, but I'm not the technological genius; that's my partner Eric. I run the business side."

"What do your robots do?"

"All kinds of things from packaging to mobility solutions, food preparation and law enforcement. It's a rapidly growing field, and a global one."

"Which is why you're supposed to be in London and not in Whisper Lake."

"Exactly."

"Well, at the end of the day your presence will make your grandparents happy. That must count for something."

"It's the only reason I'm here."

"It will be fun."

"So you've promised. I hope you don't let me down, but you certainly wouldn't be the first."

The cynical edge was back in his voice. She wondered who'd let him down. She had a feeling it was someone very close to him. "I will not let you down," she heard herself promise, hoping she wouldn't prove to be a liar.

"Tell me about yourself," Justin said, surprising her with his interest.

Up until this point, she'd written him off as someone only interested in himself, but maybe she had judged him too quickly.

"You said you're the innkeeper," he continued. "Do you work for someone?"

"The toughest boss in the world—myself," she said with a smile. "My dream of owning an inn started when I was about fifteen, but it took me thirteen years to make it happen."

"Do you have a partner?"

"No, I'm on my own, but I have investors who need me to succeed, so my success is as much for them as for me." She paused, her gaze narrowing as she saw the swelling on his face. "Your cheek is turning purple, and your eye is swelling."

"It's not a big deal."

"Do you have a headache?"

"A small one," he conceded.

She made a quick decision and made a fast right turn.

"Whoa, what are you doing?" he asked, as he braced his hand on the side of the door. "Do you want to cause another accident?"

"I didn't cause the first one, but I want to get you checked out by a doctor. You could have a concussion."

"I don't have a concussion."

"How do you know?"

"Because I've had one, and I know what it feels like."

"It will just take a few minutes."

"In my experience, no hospital visit takes a few minutes."

"I have connections. My friend is a nurse in the ER. She can take a quick look at you and get those cuts cleaned up."

"I don't need a doctor," he argued. "What I need is a phone and a computer and a few minutes to check in with my office."

"You have my phone. You can use it if you have to wait more than five minutes. But it's three o'clock on a Tuesday—we'll be in and out."

"I don't want to go to the hospital."

"Sometimes you have to do things you don't want to do for your own good," she said, hearing her mother's voice coming out of her mouth. "Damn, I can't believe I just said that."

"I can't, either," he said with bemusement. "You're not my mother."

"I didn't think I was my mother, either, but she always used to say that. I guess it stuck in my head. Has that ever happened to you? Do you find yourself saying things your parents used to say?"

"No. That never happens. But then, they didn't have much to say to me."

"You aren't close?"

"Geographically we are sometimes in the same time zone, but emotionally…a million miles apart." He sighed. "And I can't believe I just told you that. Please, take me to the inn."

"We'll get there. You might not be thinking clearly because you have a head injury. I can't take that chance."

"It's my chance to take, Lizzie. I'm not your responsibility."

"You're my guest at the inn. I take care of all my guests.

And we're here." She pulled into the half-empty parking lot by the new medical center. "It doesn't look crowded at all. Come on."

He gave her an annoyed look. "This is a waste of time."

"Come on, Justin. Do it for your grandparents. You know if they see you looking like this, they'll be worried. They'll want to know if you've seen a doctor. And if you say no, they'll be the ones driving you here."

"Damn, you're probably right," he said, as he unbuckled his seat belt. "Fine, I'll see the doctor. But if the wait is more than ten minutes, I'm out of there."

She blew out a breath of relief as she got out of the truck and walked into the ER with him. The nurse at the desk, Monica Albright, was one of Hannah's friends and Lizzie had had drinks with her on a few occasions.

"Hi, Monica," she said. "My friend was in a car accident, and he needs to get checked out. Is Hannah here?"

"She's just finishing up with a patient." Monica turned her gaze to Justin. "Are you in pain, sir? Are you experiencing any dizziness, nausea?"

"No, I'm fine," he replied. "This really isn't necessary."

"I just want to make sure he doesn't have a concussion," Lizzie interjected.

"Do you have an insurance card?" Monica asked.

Justin pulled out his wallet and handed her his card. As Monica made a copy of the card, Hannah came through the clinic doors and gave Lizzie a surprised look.

"Lizzie, are you all right? Are you hurt?"

"No, he is." She tipped her head toward Justin. "He was in a car accident."

"It wasn't an accident; I just hit a fence," Justin said.

"With his car," she added. "The windshield shattered, and the airbag deployed."

"Got it. Were you in the car as well, Lizzie?"

"No, she was driving the truck that slammed on its brakes," Justin interjected.

"It's a long story," she told her friend. "Can you check him out?"

"Of course," Hannah said, with a curious gleam in her brown eyes. "And Dr. Melnick should be free shortly. Come with me, Mr...."

"Blackwood. Justin Blackwood."

"Well, you're in good hands, Mr. Blackwood."

"I really don't need to be here," he said.

"Good, then this won't take long," Hannah replied.

As they disappeared through the double doors, Monica handed her Justin's insurance card. "Do you want to hang on to this for him?"

"Sure."

"So, he's pretty cute," Monica said with a pointed smile.

"Really? I hadn't noticed."

"Then maybe you're the one who should be getting her head checked."

Fortunately, she didn't have to come up with a reply as the ringing phone drew Monica's attention away from her. She walked into the waiting room and sat down, wishing she had her phone, but it was now in Justin's pocket. Hopefully, this wouldn't take too long. He wasn't the only one who had work to do. But she'd made the right decision in bringing him here.

She couldn't take the chance that some serious medical problem might show up down the road. She liked his grandparents a lot, and he was one of her guests, so she wanted him to be all right. Then she could put this entire incident behind her.

She had to admit that Justin was nothing like his grandparents. Benjamin and Marie were lovely, warm, charming people, who were kind, friendly and very easygoing. Justin didn't appear to be anything like them. He was attractive, though. Monica was right about that. But he was just a stranger passing through town on his way to somewhere else, so she wasn't going to think about how his compelling blue eyes made little shivers run down her spine. Instead, she reminded herself that her life, her inn, everything she wanted, was in this town. And once the doctor said Justin was all right, she could let go of her concern for him and go back to just being his friendly innkeeper.

Justin didn't know how he'd ended up in a hospital exam room, but he was beginning to realize that when Lizzie Cole wanted something, she got it. Fortunately, she hadn't lied about the examination being quick and painless. The pretty, redheaded nurse had barely gotten him onto the table when the doctor arrived. After asking several questions and putting him through a series of simple tests, Dr. Arthur Melnick, a middle-aged man with friendly light-blue eyes, determined that Justin was concussion-free and left Hannah to tend to the cuts on his face.

"This might sting a little," she warned.

"Do your worst."

"You should never say that to a nurse," she teased. "You have no idea what kind of pain I can inflict on you."

He liked her sharp smile. "Fair point. Don't hurt me too much."

"That's better. How do you know, Lizzie?"

"I don't know her. We met when she slammed on her brakes, and I swerved to avoid hitting her truck and ended up against a fence. Lizzie told me she was giving me a ride to the inn but made a sudden decision to come here instead. Apparently, my bruises started to make her nervous. The next thing I knew, we were on our way to the hospital despite my assurances that I was fine."

"Lizzie can be a force of nature," Hannah said with a grin. "I sometimes end up places I never expected to be when she's

involved. But in this situation, she made the right call. Sometimes people don't think clearly after an accident. It's always
good to get checked out."

"But I am fine," he reminded her.

"You are, but you may also find yourself in a bit more pain
tomorrow."

"I can handle it."

"You said Lizzie was supposed to take you to the inn—you're
staying there?"

"Yes, I'm in town for my grandparents' vow renewal
ceremony."

"Marie and Benjamin's ceremony?"

"You know my grandparents?" he asked with surprise.

"I met them at the inn and then we got better acquainted
when your grandfather brought Marie into the ER the day after
Valentine's Day. They were in town that weekend, and she had
gotten a nasty spider bite. One of her eyes swelled shut."

"I didn't hear about that."

"Well, she was okay. She's a sweetheart, and your grandfather takes very good care of her."

"He always has."

"I'm glad they decided to renew their vows. They were
talking about it when they came in. They wanted to do it here on
their wedding anniversary. They said that this town is one of
their favorite places."

"I know. They've started coming like four times a year," he
said. "I'm not sure how they discovered it, but once they did,
they were hooked."

"That happens a lot. It's why the population has tripled in the
last five years."

"Really?"

"Yes. We have snow action in the winter and lake activities in
the summer, along with as many festivals and parties as you
could possibly imagine. There are new housing developments

going up on every shore of the lake. I'm not sure when it will start to feel crowded, but right now, it's still pretty perfect."

"Did you grow up here?"

"I did. I left for a while, but I found my way back. Where are you from?"

"California."

"Do you live near your grandparents in Los Angeles?"

"No. I grew up in LA, but I'm in San Francisco now."

"I've been there. Beautiful city."

"It is."

"Well, Whisper Lake has its charm, too, and you'll love the Firefly Inn. Lizzie takes extremely good care of her guests. You're in good hands."

"I don't expect to be needing much. I'll be working when I'm not with my grandparents."

"Too bad. The town has a lot to offer. You should find time to enjoy it." She stepped back, as she finished applying a bandage to his forehead. "You're done. The swelling on your face should go down by tomorrow, but you might want to use an ice pack tonight."

"Thanks." He slid off the table and followed her out of the room and down the hall. She ushered him into the waiting room.

Lizzie jumped to her feet when she saw him, and an odd feeling ran through him at the concern in her eyes. She seemed genuinely worried about him, and that wasn't an emotion he was used to seeing on anyone's face.

"Do you have a concussion?" she asked.

"I do not. I told you that in the car."

She let out a breath of relief. "Well, I'm happy to have it confirmed." Her gaze moved past him to Hannah. "He's not lying, is he?"

"No, he's fine," Hannah said with a smile. "I better get back to work."

"Thanks, Hannah," Lizzie said. "I'll see you tomorrow at happy hour, right?"

"I wouldn't miss it."

As Hannah left, Lizzie's gaze swung back to him.

"Did you really need confirmation from the nurse?" he asked. "I'm not a liar."

"I don't think you're a liar, but I suspect you like to spin things into whatever you want them to be. And if it's in your best interest to be fine, then that's what you'll be."

He couldn't argue her point, so he didn't try. "Let's go. I have calls to make."

"You also still have my phone."

"I'll give it back to you at the inn. I realize now I should have used that leverage before we came here."

"It wasn't that bad, was it?" she asked, as they walked toward the door. "You don't have to worry about that cut getting infected now."

"I wasn't worrying before."

"Do you ever worry?"

"If I do, it doesn't last long. I fix whatever is bothering me."

"And you can always fix it?"

"Most of the time. Or I let go and move on."

"You and I are very different," she commented. "I worry about everything, most of which I can't control or fix. And letting go is almost impossible. I don't like to quit even if I probably should."

A serious expression ran through her gaze, darkening her green eyes. He had a feeling she'd gone to an unhappy place, which surprised him, because it was quite a contrast to the peppy cheerleader who was planning to make lemonade out of her slightly bruised lemons. But then almost immediately, her face lightened, and determination reentered her gaze.

"At least I don't have to worry about you anymore," she said. "That's one item off my list."

"You really didn't need to be concerned."

"You weren't looking at your swollen face; I was. Anyway, let's get you to the inn so we can start turning your obligation into a vacation."

"And I can get back to work."

"That, too," she said, giving him a smile that warmed him all the way through.

He felt a little bemused by his reaction. He didn't want to like her. She'd caused his accident and forced him to see a doctor. She was bossy and pushy, a ridiculously determined optimist, and she'd already given him a big headache. On the other hand, she was also beautiful, and caring and generous. He frowned. *Not that any of that mattered.* He would only be in Whisper Lake for five days. She was his innkeeper. He was her guest. It was not going to be anything more than that.

CHAPTER THREE

As LIZZIE DROVE him to the inn, Justin used her phone to call Eric. Fortunately, he'd had Eric's number memorized since he was eighteen years old.

When Eric answered, he said, "It's me. I had to borrow a phone."

"Why? You're never detached from your phone," Eric said, surprise in his voice. "I almost didn't answer. I thought you were a telemarketer."

"It's a long story. I had a small accident with the car. My phone and computer were damaged."

"What about you? Are you all right?"

"I'm okay. I'm more concerned about Anthony and the London trip. Is he on board?"

"Yes, and we were wondering why you weren't returning our calls or texts," Eric said. "Anthony is booked on a flight tonight, leaving San Francisco at ten p.m. I've brought him up to speed on what I know. He has cleared his schedule for the rest of the day, so he can go over everything with you."

"Good. I need probably thirty minutes to an hour to find a computer and download my notes from the cloud. I'm hoping everything is there. Let Anthony know that I'll be calling him shortly. How's he feeling about everything?"

"He probably has more confidence in his abilities than either of us do," Eric said dryly.

"I like his confidence, but I want to make sure he can back it up with substance."

"Agreed. So, what happened? You got in an accident? Anyone else involved?"

"No one else was hurt. I had a run-in with a fence."

"Probably because you were speeding. I keep telling you to slow down."

"Well, right now, I'm going very slow." Lizzie couldn't seem to get the truck past thirty miles per hour.

"Maybe that's what you need."

"What I need is to get back to work. I'll be in touch." He ended the call and slipped the phone back into his pocket. "Any chance you could give this baby more gas?"

"This baby is getting plenty of gas. She just doesn't like to run. She's old and tired."

"Maybe you should invest in a new truck."

"I'll put it on the list," she said dryly. "Don't worry, she'll get us back to the inn."

"Hopefully before tomorrow."

"You're very impatient, Justin."

"I have a lot to do."

"So do I. Believe it or not, you're not the only one who has a job."

"It was your idea to take a side trip to the hospital."

"To make sure you were all right. But we're almost home."

He glanced out the window. Whisper Lake was not his home, but it was a picturesque mountain resort town. The downtown area filled with touristy retail attractions: restaurants, bars, gift shops, clothing stores, and antiques shops. There were also organic food cafés and markets, and a variety of coffee and juice bars as well as tea shops.

The residential streets were a mix of A-frame cabins mixed with more modern homes, as well as a few larger estates. "It feels like a town in transition," he murmured, looking back at Lizzie.

She nodded. "It's growing like crazy. We're only two hours from Denver and while we're not as fancy as Aspen or Vail, we have great skiing and an amazing lake in the summer. Our retail and entertainment options are exploding. With the ability of more and more people able to work remotely, the full-time population is also growing. It's no longer dead during the elbow seasons of September/October and April/May. It's busy all the time."

"That must be good for your business. Did you grow up here, Lizzie?"

"No. I grew up in Denver, but my grandparents lived here, and I spent a lot of summer vacations with them. I always had this town in mind as the place I wanted to settle down in, and when the inn came up for sale, I jumped on it."

"When was that?"

"Two years and ten months ago. The first year was spent in a constant state of remodel, but I'm finally getting the inn to where I want it to be. We're starting to get repeat business. Your grandparents are among some of my best customers."

"They seem quite enthralled by this town and your inn. Although, I don't love the fact that they have to drive two hours from Denver to get here. But my grandfather loves to drive, and the fact that he's turning eighty this year doesn't seem to be slowing him down."

"That's for sure. They're both very energetic people. They went cross-country skiing when they were here in February. I think they outlasted some of the younger members of the group. And I had a line-dancing class at the inn, which your grandmother excelled at. She really kicked up her heels. I was dancing next to her, and I was huffing and puffing by the end of it, but she was fine."

He smiled at her words. "She loves to dance."

"Yes. She told me when you feel the rhythm, you gotta move."

He laughed, those words ringing a very familiar bell. "She used to tell me that, too. In fact, she's the first girl I ever danced with. She made me dance with her before the ninth-grade dance. She wanted to get me ready. I couldn't get out of that lesson no matter how hard I tried." He actually hadn't tried that hard, because he'd been nervous about the dance, and the lesson had been a good distraction. It had also made him feel less alone at a time when he was spending many days and evenings by himself. Of course, things had gotten a lot worse after that. His smile faded as less happy memories filled his head.

"That must have been a sweet moment," Lizzie said. "My dad was my first dance partner. I was ten and there was a father-daughter dance at school. I remember thinking how special I felt to have his attention on me. I was the youngest of five kids, so I didn't often have that. He was a terrible dancer, though," she added with a laugh. "Nowhere near as good as your grandmother."

"I don't think I thought she was that good when I was four-teen, but she had a lot of enthusiasm. I wasn't any good, either."

"I'm sure you've improved since then. You'll get to show me some of your moves on Saturday night as there will be dancing after the vow renewal ceremony."

He groaned. "Really, dancing? It's starting to sound like a full-blown wedding reception. I thought it was supposed to be a simple ceremony."

"It's small, but I wouldn't say it's simple. There will be a few dozen people, maybe more."

"Wait. What? Who's coming?" He really did not want to hear his parents' names.

"Do you know Vanessa and Roger Holt? Your grandparents met the Holts at the inn when they were here in February. The Holts are in their early seventies, and Roger and your grandfather bonded over watching golf while the ladies enjoyed a day shopping. They've apparently stayed in touch since then.

"Fine, that's two. Who else?"

"Carlos and Gretchen Rodriguez are also coming. They met your grandparents here at the inn last fall, and I think they took a trip to Florida at Christmas together. Some of the locals in town will be coming. Your grandparents have been very friendly on their trips here, and I encourage a lot of mingling at the inn. It's part of the experience. You'll see."

"I don't think so. I don't need any more friends."

"You can't have too many friends."

"You can have enough," he countered.

"I disagree. I've made some amazing friendships with some of my guests. I'm actually going to be a bridesmaid in a wedding for a couple who had their romantic getaway weekend at the inn last year. They had a bit of a tiff and I helped them work it out."

"So, you're a marriage counselor, too?" he asked dryly.

"I told you—I wear a lot of hats," she said with a grin.

"Is that the inn?" he asked, as a large four-story manor set in a circle of trees and beautiful landscaped grounds came into the view. The house was Victorian in architecture with a round tower on one side, big bay windows, and a large wrap-around porch. There was a circular drive in front of the manor, with a sparkling fountain sitting on a diamond of grass. A small parking lot was adjacent to the main building, and there appeared to be a barn-like structure behind the manor, maybe a garage or a second unit.

"That's it," Lizzie said, flinging him a proud smile. "Every time I see it, I get a little thrill that it's mine."

"You have some land."

"It's an acre and a half. I hope one day to expand and add some small private cabins, but that's way down the road."

"This must have been a huge investment."

"The biggest one I've ever made. Fortunately, I have some backers who believe in me. I can't let them down."

The fierce note was back in her voice. He had a feeling she would fight to the end, and that kind of determination resonated deep within him. Failure wasn't an option for him, either.

"At any rate," she continued. "Your fun is about to begin. I hope you're ready."

He found himself smiling back, even though fun wasn't really on his agenda. But maybe it should be, especially if Lizzie was going to be part of that fun. She was a very pretty woman with her messy ponytail, irresistible smile and laughing green eyes. She had the kind of gaze that drew you in and wouldn't let you go. He frowned at that thought and forced himself to look away from her. It was then he saw the police car out front.

An officer was talking to an older couple. The dark-haired woman had on black leggings and a long sweater. The gray-haired man was dressed in brown slacks and a white button-down shirt. The man appeared to be in handcuffs.

"Damn!" Lizzie exclaimed, braking so fast, he had to put his hand on the dashboard to brace himself once more. "Sorry," she threw out, as she jumped out of the truck and jogged over to the group.

He couldn't help but follow, more than a little curious as to what was going on. The older gentleman didn't look like a typical criminal. Maybe it was a domestic dispute.

"He was lingering outside my room when I went out shopping," the woman told Lizzie. "And when I came back, he was standing right outside my door again. I think he was trying to get in."

"I wasn't trying to get in," the man said. "I thought you might have checked out earlier than you thought, and I wanted to find out if the room was empty, or if someone else could have arrived in your stead."

"Like who? That doesn't make sense. I want him arrested. I don't feel safe," the woman said. "I had to call 911, Lizzie. I went to the front desk, but Shay wasn't there."

The police officer looked at Lizzie. "You want to weigh in, Lizzie?"

Justin didn't know why he was surprised the cop knew Lizzie, since so far, she seemed to know everyone they came into contact with.

"Yes, this is all a big misunderstanding, Brodie," Lizzie replied. Then she turned to the woman. "Patty, I'm sorry no one was at the desk. There should have been someone there to help you. But this man is not a threat. His name is Noah Bennett. He's not stalking you. He's a guest. And I know him very well."

"Then why is he always outside my room? He's creepy."

"It's supposed to be my room," Noah put in. "You were going to check out today."

"Well, I had a change of plans," Patty said, her gaze swinging from Noah to Lizzie. "You told me it was okay for me to stay another night."

"I did," Lizzie agreed. "And I told you, Noah, that the room would be yours tomorrow."

"I always have that room this week, Lizzie," Noah said. "You know how important it is to me to be in that room for the eclipse."

"And you will be. You can move in tomorrow and the eclipse isn't until Friday. You were the one who first booked your stay starting tomorrow," she reminded him.

"Because I got the date wrong."

"Yes, but I told you that you could move rooms tomorrow when Mrs. Lawrence checks out. You shouldn't be bothering her."

"I saw her leave and I thought maybe she'd gone." He paused, cocking his head to the right as his gaze grew reflective. "I smelled her perfume, Lizzie. It was so strong. I thought she'd come back. I guess she didn't. It must have been my imagination."

Justin frowned at the old man's words. He didn't seem to be talking about Patty anymore.

"Alice has not come back. I'm sorry, Noah," Lizzie said gently. Turning to Brodie and Patty, she added, "Noah lost someone close to him. The last time they saw each other was here at the inn during a lunar eclipse ten years ago. They stayed in your room, Patty. He's hoping she might show up this week."

"I come every year at the same time," Noah put in. "I always stay in that room. I have to be there when Alice returns. She said she would come back. And I told her I would be waiting." There was a desperate note in the old man's voice now. "I've been waiting a long time."

"I know you have," Lizzie said, giving Noah a compassionate look. "And I'm sorry about the mix-up with your room. But if Alice comes back, we'll make sure she finds you." Lizzie's gaze moved to Patty. "I'm very sorry for the worry, Patty. To make it up to you, I'll comp your stay. Will that be all right?"

"Well, yes, that would work," Patty said slowly, as she gazed at the sad-looking Noah. "What happened with your friend? Why did she disappear?"

"We were in love, but she had to leave. She had obligations. We promised we would meet again in our room at this beautiful inn the same week in April. I still believe that will happen," Noah answered. "Perhaps it is a false hope, but I hold on, because our love was so strong, so powerful, and so filled with meaning. Without it, I am empty."

Justin thought Noah was crazy, but Patty seemed completely captivated by the man's moving words, her defensive and aggressive posture softening with each word.

"I am sorry for scaring you," Noah continued. "I didn't

realize you would be fearful of me. Sometimes I feel like I'm barely alive, that my existence is almost invisible. I had forgotten what it was like for someone to really see me, to have any kind of reaction to me. I hope you can forgive me."

"Maybe we can all have some tea and cookies and talk this out," Lizzie suggested.

"That would be nice. I would like to hear more about your Alice," Patty said. "I lost my husband eight years ago. I understand what heartbreak feels like. And while I know he is not coming back, I'm not unfamiliar with the desire that he could."

"I would love to tell you my story," Noah replied eagerly. "Thank you for being so kind."

Lizzie turned to the police officer. "Brodie, can you take the cuffs off?"

"I can do that," the officer said, releasing Noah's hands. "I'm assuming no one wants to press charges?"

"I don't," Patty said.

"Thank you," Noah said, rubbing his wrists.

"Let's go inside and get some tea," Patty suggested.

"You're a very kind woman," Noah told her.

As the two went up the steps and disappeared into the inn, the police officer gave Lizzie a bemused smile. "Well, you did it again. You calmed them down and turned them into friends. You have a real talent for disarming angry people."

Justin couldn't help but agree with the officer. Hannah had been right. Lizzie was a force of nature.

"Patty lost her husband a few years ago. I thought she'd understand Noah's situation," Lizzie explained.

"Looks like she did. I wouldn't have cuffed him, but before you arrived, she was pretty pissed off and I didn't know what I was dealing with."

"I know. I understand, Brodie. You were doing your job," Lizzie said.

"How's everything else going?" the cop asked. "I heard this is a big week for you."

"It's crazy busy."

"Like always." The officer turned his gaze on Justin. "I don't think we've met."

"Justin Blackwood," he said.

"Brodie McGuire," the officer replied. "Are you a friend of Lizzie's?"

"He's a guest," Lizzie cut in.

"Looks like you've been in a fight," Brodie commented.

"Only with a fence and a steering wheel, thanks to Lizzie here."

"It was not my fault," she reminded him, adding to Brodie, "A deer ran into the road. I braked suddenly and Justin had to swerve. His car landed in a ditch. I called Tom. He's going to take the car into the shop."

"Good. You get checked out, Mr. Blackwood?"

"I did, and I'm fine."

"Hannah took a look at him," Lizzie added.

"Does everyone in this town know each other?" Justin asked.

"Not everyone," Brodie said with a smile. "But if you stay here long enough, you'll get acquainted fast, especially if you hang around Lizzie."

"Brodie is my almost-brother-in-law," Lizzie put in. "He's engaged to my sister, Chelsea, and he works with my brother Adam, who is a detective. He's basically family already."

"Speaking of family," Brodie said. "I assume you'll be at Adam's birthday dinner tonight."

"Absolutely."

"Great. I'll see you then. Nice to meet you, Mr. Blackwood."

"You, too."

As Brodie got into the car, Lizzie turned to him. "I'm sorry about that. It's not usually so chaotic around here."

"Are you sure? You and chaos seem to go together."

"Sometimes it does feel that way," she admitted. "But let's get you checked in to your room."

"I'm more interested in your computer. I don't think I have time to go buy one. I need to get online." He'd completely lost track of his time issues while Lizzie was resolving the standoff between the two senior citizens. Maybe he did have a concussion; he didn't usually let anything distract him from work.

"You can use my computer and my phone. I'll set you up in my office, and I'll have someone take your bag up to your room."

"I can handle my bag." He walked back to the truck and retrieved his suitcase. Then he followed her into the inn.

His first impression of the interior was that it was warm and spacious, with dark paneled walls and slick hardwood floors covered by colorful, thick carpets. While Lizzie checked him in at the reception desk, his gaze swept the entry, which appeared to lead in two directions: one to a large living room with comfortable couches and armchairs, the other to a library with shelves laden with books and a grand piano in one corner.

Beyond the library, he could see a dining room with square wooden tables for four and a long buffet that appeared to be laden with afternoon cookies and drink options. Noah and Patty were already seated at one of those tables, sipping tea, and sharing conversation.

"You're on the third floor," Lizzie told him, handing him a large, old-fashioned, and heavy silver key.

He raised a brow. "Seriously? No key card?"

"Not here. We do have an elevator. It's around the corner. I have to warn you it can take a while. It's safe; just slow."

"I'm fine with the stairs."

"I figured. After you get settled in, come on down. My office is back there," she said, pointing to the door behind her. "I'll make sure my computer is ready to go."

"Great." He paused. "Your computer isn't as old as this key, is it? I need video options."

She smiled. "It's less than a year old. It should have all the bells and whistles you'll need. Are you sure you don't want someone to carry your bag?"

"I've got it. I travel light."

"I bet you do."

As he turned to go up the stairs, his stomach rumbled from the delicious smell of cinnamon and vanilla. "Something smells amazing."

"My cookies. They may not be world famous, but they are Whisper Lake famous. I'll set you up with a plate in my office. Do you want anything more substantial to eat? We don't have dinner service, but I can get you a sandwich or some cheese and crackers to keep you going."

He should say yes to something more substantial. He rarely ate sugar. He couldn't remember when he'd last had a cookie, but in light of his headache, he found himself thinking that sugar might be exactly what he needed. "Cookies will be fine."

"If you're sure. There's a list of nearby restaurants in your room, but if you need more personal recommendations based on what you'd like to eat, feel free to ask."

"I will."

As he finished speaking, an Asian woman with long black hair came out of the back room.

"Lizzie, finally!" she said. "Where have you been? I've been texting you for the past hour. I need to talk to you."

"I didn't have my phone."

At her words, he was reminded that he still had her phone. He took it out of his pocket and handed it to her. "Sorry about that. I keep forgetting to give this back to you."

"It's fine," Lizzie replied. "Justin, this is Shay, my manager—Justin Blackwood."

"Marie and Benjamin's grandson. So happy you're here," Shay said, giving him a friendly smile.

"Thanks," he said, wondering when he'd last seen so many

people smiling at the same time. And it seemed to be contagious. He found his lips curving upward as he went to his room. But then he glanced at his watch, which instantly reminded him of how much work he had to do and how much time he'd lost. He needed to get back to business. Lizzie had already distracted him far too much.

―――――――――

Lizzie's smile faded as she faced Shay. She could see the wary look in Shay's gaze, which meant there was yet another problem to be handled. Her day seemed to be getting worse by the minute, but at least Justin wouldn't be privy to whatever new challenge was about to be revealed. "What's wrong?"

"Nothing's wrong. Actually, it's good news."

Relief swept through her. "Well, don't hold back. I could use some good news."

"Kyle wants me to meet his parents."

"It's about time." Kyle and Shay had gotten engaged a month ago and had been dating for a year prior to that, but she'd never had a chance to meet his parents, who resided in Australia.

"I know. But there is a small problem," Shay said.

Her heart sank. "I thought you said nothing was wrong."

"Kyle wants me to meet them tomorrow in Denver. They're only going to be there for twenty-four hours. They're basically extending a layover on their way to New York where his father is speaking at some medical conference. It's as close as they'll be to us for the next year, and it saves me from having to make a trip to Melbourne."

"Wow, that's crazy. They just found out about this trip?"

"Apparently, they didn't want to say anything until they knew if they could make the Denver layover work. I know it's bad timing, Lizzie. It's a busy week, but I can't say no. It's just the day and one night. I'll be back Thursday morning, by eleven at the latest."

This was probably the worst possible week to lose Shay for twenty-four hours. But Shay wasn't just her employee; she was also her friend. "You have to go. We can make it a day without you."

Relief filled Shay's gaze. "You're the best, Lizzie. Thank you. So, what took you so long? I thought you were going to be back an hour ago, and why did Justin Blackwood have your phone?"

"It's a long story. I have a better question—where were you when Patty Lawrence called the police on Noah Bennett?"

"What?" Shay asked in surprise. "When did that happen?"

"Like ten minutes ago. Brodie had Noah handcuffed out front when I arrived."

"I had no idea. I went to the market to pick up some grocery items for Naomi. I just got back. What happened? And didn't I just see both of them having tea in the dining room?"

"Patty thought Noah was stalking her, because he was lingering outside her room. I guess she called 911. But she should have not had to do that herself. Someone should have been at the desk when she came down."

"Victor was supposed to stay at the desk while I was gone, but I did just see him outside smoking a cigarette and looking at his phone. I was hoping that he'd only stepped out a second ago."

She frowned with annoyance. Victor was a recent college graduate and a local kid who'd told her he was interested in learning about the hotel business, so she'd given him a part-time job. But he was turning out to be a slacker, and more interested in swiping left or right on his phone than taking care of business.

"I'll talk to him," she said.

"Again? How many chances are you going to give him?"

"Just one more. It's a busy week."

"I hear you, but I wouldn't expect a miracle." Shay paused. "If Patty called the police on Noah, how are they now friends?"

"I explained the situation with his lost love, and Patty felt sorry for him. She's a widow, and I think she understands his loneliness. I suggested they talk, and it seems to be going well."

"They were laughing when I walked through the dining room, so I'd say it's going great."

"Good."

"I'll go get Victor."

"Thanks. I'm going to set Justin up in my office. He needs to use my computer for a video conference. I told him he'd have privacy."

"No problem."

As Shay left, Lizzie walked into her office. It was a bit disorganized, but she didn't have time to clean it for Justin. While it was messy, she knew where everything was, and filing was the least of her concerns these days.

She did, however, take a moment to clear space on her desk. Then she opened her laptop. Seeing three bills pop up on the screen, she quickly closed those windows, not just because she didn't want Justin to see them, but also because she didn't want to be reminded of her increasingly growing financial problems.

She just needed to get through this week. The inn was full, and her happy guests would hopefully ease some of the pressures for at least the next month.

She sat down in her worn, creaky chair and let out a breath. She had a lot on her plate, but she still felt happy to be in her office, in her inn, running her dream business. That's what she had to remember. She was doing exactly what she wanted to do, and she would make it work. She didn't just have herself to worry about; she had all her investors, her family members, who had put their trust in her and their money into the inn. She couldn't let them down. She just wished the problems were getting smaller instead of bigger.

Closing her eyes for a moment, she drew in several deep breaths, trying to remember the yoga mantras that would clear her mind and release her stress. But in the darkness, she couldn't see her normally calm mountain meadow image; she saw Justin Blackwood's very attractive face and his especially penetrating blue eyes that could be both fiery and angry as well as cold and calm.

She'd seen quite a few emotions run through his gaze over the past few hours, and she wasn't really sure exactly what she thought of him. Except that when he smiled, it felt shockingly amazing and made her want to make him smile again. Although, that would be an uphill battle. He clearly wasn't the kind of person to find joy in the little things in life.

He was supposed to be in Whisper Lake for his grandparents, but all he seemed concerned about at the moment was his work problem. Hopefully, he would get that resolved, and then he could concentrate on Marie and Benjamin and really be present for them when they arrived. She knew how important it was to them that Justin be at their vow renewal, since apparently their son and daughter-in-law, Justin's parents, couldn't or wouldn't make the big event. She knew there were some tensions in the family, but she wasn't quite sure what they were about. Not that she needed to know. She just needed to make sure everyone had a great time, and that included Justin.

She would find a way to put a smile on his face.

And then she would have to find a way to stop that smile from sending unwanted butterflies through her stomach. It had been a while since she'd felt those butterflies, and she didn't need to feel them for a man who was only passing through town on his way to somewhere else. She needed to fall for someone who wanted to stay in Whisper Lake forever. That wasn't going to be Justin Blackwood.

A knock came at her half-open office door and her eyes flew open as Justin walked into the room. He'd changed into a maroon polo shirt and faded jeans. The casual wear made him even more appealing than his very expensive suit. His face was still bruised, but that only gave him a more rugged, masculine look.

"Are you ready for me?" he asked.

She wanted to say no, because her heart was already beating faster, and her palms were starting to sweat. But he was just talking about her computer, and she needed to get a grip. "Yes," she said, forcing out the word.

She got up from the chair and tried not to brush against him as they each moved around the desk, but the brief touch of their arms sent a rush of warmth through her. She definitely was not ready for him, not in any way, so she moved toward the door.

"Take as much time as you need," she told him.

"You don't need to work in here?"

"No, I'll be somewhere around the inn," she said vaguely. "There's a landline, so I think I'll hang on to my phone."

"All right. Lizzie?"

His question forced her gaze to his. "Yes?"

"Thanks."

She was surprised. "You're welcome."

"I realize I've been a little…"

"Annoyed, irritated, angry, impatient…" she offered when he couldn't seem to come up with a word.

He smiled. And just like that, the butterflies danced again. "All of the above."

"Well, it's been a rough day," she said.

"It has. Didn't I hear something about cookies?" he asked hopefully.

"I'll get you some. What would you like to drink?"

"Coffee?"

"Coming right up."

"I don't want to put you out."

"It's what I do. I take care of my guests. Make your call. I'll try not to disturb you when I come back."

"Somehow, that seems unlikely," he said dryly, and as their

gazes met, she thought he might be just as aware of the simmering attraction between them as she was. But he wouldn't be interested in pursuing that attraction, either. They might not have a lot in common, but she had a feeling they'd be in agreement on that.

She slipped out the door and ran into Shay and Victor. Judging by the worried look on Victor's face, she had a feeling Shay had already given him a heads-up.

"Victor, we need to talk," she said.

"I know. I can explain," he said.

"Hold that thought," she said, turning to Shay. "Would you mind getting Mr. Blackwood a plate of cookies and some coffee and then take it into the office?"

"Of course," Shay said, leaving the two of them alone.

"Let's go outside," she told Victor, leading him toward the patio door. When they stepped out onto the bricks, she made sure they were alone and then said, "Why weren't you at the desk while Shay was at the store?"

"I was there most of the time. I just took a quick smoke break," he said defensively. "And nothing was going on. It was slower than slow." He ran a hand through his long brown hair, his gaze defensive.

At twenty-eight, she was only six years older than Victor, but right now she felt a million years older than him. And she'd been working in the hospitality business since she was in high school. She knew what was expected. She also knew when someone had it or they didn't, and she didn't think Victor had it.

"It's slow until it's not," she said. "That's how it works. But you had other tasks you could have worked on while you were at the desk. You could have updated the website, posted on our social media platforms, checked in with the guests to make sure they didn't need anything. There's always something to do."

"I'm sorry, Lizzie. It was just a few minutes."

"Do you want to continue working here?" she asked curiously. "Because if this job isn't for you, maybe you should look into getting something else."

"No. I like it here. I'll do better. I need to stay in Whisper Lake. My girlfriend just found out she's pregnant. I came out here to call her, because she was freaking out about how her parents will react. I was trying to calm her down. I can't afford to lose my job, especially not now. I will do better," he promised.

"I hope so." She knew she should probably fire him. *But how could she do that now?* Her anger diminished as she looked into his worried eyes. "Go see your girlfriend. Tell her you'll be there for her but not during work hours. You'll only be texting her on your breaks unless it is truly an emergency."

"Got it. Thanks, Lizzie. You're the best."

She was beginning to think she was only the best because she kept giving in to her employees. She'd always promised herself that when she was a boss, she'd be understanding, reasonable, and kind. Unfortunately, she was beginning to realize that sometimes being all those things was not very efficient or profitable.

Victor had one more chance, she told herself, knowing deep down that she'd probably already given him one more chance too many times. However, she needed to get through this week, which required his help, especially now that Shay would be gone for the happy hour tomorrow night. Hopefully, Victor would get his act together and be the right hand she desperately needed. Otherwise, she was probably going to have to bring herself to do something she hadn't done before—fire one of her staff, even one with a pregnant girlfriend and a sob story. She really hoped it wouldn't come to that.

CHAPTER FOUR

JUSTIN SPENT two hours in Lizzie's office. By the time he ended his meeting with Anthony, it was seven, and his stomach was rumbling. The cookies now seemed like a very distant memory. He needed some real food. Closing Lizzie's laptop, he walked out of the office. Shay was sitting on a high stool at the front desk, working on her computer. She gave him a smile. "Is your work done?"

"For now. But it's never really done."

"You sound like Lizzie. I practically had to force her out of here tonight for her brother's birthday party."

He was wondering where Lizzie had disappeared to. "I've missed more than a few birthdays," he admitted. "I think she said her brother is a police detective?"

"Yes. Adam is a cop and a great guy. He and Lizzie are nothing alike, though. Adam is serious and quiet, intense at times, a little broody. Whereas Lizzie is an outgoing, friendly, whirlwind of creativity and wild ideas. She rarely stops moving or thinking or even talking, but I've never met anyone who doesn't love her." Shay smiled. "She's just one of the most special people you'll ever meet."

"Her friend Hannah called her a force of nature."

"That's a good description."

"And Lizzie has a sister in town as well?" He wasn't normally curious about the people who ran the hotels he stayed in. But then, he'd never stayed in a place like the Firefly Inn.

"Yes, Chelsea is a country music artist. She's actually pretty famous. She took a break from singing for a while, but now she's building a recording studio here in town and is working on a new album. She's engaged to a police officer."

"I met him earlier. He had one of your guests handcuffed."

"Oh, right. I forgot about that. I had only left the inn for a few minutes." Shay paused, giving him a helpless smile. "I had no idea all that would go down while I ran to the market. But I'm glad it worked out."

"Lizzie worked it out. She defused the situation very quickly."

"She's good at that. So, what are you up to tonight?"

"First thing on the list is dinner. I need to get some food."

"What do you like to eat?"

"I'm not picky."

"Well, there's the Blue Sky Café run by the lovely Chloe Morgan, who serves up very hearty meals that will remind you of home. Although, Chloe will probably be at Adam's birthday party. Still, her cook is amazing."

Since he could barely remember living in a house where someone cooked him dinner, he said, "What else?"

"Burgers and wings are pretty fantastic at Micky's Brewery, and if you like beer, they have a lot of choices. Italian at D'Amico's. Mexican at Taco Pete's, Mediterranean at Kabul is awesome, and there's a new Indian restaurant named Roti's if you like spicy curry."

"Sounds like I can go around the world and never leave Whisper Lake," he said, a little surprised at the choices.

"Our food scene has improved the last several years. We've

had a lot of new housing developments and big estates going up around the lake, as well as celebrity visitors, and wealthy individuals who want to escape the touristy mountain resorts. All that traffic has brought some very talented chefs our way. We're still hoping to start providing dinners here at the inn, but we haven't quite gotten there. However, we do have a fantastic breakfast, which I hope you'll check out while you're here."

"I will definitely do that. The cookies were amazing, so I'm sure breakfast will be as well. I think I'll head into town and see what I want to eat."

"Do you need directions?"

"No. I'm just going to play it by ear."

"When you leave the inn, go to the right. You'll find the downtown area and quite a few of the restaurants I just mentioned within about a ten-block area. You can also use one of the online restaurant apps."

"I've got it."

"Have fun."

After a quick stop upstairs to grab a jacket, he walked out of the inn, heading toward downtown. It was a Tuesday night and while the sun had gone down, the temperature was still in the sixties, making it a nice evening for a walk. When he got to the Indian restaurant, he saw a line out the door, so he kept on moving. The Blue Sky Café was just as crowded, and also not that big. But when he got to Micky's, there were plenty of barstools available as well as small tables. He also liked the friendly, somewhat noisy, and cheerful atmosphere. This was the kind of place where he could blend into the crowd and not feel compelled to be friendly.

He slid onto a stool and asked the bartender for a menu. A few minutes later, he ordered a grilled spicy chicken sandwich with sweet potato fries and a deep gold ale called the Bombay Bomber. While he was waiting for his order, he checked out the basketball game on the screen behind the bar. The Denver

Nuggets were playing the Los Angeles Lakers, but were behind by sixteen points. It wasn't much of a game.

He reached into his pocket to grab his phone, realizing belatedly that he no longer had a phone or a computer. Tomorrow, he would need to replace both. It felt strange to be without his phone. He couldn't remember a time when he hadn't had it. It was his tether to his business, his life. But he was on his own now. That felt both freeing and terrifying. He liked to be in control. Without his phone, he felt a little lost, and somewhat off-balance. Although, those feelings might have something to do with his quirky innkeeper and this admittedly charming small town.

He smiled as the female bartender set down his beer and his sandwich. At least he could distract himself with food. And that food was very good. The chicken was hotter than he'd expected, but the mix of spices was delicious, and it didn't take him long to clean his plate.

As he finished everything off with a long draught of beer, he heard a commotion behind him. Turning on his stool, he saw a big group of people at a large table on the other side of the room. They were laughing and talking, all at the same time. His heart skipped a beat. There in the middle of the group was Lizzie.

Her hair was out of its ponytail, falling in soft light-brown waves past her shoulders, the blonde highlights sparkling under the lights. Her smile was as big as ever. When she laughed at something the man next to her said, he felt a squeeze in his chest, almost as if he were a little jealous. But that was ridiculous. He barely knew Lizzie. And, of course, she would be with a guy. He would have been more surprised if she were alone.

But as he watched the group, he wondered if she was actually with the brown-haired guy next to her. When that man put his arm around the blonde sitting on the other side of him, an odd relief ran through Justin.

He shouldn't care that she wasn't with that guy, but he did. And that was bad.

He was only going to be in Whisper Lake a few days, and while most of his relationships didn't last past a few days, he didn't think messing around with Lizzie was a good idea. While they might share a passion for business, she was emotional and talkative and a little chaotic. But she was also fun and friendly and sexy as well, with curves in all the right places. He'd felt a spark back in her office, and he was sure she'd felt it, too. But that was one fire he should probably not light.

As he took another sip of his beer, Lizzie suddenly looked in his direction and caught his gaze. Surprise moved through her expression. He tipped his head. She hesitated and then got up from her chair.

His gut stiffened at her approach. He hadn't thought she'd leave her friends and family to say hello, but she was probably just trying to be a good innkeeper.

"Hi," she said, her pretty green gaze meeting his. "I didn't see you here. It looks like you ate."

"I did. It was very good."

"Micky's is always great."

"So, which one is your brother?"

She turned and waved her hand toward the table. "The guy sitting at the head of the table, brown hair, blue eyes…"

"Giving us a curious look," he finished.

"Adam is a detective. He was born curious."

"And your sister? Is she next to Brodie?"

"Yes, the woman with the long hair, the gauzy top, and the soulful eyes."

"She's pretty."

"Always has been," Lizzie agreed.

"Shay mentioned she was a country star."

"One of the best. I'm incredibly proud of her. She's only fifteen months older than me, so we've always been close. Plus, we had to hang together, just to hold our own with our three older brothers."

"Sounds like a fun family."

"Yes, and I'm thrilled to have at least two of my siblings living nearby."

"Who's the guy you're sitting next to?"

"That's Zach Barrington. He's an architect and married to my friend Gianna, the blonde on his other side. Across from them are the Morgan's—Chloe and Kevin, who are celebrating a rare night out away from their ten-month-old son, Leo. Next to Chloe is Keira. She's a real-estate agent."

He felt happy once more that there didn't appear to be a man in the group who was attached to Lizzie. "Where's Hannah?"

"She's still at work, but she's hoping to stop by later. Hannah, Keira, Gianna, Chloe and Kevin all grew up here together. They were nice enough to welcome Chelsea, Adam and me into their group, along with Brodie and Zach." She paused. "And I'm sure you're not at all interested in any of this. You might have noticed that I sometimes talk too much."

"You are very friendly."

She shrugged. "It's just who I am."

"Brodie looks familiar to me; I'm not sure why."

"He was a world-class skier. He won everything except Olympic gold when he suffered a horrific crash on a practice run."

"Right. I remember that. One of my college friends was a huge skier and snowboarder. He took me to Aspen when McGuire was training there. Brodie inspired everyone on the mountain that day. He was fearless and fast. I'm sorry he didn't get a chance at the Olympics." He shook his head, a little surprised by the path Brodie had taken. "Now he's a police officer in a small town... That doesn't seem like a natural next step."

"Brodie couldn't go back to professional skiing, so he had to change his life around. His grandfather was chief of police here for a long time, and he encouraged Brodie to go into law enforcement. Aside from being a cop, he is also part of the town's new search and rescue team, which was busier than anyone hoped for this past winter. We had a bad avalanche, but fortunately no one died. Brodie and his team were able to rescue two men who got caught in it."

"So, he still does some skiing?"

"Some. Now, he's more tied up in wedding planning. He and my sister are getting married in August. They fell in love last summer, and in the nine months since then, they have bought a house together and built a music studio in the back of their property. It's very cool. I'm so happy to have Chelsea make Whisper Lake her home base. She used to travel all the time. Now, she'll tour, but when she's home, she'll be here." She paused. "What about you, Justin? I know your grandparents live in Los Angeles. Do you as well?"

"I'm based in San Francisco, but I travel half the year."

"Do you enjoy that?"

"For the most part. I go where the business takes me."

"Then business must be good."

"Opportunities are presenting themselves around every corner. While I'm missing London this week, I'm scheduled to go to Tokyo next week, then Australia after that."

"I'd love to go to both those cities."

"Have you traveled much?"

"Not internationally. I've done a tour of inns that has taken me through New England and the South: Charleston, Savannah, and New Orleans. I have been to San Francisco and Los Angeles. I actually worked in LA for a year at a big hotel chain. I liked the beach, but I missed the mountains of Colorado. And I knew that I had to get back."

He was surprised she'd traveled as much as she had. He'd had the idea that she'd just been in Denver and then Whisper Lake, but clearly there were a few more twists and turns in her story. "There's still a lot more for you to see. I'm sure there are charming inns all over the world."

"One day, I hope to see them all, but for now I'm spending all my time at the Firefly. My business is my life."

"I know what that feels like," he said, finding himself relating to her more than he'd imagined he could at their first meeting.

"I wouldn't even be here tonight if it wasn't my brother's birthday," she added. "I keep thinking I'll reach a point where I have better control, where I can slow down a bit, but I don't know when I'll get there. Have you reached that point?"

"Theoretically. But there's always more to accomplish."

"You keep moving the goal post," she said, an understanding gleam in her eyes. "I do that, too."

"It keeps life exciting."

"And exhausting."

"It's up to you how fast you want to run and for how long. That's the beauty of owning your own business. You're the boss. You call the shots."

"I wish that were true. I am the boss, but a lot of external problems seem to be calling the shots." She brushed her hair out of her face. "But I'm not going to think about those problems tonight. I should probably get back to the group."

He knew she was right, but he didn't really want her to leave. He liked talking to her. She was a beautiful mix of soft and hard —the friendly, optimistic cheerleader and the driven business-woman. He wanted to know more, but she wasn't here with him. She had a whole table of people waiting for her to come back. "Don't let me keep you," he said.

She hesitated. "Do you want to join us, Justin?"

He was surprised by the invite. "You're with your family and your friends."

"There's always room for one more. And I don't feel right leaving you sitting here alone. You're my guest."

"You run the inn where I'm staying. That doesn't make you responsible for me," he said, a little bemused by that idea. But then, he usually stayed in five-star luxury hotels these days and rarely did he know any of the staff by name. He certainly didn't know anything about their families.

"I'm not responsible for you, but I am interested in your well-being, and I promised you that we would turn your obligation into a vacation. Since your grandparents aren't in town yet, you're at loose ends. Come on, join us. You've been working all afternoon, and I know you don't have a phone or a computer to get lost in."

"That's true. I need to get those items tomorrow."

"You can absolutely do that, but not tonight. Nothing is open now. Join us."

A small voice inside his head suggested that no would be a better answer than yes. But there was something about Lizzie that made it impossible for him to refuse.

It wasn't a big deal. And without his electronics, he was looking forward to a long night of nothing. There wasn't even a television in his room. Although, there was a bookshelf in his room with a variety of novels and nonfiction books, as well as a library downstairs. Apparently, Lizzie liked to encourage reading.

"Come on, Justin," she said. "It will be fun. And you seem like someone who could use some fun."

"I can be fun," he said defensively.

"You can be, but are you?" She gave him a doubtful look. "I think you're going to need to prove it."

"You might regret that challenge. I might be more fun than you can handle."

She laughed. "You're not short of confidence in any area, are you?"

"Why should I be?" he asked, knowing he sounded cocky as hell, but she seemed to like it. He slid off the stool and followed her over to the table.

As Lizzie introduced him to her friends, he received a lot of friendly smiles and speculative looks. Zach was quick to pull over a chair, so he could sit between him and Lizzie. He was more than happy with that scenario.

"So, Justin, I have a question for you," Keira said from across the table. He could see the amusement in her sparkling brown eyes.

"What's that?"

"Do you sing?"

"Uh…I was not expecting that question."

"It's karaoke night," Lizzie explained, as she poured him a beer from the pitcher on the table. "It starts in about ten minutes."

"Got it. No, I'm not a singer."

"Are you sure?" Keira asked. "We need some men to get up there for a change. And these guys swear they can't carry a tune, although I think some of them are lying, or maybe all of them."

"Chelsea and Lizzie got all the talent in my family," Adam said.

"We're not having Chelsea sing," Keira said, with a shake of her head. "She's too good for karaoke. She'll make the rest of us look terrible."

"None of you are terrible," Chelsea put in with a laugh. "But I am resting my voice tonight. I'm going to start recording tomorrow."

"That's exciting," Lizzie said. "Is the studio completely finished then?"

"It's close enough for me to start laying some tracks. And Brodie will be happy to have me do something besides talk about the wedding. I never thought I'd be one of those brides, but it turns out, I might be."

"Not at all," Brodie said, his arm around his fiancée's shoulders, his fingers gently stroking her neck. "You're nowhere close to a bridezilla, babe."

"I've been a little obsessed. Now I can see why you and Zach eloped," Chelsea added, giving Gianna a pointed smile.

Gianna shrugged. "I'd already planned a few weddings that didn't happen; I didn't want to go through all that again. Zach and I got married on New Year's Eve," she added for Justin's benefit. "We had a babysitter for his daughter, Hailey, so it seemed like the perfect time to do it. Lizzie threw us a reception at the inn a few weeks later."

"Which was amazing," Zach said. "You are the party queen, Lizzie."

"I like being the queen of anything," she said with a laugh.

"I think we need another round," Kevin said, getting to his feet. "Who's in?"

"We should probably get going," his wife Chloe put in. "Leo has a cold, and I don't want to stay out too long."

"Leo is fine," Kevin told his wife. "And he's with his grandparents. How often do we get a night out? I'm going to order another round for the table." He headed for the bar.

Justin couldn't help noticing the irritated expression that moved across Chloe's face. Adam also gave her a concerned look.

"Everything okay?" Adam asked.

"It's fine," Chloe said quickly, masking her disappointment. "Kevin is right. We haven't had much fun lately."

"Then let's get this party started with some karaoke," Keira said, a forceful note in her voice.

Justin had a feeling that when Keira went after something, she got it. She was definitely the most hard-edged of this group. Chloe seemed softer, quieter, more of a follower than a leader. Chelsea had a free-spirited, bohemian vibe. He hadn't quite figured out Gianna yet, although her comment about having planned three weddings intrigued him.

Shay had mentioned that Adam was the complete opposite of his sister Lizzie, and on first impression, he definitely appeared to be the night to her day. He had an intense, more serious vibe to him. He also appeared to be opposite to Brodie, who couldn't seem to stop smiling. Although that might have something to do with the beautiful Chelsea. And then there was Zach, who appeared to be as entranced with his phone as Justin normally was. He couldn't help noticing that Zach kept checking his texts.

"Let's not be first up," Lizzie said. "Let's see how good the talent is tonight."

"Are you kidding?" Keira asked. "It's way better to be first. The bar has not been set yet. Plus, I don't want you guys to back out if someone great hits the stage before us."

"Don't waste your breath arguing, Lizzie," Gianna interjected. "If Keira wants us to sing, we will sing."

Keira gave a careless shrug. "You guys always complain and everyone always has a good time in the end."

"All right, all right," Lizzie said, getting to her feet. "Come on, Gianna, Chloe. Let's do this."

"Not me," Chloe said. "I want to call home and check on Leo." She pulled out her phone, got up from the table and headed to the door, leaving a somewhat tense silence behind her.

"What is going on with them?" Lizzie muttered.

"Kevin is being an ass," Adam said tersely. "In case you haven't noticed."

"He's just finding his way back into the group," Lizzie said.

Adam gave his sister a disbelieving look. "You always look for the positive spin, but in this case, there might not be one."

"I hope that's not true. They have a baby to raise together."

Adam got up from his seat. "I'll be back."

Justin didn't know if Adam was more annoyed with the

missing Kevin or with his overly optimistic sister, but he disappeared into the crowd.

"What is with him?" Lizzie asked.

"Forget him," Keira ordered. "Let's sing. This is supposed to be a party."

"Adam's party," Lizzie reminded her.

"He'll be fine," Chelsea put in. "Go sing."

Lizzie, Keira and Gianna left the table, leaving Justin with Chelsea, Brodie and Zach.

"How's your head?" Brodie asked.

"It's fine." He still had a dull ache in his temple, but the beer was helping with that.

"What happened?" Chelsea asked.

"I was driving behind your sister, Lizzie, when she braked very fast to avoid a deer. I swerved to avoid the back of her truck and ended up in a ditch."

"I saw Tom earlier," Brodie put in. "He said your car was totaled."

"Well, it was a rental car, so hopefully insurance will take care of it."

"And now you're staying at the inn?" Chelsea asked.

"Yes. I'm here for my grandparents' vow renewal ceremony this Saturday. They got delayed, so they're not arriving until tomorrow."

"Where are you from?" Zach asked curiously.

"San Francisco."

A gleam entered his eyes. "I used to live there. I had a condo south of Market. What about you?"

"I'm in Russian Hill."

"Great area."

"What brought you to Whisper Lake?" Justin asked.

"I was doing a remodel at the summer camp for a buddy of mine. I ran into Gianna, and that changed everything. We'd actually met at that camp when we were kids. A decade or so later, we end up back at the lake at the same time, and now we're married. We got a second chance, and we took it."

"And you run your business from here?"

"Yes. It's actually not that difficult. I visit job sites when I need to, but the rest of the time I'm here. I have an eight-year-old daughter, and this is a good place for her to grow up. I have to say this lake really changed my life."

"Mine, too," Brodie said. "It gave me a second chance, too. I had to reinvent myself, and I was able to do that here."

"I saw you ski once at Aspen," he interjected. "You were amazing."

"I used to be," Brodie agreed with a matter-of-fact nod of his head. "But that part of my life is over." His gaze moved to Chelsea. "I can't say I'm sorry, because it brought me here. It brought me Chelsea."

She gave him a soft smile. "I feel the same way." Dragging her gaze away from her fiancé, she added to Justin, "I also got a chance to start again."

"That seems to be a theme around here."

"It is," she said. "If you stay more than a few days, you might find yourself changing in a way you never expected."

"I'm happy with the way I am."

Brodie grinned. "I thought the same thing."

"Me, too," Zach said. "Talk to us when you've been here a week."

"I didn't come here to change or reinvent or heal. I just came for a wedding. Maybe if I was looking for something else, I'd find it, but I'm not." He didn't know why he felt the need to tell them that so forcefully. Perhaps because their words scared him just a little. He only liked change when he was in complete control of that change. Anything else brought back a feeling of helplessness from his past that he never wanted to experience again. Seeing the thoughtful looks coming back at him, he felt a little too exposed, so he refilled his beer mug and then passed the pitcher to Zach. "Might as well finish it off. Looks like we have another two coming," he added, seeing Kevin heading to the table.

"Who needs another drink?" Kevin asked, setting the pitchers down on the table. "And where did everyone go? Where's Chloe?"

"I think she went to the ladies' room," Chelsea said.

Kevin nodded and sat down, wincing a little as he did so.

"Still feeling that knee?" Brodie asked.

Kevin shrugged. "It's fine. Everything is good. I keep telling Chloe that, but she wants to make problems where there aren't any." He stopped talking. "Sorry, I don't know why I said that." He poured himself a full glass and drained half of it in one long swallow. Then he stood back up again. "I'm going to find Chloe. I know she's on the phone. She can't trust anyone with Leo, not even my parents."

As Kevin left again, Chelsea let out a sigh and shook her head. "I want to help, but what can we do?"

"Nothing," Brodie advised. "Kevin and Chloe have to work out their own life." Brodie looked at Justin. "It's a long story."

"You don't have to tell me," he said, realizing he was getting very caught up in the lives of Lizzie's friends.

"Kevin is on medical leave from the army," Chelsea put in. "He went through a rough time, and while he's been back almost ten months now, he's still not fitting into his old life."

"My father always had a hard time when he was home in between deployments," Zach put in. "I see a lot of my mother in Chloe. But Chloe has her husband back. Hopefully, he'll realize that being home with her and his son is where he needs to be and where he wants to be."

"Looks like the girls are up," Chelsea said, drawing their attention to the small stage where Keira, Lizzie, and Gianna were standing in front of a microphone.

As the women began to sing, Justin realized one thing very

quickly—they were good, especially Lizzie, who was front and center. While she'd expressed reservations about singing, she didn't look at all uncomfortable. And in the glow of the stage lights, her beautiful face, framed by a cascade of silky brown waves, hit him like a sucker punch. He had to force some air back into his body, shocked at his reaction to her.

But who could resist that laughing, inviting smile, or the way she moved her hips with the rhythm of the song? It felt like she was looking right at him—singing Whitney Houston's hit, "*I Wanna Dance With Somebody.*"

And damn if he didn't feel like dancing with her.

Not just dancing. He wanted to kiss her mouth, run his hands along her curves and through her hair. And then he wanted to get even closer.

He told himself to look away. Better yet, he should get up and walk away. He didn't need to get tangled up with a small-town innkeeper with a cheery personality and a heart of gold. They wouldn't be a good match at all. She was emotion; he was logic. She was warmth; he was cold. They were complete opposites.

But he couldn't quite get himself to move…

CHAPTER FIVE

JUSTIN WAS STILL TRYING to pull himself together when Lizzie returned to the table. She gave him another dazzling smile, and he had to shove his hands into his pockets, so he wouldn't do something crazy like grab her and kiss her in front of her friends and her family. The impulsive idea was completely out of character for him. He really needed to get a grip.

"What did you think?" she asked, as she sat down next to him. "Did we sound better than a bunch of squealing cats?"

"Hey, set the bar a little higher," Keira complained.

"You sounded great," he told them all.

"And you're probably just being nice," Lizzie said.

"I'm not really known for that."

She tilted her head, giving him a thoughtful look. "It's not a bad thing to be known for. I'm nice."

She was many more things than nice, but he wasn't going to get into that.

"Where is everyone?" Lizzie asked. "Chloe, Kevin, my brother?"

Chelsea sighed. "Chloe and Kevin are fighting. Adam

seemed to be annoyed by that. I'm not sure what's going on, or if anyone is coming back."

"I think they'll be back," Brodie said. "Maybe. But we can have fun without them. I'm thinking about singing a song."

"You are?" both Lizzie and Chelsea said at the same time.

"Yes. Justin, Zach, you two in?" Brodie asked.

"I gotta go," he said quickly.

"I thought you were going to show me how much fun you can be," Lizzie said pointedly.

"I don't sing well."

"You don't have to sing well. You just sing," she told him.

"Come on, join us," Brodie said, as he got to his feet. "We'll find a good song."

Somehow, he found himself propelled to the stage with two guys he'd met less than a half hour ago. "What are we going to sing?" he asked. "No sappy love songs, or you two are on your own."

Brodie laughed. "No love in your life?"

"Not at the moment." He perused the list of song choices, trying not to wince at the older couple on stage currently attempting to sing *"Just The Way You Are"*.

"Here's one," Zach said, putting his finger on the page. "What do you think?"

He read the title and grinned. "I like it."

Brodie laughed. "Let's do it."

A moment later, they took the stage and pounded out the lyrics to *"Born To Be Wild."*

Being on stage with the lights in his eyes, and the pulsing beat of the song running through his body, he felt wilder than he had in a long time. He wasn't in a business suit. He didn't have a tie choking his neck. He wasn't talking to investors or engineers. He was belting out a song in a bar in a town he'd never been to before with a couple of guys he'd just met. It felt both good and unsettling. *If he wasn't himself anymore, who was he?*

That question left his head when his gaze met Lizzie's. She was wide-eyed, as if she couldn't quite believe what she was seeing. And that made him want to shock her even more. He grabbed the microphone and rocked backward on the last chorus, practically knocking over Brodie and Zach as he busted out the line: *"We were born, born to be wild."*

The bar erupted as the song ended. Brodie slapped him on the shoulder. "Nice job turning us into your backup singers."

Despite his words, there was no anger on Brodie's face, just amusement.

"I was fine with it," Zach put in. "I could feel myself singing out of tune."

"You were great, both of you," he said. "I just felt like letting loose, which I don't actually do that often."

They moved off the stage as the next group stepped up. When he returned to the table, they were met with applause. Adam, Chloe, and Kevin had also returned, and seemed to have eased whatever tension was brewing among the three of them. He grabbed his beer and took a long swig, then he gave Lizzie a challenging smile. "How fun was that?"

"Really fun," she said with an approving gleam in her eyes. "I didn't know you had it in you."

"To be honest, I didn't, either."

"You have a great voice, Justin," Chelsea put in. "You can definitely sing."

"Hey, what about me?" Brodie complained.

Chelsea leaned over and gave her fiancé a kiss. "You can sing, too."

Brodie grinned. "I can't, but I just wanted the kiss."

Justin smiled at the sexy banter between them. They certainly made love look easy, which was not his experience. "I should get going," he said, thinking it was past time for him to head back to the inn. "It was nice to meet all of you."

"I should go, too," Lizzie said. "I'll walk back with you, Justin."

He was surprised at her words, but he could hardly say no.

"You're leaving, Lizzie?" Keira said, disappointment in her eyes. "It's early. Hannah isn't even here yet."

"Tell her I'm sorry I missed her, but I'll see you tomorrow at the inn's happy hour, right?"

"I'll be there," Keira said. "In fact, I'm going to bring someone. I should probably talk to you about that."

"That's fine. The more the merrier."

"But—"

"We'll talk tomorrow," Lizzie said, cutting off Keira. "Have fun everyone."

After a round of good-byes, they left the restaurant.

When they stepped onto the sidewalk, Lizzie let out a breath. "It feels good to be outside. It's not so noisy."

"I thought you like noise and action."

"I do, but I also like quiet." She paused, giving him a speculative look. "So, were you really born to be wild?"

He laughed. "No, I think I was born to be boring."

"I haven't seen boring yet. Impatient, annoyed, driven, a little isolated, yes. But boring? No."

"That's how you see me, huh?"

"It was before you decided to rock and roll it out on the stage."

"Maybe your first impression was wrong."

"I'm thinking it might have been," she admitted. "Are you glad you joined the party?"

"Yes. Your friends are great, very down-to-earth, friendly, welcoming. Well, most of them anyway. I don't know what was going on with Chloe and Kevin or your brother, but they were not in the best moods. Is there some kind of love triangle?"

She frowned at that question. "Chloe and Adam got really close while Kevin was on his last deployment. He was pretty much gone for eighteen months straight. But my brother respects their marriage. And I don't believe he has ever acted inappropriately, but there's a part of me that thinks he might be in love with her, and I don't see that ending happily. She's taken. She has a baby with Kevin, and she's been with Kevin since she was a teenager. I think they're just going through a rough patch."

"Have you talked to Adam about it?"

"God, no. My older brother does not discuss his love life with his sister."

He nodded. "I probably wouldn't, either."

"I just don't want him to get hurt. But what can I do?"

"Nothing. He's his own man. And you should stay out of it."

"I agree, but it's difficult for me to do nothing when people I love are hurting."

"He seemed more pissed off than hurt to me."

"Men always act angry when they're hurt. I think it's some kind of defense mechanism. I bet you do it, too."

He thought about that and realized she was right. "Maybe occasionally."

She gave him a knowing look. "Probably more than occasionally. Anyway, what do you think of Whisper Lake so far?" She waved her hand toward the street.

"It's charming. It feels like a small town, but there's actually quite a bit of business here. More than I would have expected."

She paused as they stopped at a corner. "Do you feel like taking a walk down to the lake? It's less than a mile, and there's a lovely park to go through on the way."

Alarm bells went off in his head at her suggestion. Taking a walk in the moonlight with this beautiful woman seemed a little dangerous, but her inviting smile made it impossible for him to say no. "Sure," he said. "I haven't actually seen the lake up close yet. And to be honest, I'm not sure what I'll do back in my room with no electronics."

"You could always read. We have a great selection of books in the library."

"And in my room."

"Which were all handpicked for you."

He raised a brow. "Seriously? How would you know what I like to read?"

"I asked your grandparents when they booked your room. They said you used to be into spy thrillers. They weren't sure if you read for pleasure anymore, but that you might be tempted to pick up a book with a fast-paced, techno-thriller plot, so that's what I put in your room."

He was incredibly impressed by her attention to detail. "I can't believe you give such personal attention to a small detail like what book to put next to someone's bed."

"It's all part of the Firefly Inn experience. I want you to feel so comfortable that you never want to leave."

"I'm beginning to see why my grandparents love your inn so much."

"They're becoming two of my best customers," she said with a laugh. "Oh, and the book I picked out for you came out two months ago, and the author was someone my mother found in the slush pile. She works for a literary agent in Denver. She told me about the book the second she read it. She said it was amazing and that she thought it would be a bestseller. Luckily, the agent she works for agreed, and managed to get the author a good deal. I'm not sure it has hit any lists, but she's still very proud of her find. She's always looking for the diamond in the rough, but she doesn't find them that often."

"That sounds like a fun job, if you like to read."

"Which she does."

"What does your father do?"

"He's a tax accountant. He's very much about the numbers and things adding up. I do not take after him, unfortunately, but I have other skills."

"Does he help you with your financials?"

"No. I have an accountant here in town. However, my parents are two of my investors, so I will have to show them the books for this year when they're finalized, which will be soon, and possibly depressing. So, let's not talk about that. Tell me about your parents. Your grandparents mentioned that there was some tension in the family, but they didn't seem inclined to explain."

"That's an understatement," he said dryly.

"Are they together?"

"Oh, yeah, they're together. They've always been their best selves with each other and probably their worst selves with the rest of us."

"Do you have any siblings?"

The question shouldn't have caught him off guard, but it did. "My grandmother didn't tell you about Sean?"

"No. Who's Sean?"

"He's my half brother. My mom had Sean when she was seventeen. One of those accidental one-night stand kind of pregnancies. When Sean was five, she married my father, and I came along a year later."

"Were you and your brother close?"

"Very close. There was six years between us, but he was my big brother from the first second he held me. At least that's what my parents told me. And I certainly don't remember a time when he wasn't there for me." He paused. "Actually, that's not true. There did come a time, but it was years later. Do you mind if we don't talk about Sean?"

"Of course not. Sorry if I was prying."

He shrugged. "It's fine. You said you used to vacation here with your grandparents. Are they still here?"

"Sadly, no. They both passed on—my grandfather about ten years ago, and my grandmother five years ago. I wish she could have seen me buy the inn. We used to walk by it when I'd visit, and I'd tell her one day it was going to be mine. Sometimes, I can hardly believe it is mine." Lizzie cleared her throat. "I think my nana would be happy that I ended up here. She loved Whisper Lake, and so do I."

"How did the lake get its name? Is there a story?"

"Of course there's a story," she said with a smile, as they reached the shore of the lake. She took a seat on a nearby bench and he sat down next to her, somewhat amazed by the vast body of water in front of him.

"I didn't realize the lake was so big," he commented.

"It takes almost an hour to drive all the way around it. It's very clean and very cold. It doesn't really warm up for swimming until July. But you asked about the story…"

"I did," he said, seeing the gleam in her gaze.

"Have you ever heard of the orphan trains?"

He shook his head. "No."

"The trains took homeless children from New York City to points across the Midwest and rural America, dropping them off to work on farms. This was in the late eighteen-hundreds until 1929. One of the trains broke down on the northern shore of the lake on its way to Denver. There wasn't much of a town then, just a bunch of farms."

He smiled at the passion in her voice. Clearly, this was a story she liked to tell.

"But that night," she continued, "the farmers heard the cries of the children on the broken-down train, and they went to rescue them. There were about thirty of them plus a few adults to run the train and chaperone. It was a long winter, and no one could get in or out of town. When spring came, and they were able to fix the train, the families at the lake wouldn't let the kids go. They were part of their families. And a town was born."

"That's a cool story."

"Yes. There's a little more."

"Go on."

"The kids said during their journey across the country that

every night they would whisper prayers for a new family, and that's where they came up with the name Whisper Lake. It was the place where they'd found their families. Ever since then, the lake has been known to be a refuge to all who are needy, who are lost, who are looking for something new. There's a summer camp on the eastern shore that my cousin remodeled and reopened, and it embodies the spirit of those kids. They bring in underprivileged children from all over the country for at least several months a year."

"Interesting. I thought you were going to say something about hearing whispers in the wind."

"Oh, sure, that is part of the lore. A couple of the kids didn't make it through that first winter, that's the sad part of the story, and sometimes at night, people swear they can hear their cries. When I was a teenager, I went to the lake one night to drink tequila sunrises, and I don't know if it was the tequila, or the ghost stories we were telling each other, but I definitely heard something on the wind."

"It was probably the tequila."

"You don't believe in ghosts?"

He hesitated. "No, but sometimes I wish I did. Unfortunately, my logical brain doesn't take me there."

"There's supposed to be a ghost at the inn."

"Really?"

"Yes, in room ten. Guests have reported odd things: the stirring of a curtain, a ticking clock, a rocking chair, footsteps in the night. I forced myself to sleep in there twice, and my imagination was working overtime. I didn't really hear anything, or I didn't want to admit I did."

"Then you did hear something?"

"Maybe. Or it could have been in my head."

He smiled, thinking that was the more likely scenario. Clearly, Lizzie had a big imagination. "Where is room ten? Is someone in it now?"

"No, it's in the attic. It's our least popular room, and I leave it open for emergencies, just in case I get a late booking, or someone can't get out of the area because of a snowstorm. It has low ceilings, so it's not comfortable for very tall people." She paused. "The previous owners of the inn told me that the ghost is alleged to be the daughter of the first couple who lived there. She died as a teenager. She was thrown from a horse, apparently. That was back in the nineteen-forties. That was her room."

"I'm surprised you don't have people who want to stay there just because there might be a ghost."

"We have had a few ghost hunters come by," she admitted. "The ghost was mentioned in an article about ghostly inns in a travel magazine about five years ago, and I've had two people stop in specifically to stay in that room, but they never heard anything."

"You can still use the story as a drawing card. It's legend, and who doesn't like a good legend?"

"Some people specifically ask not to stay in any room that might be haunted."

"People really ask you that?"

"Yes, all the time."

"I can't even imagine that question coming to my mind."

"I doubt you stay very often in small inns."

"That's true. I'm usually in very busy, populated cities."

"Well, hopefully your experience here will make you appreciate being in an inn that makes you feel like family and not just a business traveler."

He didn't know what being part of a family felt like. If he had known at one time, he'd forgotten, but he didn't want to get into that with her. "Tell me how you came to be the owner of an inn."

"Are you sure you want to know? I'm thinking it's probably time for me to stop talking."

If she stopped talking, he'd probably have to answer her

questions, and he'd rather not get into his personal history. "I'm always interested in origin stories for business owners."

"Well, all right. I wanted to run an inn since I was a little girl. Every pretend game in my childhood involved a hotel, and I was in charge. My friends would be the guests, or the other workers, but I was always running the place."

"How did you get from the dream to here?"

"I started working in hotels when I was fifteen as a maid. And since then, I've done every job. In addition to housekeeping, I've been a desk clerk, room service operator, laundry worker, concierge, banquet server. I've even parked cars for valet. I did eventually get a degree in hotel management, but in some ways, I think my practical experience has served me better."

"I'm impressed. A lot of managers don't want to start at the bottom and work their way up. They prefer to jump into the top spot right away."

"Because I started young, the bottom was the only place available to me. But working hard is something that has also been ingrained in me since I was a kid. Anyway, when the opportunity to buy the inn came up, I was lucky enough to have some family members willing to jump in. They knew how hard I had worked to get ready, and they wanted to invest in me."

"That's great, but it also adds pressure."

She nodded in agreement. "Unbelievable pressure. I can't let them down. It's not just my parents. All my siblings bought in, as well as some of my cousins. I can't fail."

"Do you think you will?"

Her lips tightened, and she clearly didn't like his question. "No. Why would you say that?"

"Because there's something in your voice, an edge of desperation."

She ran a hand through her hair, tucking it behind her ears as she looked out at the lake. "It's been a rough few weeks, but I'm not giving up. I'm too stubborn for that."

"You need stubbornness to build a company. I have plenty of that as well."

She turned her gaze back to him. "I noticed."

"And I have investors, too, not family, but people I don't want to let down."

"You know how I feel then."

"Yes. That's why I was so needy to get a computer today. I have a big presentation happening in London that I should have been going to, but I couldn't say no to my grandmother, so here I am."

"I heard you talking about that on the phone earlier. But don't you run a big company? Surely there are other people who can make the deal."

"I had a good person lined up, but she had a family emergency, so I'm going with someone smart but green. Hopefully, he'll come through. I tried to tell him everything he needs to know, but I'd rather be doing it myself."

"It's hard to let go of the reins when you have a lot on the line."

"And even when you don't, if you like to be in control."

"True," she said with a nod. "I like to excuse my need for control as a result of my dedication to my investors, but it's been around longer than I've had investors." She blew out a breath as her gaze returned to the lake. "But when I come down to the water, when I take a minute to just enjoy the moment, I'm reminded that I'm exactly where I want to be, problems and all."

"Do you take many minutes?" he asked doubtfully.

"Not many, but some. What about you?"

"Hardly any."

"How do you keep up the pace?" she asked, gazing back at him.

"I just never stop, so there's never a difference. I'm always on the run. It's my normal."

"You're not running now, Justin."

"I should be. I don't usually waste time like this."

"You're not wasting time. You're here by the water. Look around, breathe deep. The lake can be healing."

"I don't need healing."

She gave him a thoughtful look. "Are you sure about that?"

He frowned. "Why would you ask me that?" He couldn't help but repeat her earlier question to him.

"Because you're wound very tight, and when people are constantly on the run, I can't help wondering what they're running from."

"I'm not running from anything; I'm running toward my future."

"Okay, have it your way."

"It's the truth." He didn't know why he felt the need to convince her, especially since maybe it wasn't really the truth. He lifted his gaze to the sky. "I have to admit I haven't seen so many stars in a long time. I feel like I'm in one of those shows at the observatory where you sit back in your chair, they turn out the lights, and there are a multitude of stars and planets overhead."

"It does feel that way. But this is better, because it's real."

Was it real?

He felt like he was having an out-of-body experience, as if the bump on his head earlier had changed him into someone else—someone who wanted to walk with no real destination in mind, someone who wanted to share about his family and kiss the pretty woman next to him, when he knew better than to start something he couldn't finish.

On the other hand, he'd always been a man who went after what he wanted. And if he wanted her, and she wanted him… *Why should anyone say no?*

As he moved his gaze away from the sky to her face, she looked back at him, and something in her expression shifted. The gleam in her eyes grew wary.

"It would be a bad idea," she warned.

"Probably," he agreed.

"Unless we're not talking about the same thing?"

"I think we are."

"There's something…" she began.

"Between us," he finished.

"It's unexpected. And crazy. We don't know each other at all," she said.

"Sometimes it's better that way. It becomes very simple. Desire, want, need."

She swallowed hard. "It's never as simple as that. At least, not for me."

"Nothing has to happen."

"I know that."

Despite their agreement, neither one of them seemed able to look away, to break the connection. The air between them grew tense and filled with electricity. He felt an irresistible pull to Lizzie, and he didn't feel like fighting it, especially not when he could see the same hunger in her gaze. Just a kiss. *What was the harm?*

Before he could let an answer come to mind, he leaned forward, putting one hand behind her head as he pressed his mouth against hers. Her lips were sweet and hot, and they parted eagerly for his kiss. With her hunger matching his own, he angled his head and took the kiss deeper. It felt so easy, so familiar, so perfect… Which almost made him pull back, because perfect scared him. But she tasted too good, and he felt like he'd been needing this kind of a kiss for a long time.

Finally, Lizzie pulled away, stopping the madness. She gave him a breathless smile, her eyes lit up in the moonlight. "So… that happened."

"It turns out it was a good idea after all," he said.

"For now."

"Do we have to worry about any other time but now? You

just said I should take a minute once in a while. I was just following your advice."

"That wasn't what I had in mind. But it was…nice."

He didn't particularly care for the lukewarm adjective, but she was already on her feet.

"Are we leaving?" he asked, as he stood up.

"I need to get back to the inn. My minute is over."

"All right."

He followed her down the path, feeling awash in a swirling silence of emotions, unspoken words, and a conflicting desire to turn back time or just stop and kiss her again.

Maybe giving in to his desire hadn't been a good idea after all, because now he wanted more.

CHAPTER SIX

SHE SHOULD SAY SOMETHING, but she didn't know what to say. Lizzie dug her hands into the pockets of her jacket as she walked back to the inn with Justin. He didn't seem to know what to say, either, and quiet surrounded them as they made their way through the park. It was getting colder, too, or maybe it just felt that way with the new tension between them.

She'd never expected their walk to the lake to end in a fairly spectacular series of kisses. One minute they'd been chatting about family and work stuff, and the next minute they were tangled up in each other's arms.

Justin had kissed like he did everything else, with a confident, hungry impatience, and that hunger for her had ratcheted up her own desire. She hadn't felt so caught up in a man in a very long time, and the attraction had swept her away in a tidal wave of feeling.

Passion had not been part of her life this past year. The few dates she'd had, the couple of men she'd kissed, now seemed rather pale in comparison to Justin. Those kisses had been nice but not heart-stopping, and while she'd told Justin his kiss was nice, too, it was only because she hadn't been able to come up with a better word or a way to describe just how he'd made her feel.

Justin had woken something up inside her, and she really, really hoped she could get that something to go back to sleep, because this was the wrong man, the wrong time, the wrong place, the wrong everything…

At least she'd had the willpower to stop things from going any further. When they got back to the inn, Justin would go his way, and she would go hers. Their kiss would just be a memory of an impulsive, moonlight moment that would never be repeated. Maybe Justin was a world-class kisser, but he would never be part of her world. While a fling could be fun, she didn't have time for that, and deep in her heart she knew that she wasn't really a fling kind of girl. Although, maybe she should be. She worked hard. She deserved some fun, too.

Not that kind of fun, she told herself, wishing her brain and her body weren't suddenly at war. That wouldn't be helpful. She needed to focus on her work, on her dream. Getting distracted now could be a disaster.

As they walked up the steps to the inn, Justin suddenly broke the silence.

"Do you want me to apologize, Lizzie?"

She paused in front of the door, looking him straight in the eye for the first time. "No. It was just a kiss, a really good kiss," she found herself admitting.

"I thought so, too. And I like *really good* better than *nice*, which is what you said before."

"I might have been trying to downplay it," she admitted. "The thing is, Justin, I'm not interested in a one-night stand, and that's all this could be."

"I am here for five nights," he said lightly. "We could have a lot of fun in five nights. And I think you challenged me to fun earlier."

"That was for karaoke, and while you did rise to my challenge, I can't take it any further. I have so much work on my plate right now. I'm juggling a lot of balls in the air. You, of all people, should be able to understand that."

"I do understand. I've actually said the very same thing."

"You're on vacation, but I'm not. I have a lot at stake, and this is a big week for the inn."

"Then I'll try not to distract you."

She had a feeling just his presence at the inn would be enough to distract her, but she wasn't going to tell him that.

"Before I say good night…" he began.

A shiver ran down her spine as she thought he might steal another kiss. *While she should push him away, would she?*

"Do you know where I can get a computer and phone tomorrow?"

His very practical question brought her down to earth, but she couldn't stop the unexpected shiver of disappointment that ran through her. "Yes. You can find just about every mobile phone retailer on Adams Street, as well as a computer store. It's six blocks away. You just head back toward Micky's but turn right on Valmont and left on Adams. Do you want me to write it down?"

"I've got it. Thanks."

He opened the door for her, and she stepped into the lobby. Shay wasn't at the desk, but she could see her manager talking to one of the guests in the living room.

"Do you need anything else tonight?" It was a question she often asked her guests, but now it seemed to take on a lot more meaning, and she could feel her cheeks growing warm.

He gave her an amused smile. Apparently, she was a little too easy to read.

"I better say no," he told her. "Because I don't want to distract you."

"I was talking about bottled water or a mint, maybe a newspaper?"

"I'm fine. I might try that book by my bed."

"I hope you enjoy it." She drew in a breath, wondering why it was so difficult to turn away. But that's what she needed to do. "Have a good night, Justin."

"You, too, Lizzie."

She forced herself to move. She walked around the desk and then through the door to her office. When she was finally alone, she let out a breath, feeling more unsettled than she had in a long time. But she'd done it. She'd walked away. She'd said no. That was the end of it.

Maybe…unless she changed her mind. Five nights of fun was rather tempting.

A knock came at her half-open door, and she jumped. It wasn't Justin; it was Shay.

"How was your night?" Shay asked, as she stepped into the room.

"Good. Everything quiet around here?"

"Yes, no problems. I've confirmed all the details for tomorrow. Naomi will be in the kitchen at six a.m. as per her usual shift. She'll take a three-hour break between eleven and two and then she'll work from two to six to provide food for the cocktail party. Karen will be working the same morning shift but will come in from four to eight to cover serving and cleanup. Victor will cover the desk from noon to four thirty and then will take over as a bartender during the event. He'll also stay until eight to help with cleanup." Shay looked down at the electronic tablet in her hand. "Sharilyn and Margarita will be on cleaning tomorrow. They'll be working from ten until three on guest rooms and the common areas." She glanced back at Lizzie. "I think that's it."

"Thank you for being so organized. I feel like I've just been putting out fires lately."

"Well, I am sorry about earlier with Patty and Noah and the police. That shouldn't have happened."

"I spoke to Victor. He knows he's on thin ice. He said his girlfriend is pregnant."

"Is that why he's been so rattled? That makes sense."

"I couldn't fire him."

Shay gave her a knowing look. "I figured, but he needs to do better."

"I hope he will."

"Anyway, I'll be leaving early in the morning, but if you have any questions, you can call me, not that you can't run this place better than anyone else here." Shay gave her a guilty look. "I feel bad leaving you with the party and an inn full of guests."

It wasn't the best timing, but Shay worked hard, too. "Don't worry about it. Enjoy the time with Kyle and his parents. That's important, too."

"I hope they don't hate me."

"They won't hate you. They'll love you. You're always a big hit with the guests. I don't think they'll be any different."

"It's just that Kyle is their only child. And I think they're going to be pretty picky when it comes to who's marrying him."

"It doesn't matter what they think, only what you and Kyle think."

"I really love him, Lizzie," Shay confessed. "I never thought I'd feel this way. I couldn't imagine it happening. I had so many bad dates for so long. I figured I'd just eventually have to settle for someone who was all right. But Kyle is so much more than that. Sometimes, I feel like I should pinch myself in case I'm dreaming."

"It's all real," she said, feeling a little jealous. This past year for her had definitely been the bad date stage, not that there had been that many dates.

"So, was everyone at Adam's party?" Shay asked.

"Everyone but Hannah. She was working."

"Is your brother dating anyone?"

"Not that he's told me, but he keeps that kind of information to himself."

"He's so good-looking. I can't tell you how many of my friends have their eyes on him. But he doesn't seem to hit the single spots up much."

She shrugged. "Like I said, I have no idea…"

"You know who else is good-looking? Justin Blackwood."

"He is attractive," she agreed, trying not to let on just how handsome she found their guest.

"He was looking for somewhere to eat earlier."

"He made his way to Micky's."

"Oh, you saw him then?"

"Yes. I actually asked him to join us. I hated seeing him eating alone."

"That's interesting. What's he like when he's not in work mode?"

"He's more charming than I first thought," she admitted. "When we first met, he was so upset about his phone and his computer, he couldn't think about anything else. But, apparently, he's gotten over not being tethered to his electronics, at least until tomorrow when he can replace them."

"Is he single?"

"I think so." She realized she didn't really know Justin's status, although hopefully he wouldn't have kissed her the way he had if he was dating someone.

"Maybe you should get better acquainted," Shay said with a wicked glint in her eyes.

"He's leaving on Sunday. I don't think we need to get any closer."

"That's almost a week from now. A lot can happen."

"I don't want anything to happen. I'm busy."

"You need to make time for a relationship, Lizzie."

"Maybe, but I don't need to make time for a man who's

leaving in a few days. And now, I really need to focus on some paperwork. I have bills waiting to be paid."

"All right. I'll leave you to it."

As Shay left, Lizzie drew in a breath. As she did so, she thought she smelled traces of Justin's cologne. Or maybe that was just her imagination. Perhaps Shay was right, and she did need to get out more and not just with her girlfriends and family members. She was a little lonely. That's why she'd gotten so swept up in Justin.

But if she was going to date someone, it would be a man who lived in Whisper Lake, not someone who was just passing through her life. She'd gotten involved once before with a man who had been going in a completely different direction, and it had almost ruined her dream. She wouldn't make that mistake again.

―――――――

Justin woke up sweating. The sun was streaming through his window, but it was only eight, and it shouldn't be so hot. *Did he have a fever?*

He rolled out of bed and stood up, feeling a blast of heat coming from the vent. He walked over to the thermostat. It was set for heat to come on at sixty-five degrees, but the room temp was up to ninety-seven. *What the hell?*

He pulled on his jeans and a T-shirt, slipped his feet into sneakers and grabbed his key. When he got downstairs, he saw a group of guests surrounding the front desk with Lizzie in the middle. She looked frazzled but shockingly pretty in a pair of white cut-off shorts that showed off her legs and a pink tank top that clung to her curves. Her hair was pulled into a high ponytail, and her cheeks were bright red. She had beads of sweat on her brow, which he suspected were coming not just from the heat but the pressure of the group.

Lizzie put up a hand, calling for quiet. "If you all stop talking at once, I can answer your questions. I just got off the phone with the furnace guy. He'll be out very soon. Something is clearly wrong with the heat, but we will get it fixed as soon as possible. In the meantime, we're going to serve breakfast in the dining room. The windows and the French doors are open, so it's a lot cooler in there."

"What are you going to do if they can't fix it?" a man asked, his tone annoyed and frustrated. "We can't stay here if it's going to be like this. Can you set us up somewhere else?"

"I'm sorry, but all the hotels are full this week for the eclipse," Lizzie explained. "But I don't want you to worry. We will get this fixed, and I will comp all your rooms for a night."

"Well, all right," the man said, his tension a bit eased by her words, but he was still not happy. "However, if it's not fixed by this afternoon, we might have to leave."

"Let's not worry about that now," she said. "Please get yourselves coffee and tea and order breakfast," Lizzie urged. "And don't forget, we'll be having our weekly happy hour cocktail party this afternoon, starting at four o'clock."

As the group moved into the dining room, he stepped forward, and Lizzie gave him a tense smile.

"Did you hear?" she asked.

"Yes. I figured the heat was broken when it was over ninety in my room."

"I don't suppose you know anything about furnaces."

He hated to dash the hopeful gleam in her eyes, but handyman repairs were not his area of expertise. "Unfortunately, no, I can't fix your furnace. But I do know something about business. Why are you offering everyone a free night?"

"Because they're inconvenienced. It's called goodwill."

"It's called being too nice. And you offered to comp that woman yesterday her entire stay because she was bothered by the old man standing outside her door."

"She was also inconvenienced and upset."

He tipped his head toward that very same woman who was laughing with Noah in the adjacent dining room. "She seems pretty good now."

"Well, she's happier because she knows I took care of her. And the others will be happier, too."

"And you will go broke making everyone happy."

She frowned. "Look, I'm doing what I have to do."

"Actually, there are other things you could have done. You could have offered everyone a free batch of cookies or some of that homemade jam you're selling. You could have offered a percentage discount." He could see by the expression on her face that she was not thrilled with his suggestions, and he should stop talking, because it was really none of his business. On the other hand, she'd expressed to him how hard she was working, and implied she was on shaky financial ground. *If he could help her, shouldn't he try?*

"In the hospitality business, making the guest happy is the number-one priority," she argued. "If I lose in the short-term, I gain in the long-term."

"I agree with that in principle, as long as you have enough cash to survive until you get to the long-term. But if you don't, then you have to stop giving away the entire store without even being asked."

She stared back at him. "I was afraid they were all going to check out. Better to lose one day than the whole week."

"Where would they go? Every hotel in town is booked. You just said so. Although, I'm not sure why the lunar eclipse is such a big draw, but everyone seems to be talking about it."

"You get a great view of the eclipse from here. Anyway, it's done. I offered the comps; I can't take them back. And I will comp your room, too."

"No, you won't."

"I want to treat everyone the same."

"I can afford to pay for the room, heat or no heat. And you don't have to take my advice. I was just trying to help."

"I appreciate that, and maybe I was too impulsive with the offer, but I felt cornered and I'm a bit of a people pleaser."

"A bit?" he queried.

She gave him a wry smile as she threw up her hands. "Fine. I'm a big people pleaser. I like people to be happy."

"And you want them to like you."

"It's more that I want them to like the inn."

"Which is an extension of you."

Her brows drew together. "Are you saying all this is because I have some desperate need to be liked?"

"Do you?"

"No. I'm already well-liked."

"Because…"

"Because I'm a nice person, and I'm a good friend." She tilted her head as she gave him a thoughtful look. "And besides analyzing me, maybe you should look in the mirror. Try a little harder to be liked."

"I don't really care if anyone likes me," he said, although deep down he was beginning to think he did care about one person liking him, and that was her.

"That's probably good, since you're not always that nice."

"I can be nice."

"Yes, and you can be fun. But as I said last night, just because you can be something doesn't mean you are. If you have to think about being nice or being fun, that implies you're not really either of those two things, or at least, it doesn't come naturally."

"Ouch," he said. "Maybe you're not as nice as I thought."

She instantly looked regretful and apologetic. "I'm sorry. It's been a rough start to the day. I didn't mean to insult you."

"You were just being honest."

"I was being stupid, because you're my guest."

"Who was getting in your business without being asked."

She met his gaze. "Well, that is true. At any rate, you should get some breakfast. You can pick from three entrees and several sides, or if you don't want anything cooked, there's yogurt and granola, fresh fruit, croissants. Breakfast is included in your stay." She suddenly frowned. "I'm sure you don't think that's a great idea, either."

"Whether it should be included in the stay depends on how rich you are."

"Not very. I've considered cutting back on the menu, but if I do, it will be difficult to keep Naomi. She's my chef, and she only came on board because I promised her a longer-term plan of offering dinner as well as breakfast, turning the dining room into a restaurant that the locals can enjoy all year long. Naomi is a fabulous cook and she's been happy enough with part-time because she has a daughter in high school, but next year her daughter goes off to college, and then she wants a full-time job. I don't want the other restaurants in town to steal her away." She brushed a tangled strand of hair off her forehead. "Anyway, those are all problems for another day. Right now, I need to open more windows."

"I'll help you."

"That's not necessary. You should eat."

"I'll let the crowd die down," he said, noting that most of the tables were taken.

"All right," she said, heading into the living room.

They made their way through the inn, opening every window and door and then moved upstairs to the guest rooms. Things slowed down as Lizzie stopped to explain to various guests the problem with the furnace and asked them to open their windows. He didn't really know why he was still following her around. He had other things to do. He needed to get dressed, go into town, and get himself a phone and a computer. Then he needed to work. But as they made their way up the stairs to the attic, he was reminded of her story from the night before.

"Is this the ghost room?" he asked, as she used her key to open the door to the only room on the fourth floor.

"Yes, but I don't think you'll see anyone." She stepped into the room and walked over to the window.

It was even hotter in this attic room tucked under the eaves. As Lizzie struggled with the window, he moved across the room to help her. They were both sweating even more by the time they got the rusty latch to move. As cooler air filled the room, he drew in a grateful breath. "That's better."

"I'll say," she agreed.

As he glanced around the room, he saw that it was decorated as attractively as all the others. There was a colorful quilt on the end of the double bed, a vase of fake flowers on the desk as well as a couple of shelves of books. There was a rocking chair across from the bed, adjacent to the window, and it moved gently back and forth with the breeze, or so he hoped.

Lizzie followed his gaze. "It's just the wind. No one is rocking."

"Are you sure?"

She put her hand on the chair and stopped the motion. Then she sat down in it. "Satisfied?"

He perched on the edge of the bed. "Hopefully, you didn't squish the ghost," he said with a grin.

"You don't believe in ghosts. Although…" She paused, giving him a speculative look. "You said something last night about maybe wanting to believe—"

"I don't remember saying that," he lied.

"Well, you said something. What did you mean?"

"I don't remember. But speaking of ghosts, tell me about Noah."

"Noah and ghosts don't go together."

"Are you sure? Isn't he roaming the inn, looking for some long-lost love?"

"She's not a ghost. She just left."

"What's his story? I saw him late last night from my window. He was out in the yard, wandering through the garden. He kept checking his watch and looking back toward the inn, to a particular room."

"The room he shared with Alice, it's on the floor below us. He'll be moving in there today after Patty leaves."

"Because he's expecting this woman named Alice to come back?"

"Yes. But I doubt that will ever happen."

"Why not?"

"It has been ten years, for one thing." She paused. "You really want to hear the story?"

"I do."

"Okay, here goes. Ten years ago, Noah and Alice stayed in room six this same week in April. Noah had come to the lake to heal. He'd spent the past year grieving the loss of his wife, and he needed to start over. His friend told him about the inn and he came here for a week. The second night he was here, there was a lunar eclipse, and he and the other guests went down to the beach. He ended up sharing a picnic blanket with Alice, who was staying in room six. They drank too much wine and during the darkness of the eclipse, they shared a forbidden kiss."

"Why was it forbidden? Wait, let me guess. She was married."

"Yes. Alice was married and living in Paris with her husband. But she came to a work conference in Denver and then afterward came up to the lake to vacation. She was deciding what to do with her life and whether or not she would stay married, since she was very unhappy with her husband. At least, that's what Noah told me."

"Not an unfamiliar explanation for an affair," he said dryly.

"Good point. Anyway, they fell hard for each other that week. Alice kept extending her stay and so did Noah. They couldn't bear to part. But then tragedy struck. Alice got word that her husband had been in an accident, and she needed to return to Paris. She told Noah she had to leave, but that one day they'd see each other again. She didn't know when, but she would come back to this magical place where she'd discovered real love and happiness for the first time. Noah said he was devastated when she left, but he understood her duty to her husband. They agreed not to speak again until she could come back, until she could leave her husband. Every year since then, during the second week in April, Noah comes back to the inn, hoping that this will be the year when Alice comes back."

He shook his head. "She's not coming back, not after all this time."

"I don't think so, either, but Noah hasn't given up."

"If he wants her so badly, why doesn't he go to Paris and tell her he's still waiting for her?"

"I don't think he knows where she is."

"He could hire someone to find her."

"He's in his seventies."

"Which means he doesn't have a lot of time to waste. He's already blown ten years."

She gave a helpless shrug. "He's a romantic. Alice said she'd come back. He thinks eventually she will."

"She could be dead. He could be waiting forever. That seems more tragic than romantic."

"It would be romantic if she came back."

"But she probably won't. And why is it just her choice?" he argued. "Why doesn't Noah get a say?"

"I don't know. I'm not really disagreeing with you, Justin."

"So you wouldn't spend ten years waiting for a guy."

"No. I don't think I'd spend ten minutes right about now."

"Ruthless," he said with a grin.

"You can't count on another person for your happiness. It doesn't work that way. You have to go out and grab what you want. Waiting seems so passive."

"I completely agree. If I wanted a woman like Noah wants Alice, I'd go get her. I'd fight for her."

"I've always wondered if Alice wasn't waiting for him to do that. But Noah seems to feel some guilt about their affair, and he believes it has to be her decision. He can't try to persuade her. But meanwhile, the clock is ticking, and Noah spends a week here every year wandering around the inn. There was a period when the inn was closed. It was locked down for almost a year before I bought it. Noah said he went crazy during that time. He used to come and sleep in his car."

"The man is crazy."

"He acknowledges that. He said love makes him insane," she said with a soft smile. "It is pretty sweet. I can't imagine being loved like that."

"I can't imagine loving anyone like that. It seems too one-sided. Needing anyone that much makes a person weak and vulnerable and desperate. Who wants to live like that?"

"Apparently, neither one of us. But it's Noah's life. He gets to do what he wants with it."

"Have you ever tried to persuade him to let her go?"

"No. It's his choice."

"I thought you wanted your guests to be happy."

"I do, but I don't meddle in their lives."

"You don't?" he asked doubtfully.

"Well, sometimes I do," she admitted. "But not in something like this. And what would I even say?" She shook her head. "It's up to him if he wants to come here every year, and I'm happy to have him. He's a lonely old man. Even if Alice doesn't show up, he gets to be in a place that brought him joy a long time ago."

"It's not enough."

"I don't think Noah wants as much for himself as you want for yourself."

"He should. Everyone should. Why settle? Why not go for what you want? That's what you're doing. That's what I'm doing. Maybe with a little encouragement, Noah would do the same."

"If you want to encourage him, feel free."

"Maybe I will."

"And that wouldn't distract you from your work?"

"Fair point." Her words made him realize how much time he'd wasted on this conversation.

"I'm surprised you're so interested in Noah," she continued. "I thought your only waking thought would be on getting a new phone and computer."

"That's at the top of the list, but I doubt the stores open before nine."

"True, but you still seem awfully caught up in Noah's story."

"Maybe I just wanted to keep you here a little longer."

Her gaze widened. "Why would you want that?"

"I like talking to you," he said simply. "Actually, I liked kissing you even more."

Her lips parted, as wariness filled her gaze. "That's direct."

"That's who I am."

"I told you last night, I'm not interested in a hookup. And I can't imagine that I'm the kind of woman you usually date."

"I have to admit you're the first innkeeper I've ever kissed."

She smiled. "And you're the first robot maker I've ever kissed. But it's not happening again."

"What happened to turning my obligation into a vacation and making sure I have a fantastic time in Whisper Lake?"

"I'd be happy to introduce you to my single friends, some of whom might find a fling more interesting than I do."

"But I don't want them. I want you. And I think you feel the same way about me. Those kisses were not one-sided. There's an attraction between us. It might not make sense, but it's there."

"That doesn't mean we have to act on it."

"Or we could and make ourselves happy."

"For a few nights? No. Not interested. I'm a relationship kind of woman, Justin. I could try to pretend otherwise, but I'd be lying."

He felt incredibly disappointed to hear that, not that he was particularly surprised. "I'm definitely not a relationship kind of man."

"Have you ever been in love?"

"No."

"But you must have been involved with someone," she pressed.

"I have on occasion dated for a few months or so at a time. The last woman I spent real time with was probably two or three years ago." He frowned, thinking maybe it was even longer than that. But he didn't care. He wasn't lonely. He wasn't unhappy with his life.

"What happened to her?" Lizzie asked.

"Nothing specific. Our schedules stopped meshing up, and too many cancellations led to the end of whatever it was. We just stopped talking."

"You both stopped talking, or you did?"

"Actually, I think it was mutual."

"You think? It probably wasn't. That's a lie men tell themselves to feel better about disappearing on a woman."

"I didn't disappear. We kept trying to set something up, and it didn't happen, and we decided to get in touch if we were ever both free, and that's where we left it. What about you? When was your last relationship?"

"Two years and ten months ago."

"That's rather specific," he said, curious about the shadows moving through her eyes.

"I remember specifically because we broke up when I decided to buy the inn."

"What happened? He didn't want to move to Whisper Lake?"

"That was one reason. But it was more than that. We met when I was working at a hotel in Denver. He actually became my manager when he transferred in from Los Angeles. We never should have started anything because he was only going to be there for three months and then he'd be taking a permanent position in New York. But I decided not to think about that. And as the time passed, and he suggested I move to New York with him, I thought maybe I would. But then I found out the inn was for sale, and I realized I could have my dream."

"But you couldn't have him, too."

She shook her head. "No. There was nothing for him here. He had much bigger dreams. He tried to talk me out of buying the inn. He showed me all the ways I was going to fail. It was a little hard to take. I suppose he was trying to give me good advice."

He winced, thinking he'd been trying to give her similar unwanted advice only a short while ago.

"But," she added, "I didn't want to hear all the reasons why I couldn't do it. I wanted to hear why I could. But he didn't believe in me. Anyway, he went to New York, and I came here. I think we're both happier. But sometimes I still hear his voice in my head, all the doubts he raised, especially when things like the furnace break, and I wonder if he was a little bit right." She shrugged, then got to her feet. "Anyway, that's my story, and I should get back to work. I can't fix the heat, but I have other things to do." She paused. "I learned my lesson, Justin. I don't start things that can't be finished, not anymore."

He slowly nodded, then stood up. "I get it. Too bad."

"I'm sure you'll survive."

He met her gaze and smiled. "I'll survive, but I'm still sorry."

"I don't think I've ever met anyone as direct as you."

"I don't play games. That's why I could never be like Noah. I would have hunted Alice down and told her how I felt and then I would have known. I would have moved on."

"Maybe Noah can't handle the truth as well as you can. Some people have softer hearts."

"I can't argue with that. My heart hardened a long time ago."

Curiosity ran through her gaze. "I've been telling you a lot of stories, but one of these days, you're going to have to tell me at least one of yours."

"I'm not that interesting."

"I doubt that. But I need to get a shower and then go downstairs."

Thinking about Lizzie in the shower made him realize that he needed a shower, too, and that it needed to be cold. Because talking to her had only made him want her more.

She flushed a little as their gazes met. "Don't picture me in the shower," she warned.

"Too late," he said with a grin, as he headed down the stairs behind her. They might want different things, but they also wanted each other. And he wasn't ready to give up on making that happen.

CHAPTER SEVEN

LIZZIE HAD trouble not picturing Justin in the shower. He'd looked hot in jeans and a T-shirt with his wavy brown hair, broad shoulders, and extremely fit body. She couldn't imagine there was an ounce of fat on him. He liked to be in control of every situation, and she suspected that covered diet and fitness as well.

She didn't know why she was so attracted to him. His cockiness should be irritating. His directness should be unappealing. His devotion to his job and his electronics should be a red flag that he was not the man for her. But then she thought about the way he'd kissed her with passion and purpose and almost deliberate restraint as if he were afraid to release the floodgates.

She shared that fear. Just kissing him had made her lose track of where she was, who she was, what she was doing. Having sex with him would be an off-the-charts distraction.

It would probably be amazing, and it had been a long time since she'd experienced amazing, but then it would be over. And she had enough self-awareness to know that she probably wouldn't handle that well. So she turned the water temperature to cold and was shivering by the time she stepped out of the shower. But it took only a few moments of the inn's rebellious heating system to put her back in the hot zone.

She slipped into a summer dress and sandals, grabbed a sweater for when she went outside, and then headed downstairs. The furnace guy said he'd be there at one, which was still two hours away. After checking on the guests, making sure that Victor would be able to man the front desk, and would be able to let in the repairman if she ran late, she left the inn and slid behind the wheel of her Prius.

She needed to pick up a few items for the cocktail party, and she also wanted to check in with Chloe at the Blue Sky Café. She hadn't liked what she'd seen the night before, and Chloe had not returned any of her texts. She decided to stop there first, then run to the market after that.

When she got to the café, she was surprised to see Adam sitting at one end of the counter. talking to Chloe. They appeared to be having a rather serious, intense conversation, which made her pause. *Was there something going on between them?*

She was almost hesitant to interrupt, but then Chloe looked up and saw her. She gave her an odd, surprised look, then forced a smile onto her face and waved her over.

"Hey there," Chloe said. "I get two Coles for the price of one."

"And now you have one. I need to get back to work," Adam said quickly, sliding off his stool. "Everything good with you, Lizzie?"

"Yes. I'm having my cocktail party tonight. Can you make it?"

"I doubt it. I'm working on a series of break-ins on the west shore. So far, they've all been empty houses, but I'm concerned at the frequency and escalation."

"That's disturbing."

"That's why I need to catch whoever is doing it," he said shortly.

She wondered if it was the break-ins that were making him tense or whatever he and Chloe had been talking about.

"Also," Adam said, pausing. "I spoke to Nathan this morning. He got into a motorcycle accident in New Zealand."

"What? Is he all right?"

"He's fine. But he needed some cash, so I wired him some money. He told me not to tell anyone, but that's not how it works in our family. Honesty is always best." Adam's pointed look swung to Chloe, then returned to Lizzie. "Don't worry about him. He's okay."

"I'll see if I can get a hold of him later," she said. "Did you tell Mom and Dad?"

"Not yet, but I will. I'll see you later."

As Adam left, Lizzie took the seat he'd just vacated, pushing his barely drunk coffee cup to the side as Chloe set down a new one for her.

"Do you want something to eat?" Chloe asked.

"Coffee is fine."

"I'm surprised you have time for coffee. You're usually extremely busy on happy hour days."

"I'm going to the store after this to pick up a few things. It was a good excuse to get out of the inn. I'm also having a tremendously bad heating problem. The furnace broke and the inn is up to about a hundred degrees inside. It's unlivable. Most of the guests have gone to the beach, or somewhere else in town for now, but if I don't get it fixed before this afternoon, my party may be a complete bust. Beyond that, guests will probably start leaving."

Chloe shook her head. "It's been one problem after another for you this month."

"I know. I'm in a bad patch."

"Is there anything I can do?"

"No, but thanks." She looked around. "It's not too crowded in here."

"Not yet. The lunch rush starts around eleven thirty." Chloe pulled out her phone and then smiled. "Look, Leo is crawling all around." She turned the phone around so Lizzie could see the video.

"So cute. He's getting big."

"I know. I miss him so much when I'm at work, but it is what it is." Her smile dimmed, as she put her phone into her pocket. "I'm lucky that Kevin's parents are here for a few months. They love to watch Leo."

"Does Kevin love to watch him?" she couldn't help asking.

"Yes. Kevin is great with him. He adores Leo. He just…" Her voice fell off. "I'm sorry, Lizzie. I don't want to talk about Kevin."

"Is that what you were talking about with Adam? Because you both looked tense."

Chloe hesitated, her gaze swinging around the half-empty restaurant, as if to make sure no one could hear them. "We were talking about Kevin."

"What's going on? Or would you rather not say?"

"We're having problems."

"I'm sorry. I had hoped things were getting better."

"They're getting worse." Chloe drew in a breath. "I saw a text on his phone, Lizzie. I think there might be another woman."

Shock ran through her. "Are you sure?"

"No, I'm not sure. But something is going on, and he won't talk about it."

"Did you ask him about the text?"

"Not yet. Adam thinks I should confront him. But Kevin has had a hard year since he was captured and injured and sent home to recover. He's not himself. I don't know if I will push him into a conversation I don't really want to have." She paused. "I have a son to consider. I can't break up this family over a stupid text."

"You know how much I hate admitting that Adam is always right, but he's right. You have to talk to Kevin."

"What if he's having an affair? What if he wants to leave? What if he gets so angry, he just flips out?"

"Is that a possibility? Are you scared of Kevin?"

"No. That's not what I meant. He would never hurt me, but his temper is much sharper than it used to be, and his words hurt. I sometimes feel like he's trying to drive me away. If we break up, he can go back to the army when he clears medical and not feel guilty about it. That's what he really wants. I asked him to get out, but he can't quite commit to doing that. He misses his team. He doesn't feel like he has a life here."

"He has you and Leo and his parents and this diner."

"He hates the diner. His parents always wanted him to run it, but he never wanted to. He asked me if I'd move somewhere else with him. I said I'd consider it, but we'd have to figure out what we would do for jobs. Sorry. I shouldn't be dumping all this on you. You have your own problems."

"That doesn't mean I can't care about you. I think you have to find out what's really going on with Kevin, even if it hurts."

"It's so easy to say that, but you don't have a child."

"That's a good point. I'm not in your shoes, and I don't know how you feel. But I have been in a relationship that wasn't honest, and it never ends well. If he is having an affair, you need to deal with it, and if he's not, then you can move past that idea and work on the rest."

"You're right. I just have to decide if I can do it. You Coles are pretty smart."

"Adam is definitely smarter than me, but I have my moments."

"I don't know why you'd say that, Lizzie. Sometimes you don't give yourself enough credit."

She shrugged. "I had to follow in the footsteps of four siblings who were much more brilliant than me. Even Chelsea, who only ever wanted to sing, got through school with much better grades. I have street smarts, but not book smarts."

"Sometimes that's more important."

She took a sip of coffee. "I think you should come to my party tonight. Leave Kevin at home if he doesn't want to participate. Keira will be there—Hannah, too. I'm going to make margaritas."

"I do love a good margarita. I'll see. If I get the courage up, I may ask Kevin to take a walk with me and see if we can figure things out."

"Whatever is best," she said. "I better get back to the inn. Call me anytime, if you need to talk, or text me. I'm here for you."

"You're very generous, Lizzie."

"And you're my friend. That's what friends do."

"Speaking of friends, that man you were with last night... very handsome."

She saw the gleam in Chloe's eyes. "Yes, Justin is attractive. No doubt about that."

"And..."

"Nothing. He's a guest. He's leaving soon. Enough said."

"Not nearly enough," Chloe said with a laugh. "You looked at him last night like he was a big juicy steak, and you wouldn't mind taking a bite."

Guilt warmed her cheeks. "I was not that bad."

"You were, especially when he started acting like a rock star on stage."

"That did surprise me. When I first met him, he was in a suit and tie. I did not think he had an inner rock star inside him. But, like I said, he's only here for a few days, and I don't have time for men. They're always distracting. I have bigger plans for my life."

"A man doesn't have to get in the way." Chloe paused. "Okay, I have to admit they often get in the way, but sometimes that's a good thing. You don't want your life to be only about work."

"It's what I do best." She stood up. "I'll see you later. And, Chloe, whatever you decide to do, you have my support."

"Thanks. Don't say anything to anyone else."

"I won't. And I know Adam won't either."

"No, he wouldn't. He's such a good man, Lizzie. I don't know why he's still single."

"I guess he hasn't found the right person." As she left the café, she couldn't help thinking that Adam might have found the right person for him, but she was already taken. And no matter what happened with Chloe and Kevin, their relationship was not going to end any time soon. They had a baby together. Chloe would fight hard to make her marriage work.

Maybe she should find someone to introduce Adam to, get him looking in another direction. She really wanted him to be happy.

She smiled to herself at that thought. She was a people pleaser. Well, it wasn't the worst thing in the world. She just had to remember that she couldn't solve everyone's problems. However, it was a lot easier worrying about their problems than her own.

After picking up a new laptop computer and a phone, Justin spent several hours at Harvey's Coffee, which had a great selection of coffee and tea as well as sandwiches, salads, wraps and pastries, as well as a dozen tables at which to work. Apparently, he wasn't the only one in Whisper Lake who also needed to be on a computer.

It was a lot cooler at the coffeehouse, and he felt better after downing a couple cups of coffee and getting some work done. He'd sent Anthony more information to study before the presentation, trying to make it as easy as possible for him to do the pitch without any mistakes.

He'd also gone through most of his emails and taken care of the more pressing questions, some of which pertained to his upcoming trips to Tokyo and Melbourne.

Normally, he got a buzz of excitement thinking about the next trip, the next deal, the next step forward in his drive to take his company as high as he possibly could, but he felt more removed from his business here in Whisper Lake. The frenetic energy, the relentless drive that usually accompanied his workdays seemed to be diminished. He couldn't concentrate. He was constantly being distracted by people coming in and out of the café. And that was unusual, too, because he could usually tune everything and everyone out. He'd always prided himself on his tunnel vision. While some people saw it as a negative trait, it also had a flip side: he could get work done no matter where he was or what was happening around him.

But not today. His mind kept drifting back to Lizzie, to all the random things they'd talked about: Noah and the missing Alice, the ghost in room ten, and Lizzie's break-up story. He'd seen pain in her gaze when she'd spoken about the man who had refused to follow her to Whisper Lake. Although, he didn't think it was that decision that had bothered her. Her boyfriend hadn't believed in her abilities and that had stung.

He couldn't totally relate. He hadn't ever considered what anyone else thought about his skills. He'd grown up having to be independent. He had never been surrounded by a lovely family of cheerleaders, ready to applaud his every effort, regardless of the actual achievement. But Lizzie had grown up differently. She was close to her parents and her siblings, and it seemed that she had a lot of family support. But she also cared too much about what people thought of her. He wondered where that insecurity came from, especially since she did have support. There was something that he didn't know about.

Not that he needed to know. She'd made it clear she wasn't interested in a hookup, and that's really all he had to offer. He needed to back off; he just wasn't sure he could actually do that. He hadn't been this interested in a woman in he couldn't remember when...

He turned his head as a man approached his table. It was Brodie, wearing his police uniform. He had a coffee in his hand.

"Hey," Brodie said with a nod. "Am I interrupting?"

"Not at all. Have a seat." He pushed out the chair next to him. "You must be on a break."

"Yep. And Harvey has the best coffee in town."

"Everything is good here. I've been sampling."

Brodie grinned. "I've had everything, too, but I'm saving room for what Lizzie is serving up tonight."

"I heard something about margaritas and chips and guacamole," he said.

"Great. I love Lizzie's margarita parties." Brodie sipped his coffee. "When do your grandparents get in?"

"Tonight. Their flight got canceled yesterday, so they had to wait to get on another one."

"That's a drag. I met them when they were here in February. Great couple."

"They seemed to have met a lot of people in this town."

"Well, Lizzie likes to merge the guests at the inn with the locals. She thinks it enhances their stay if they feel a part of the town. So, Chelsea and I get a lot of invitations to the inn. I can't complain. Lizzie always puts on a good party."

"She certainly works hard at treating her guests well and giving them a first-class, personal experience."

"Chelsea said Lizzie was always like that. Even as a kid, she'd bring home strays—not cats or dogs—but other children who were not quite fitting in. If someone was getting bullied, they were getting an invitation to the Cole house for a family dinner. Chelsea told me that it was the odd night that Lizzie didn't have someone in the chair next to her who she was trying to make feel better about something."

He could totally see her doing that. She seemed to feel a need to make sure everyone was feeling included and happy. It was a very sweet trait. Damn! He needed to find things *not* to like about her. "It's good her parents went along with that. You'd think with five kids, they wouldn't enjoy having an extra child for dinner."

"They were cool. They always have room for one more. Lizzie's dad is one of the friendliest guys you'll ever meet. And he has the heartiest handshake. First time we met, I thought he was testing me to see if I was strong enough to take on his hand-shake and his daughter."

Justin grinned. "Apparently, you passed the test."

"Without a wince. But, honestly, I think as long as I was putting a smile on Chelsea's face, they were okay with me. They love their kids to death, and they're very involved, but not too much. They're big believers in letting their children do their own thing, have their own successes or their own failures." Brodie paused. "My father was nothing like Chelsea's dad. He got so wrapped up in my skiing career that my failures became his fail-ures—same with my successes. He really had trouble when that career ended. But we're better now. With more separation, we actually seem to be getting closer."

He nodded, surprised that Brodie was volunteering so much personal information. But then, everyone he met in this town seemed to treat him like he was already a long-time friend. It was both strange and appealing at the same time. Most of his friends were tied to his business these days and he realized now how often those meetups turned to business talk. They never got personal, which he had always been fine with. But now…well, Brodie reminded him a little of his brother, who'd also had a rambling, over-sharing personality. And he realized how much he'd missed this kind of easy chatter.

"So," Brodie said. "Tell me more about your company. Do you provide law enforcement robots?"

"We do. Does the department here have any?"

"Unfortunately, no. But I've heard they're being used in a lot of creative ways in bigger cities."

"Everything from disarming a bomb, to infiltrating a hostage situation, clearing obstacles, and aiding in search and rescue operations. A robot can go where a man can't. But, of course, it requires some technological skill that some departments don't have."

"And money," Brodie said dryly.

"That, too, but we offer a lot of discounts for anything that can improve public safety and help first responders."

Brodie nodded. "That's good to hear. How did you get into it?"

"My brother was very into robots when I was young. I didn't know what I was going to do with them, but here I am now."

"You must have some brilliant people working for you."

"I do. I started the company with my freshman-year college roommate. He was an engineering major. I was business. It was a good match in a lot of ways."

"So, you started when you were eighteen."

"Pretty much. Eric and I built the company together."

"Did you ever think it would get so big?"

He smiled. "I always thought that."

Brodie grinned back at him, understanding in his eyes. "Yeah, I get that. People used to ask me if I ever imagined being as good as I was at skiing."

"And you had to say yes?"

"I saw myself on the Olympic podium from the first time I raced down a mountain. I was about eight. Unfortunately, I never got that moment, but I did stand on a lot of other podiums, and I skied the most incredible mountains in the world, so I can't really complain."

He was impressed that Brodie wouldn't complain about being deprived of a gold medal that would have been the pinnacle of his career. "You have a good attitude about it. I don't think I'd be so chill if I'd gone through what you did."

"Oh, it took me a long time to get to a place of acceptance. In fact, last year, I had the opportunity to get back into the skiing world in a different way, and I was tempted, but in the end, I knew that I'd moved on. I like being a cop. I actually help people. I'm not nearly as selfish as I once was. And then there's Chelsea…"

"When are you getting married?"

"August. But it feels like we're already married, like we've known each other forever."

"Love at first sight?"

Brodie laughed. "No. Chelsea was not easy. But she was going through a lot of stuff that she had to deal with. And in some ways, I was too. We both came to Whisper Lake to start over, but it didn't go quite as we planned; it went better." He checked his watch. "I better get back to work. I'll probably see you at the inn later."

"I'll be there," he said.

After Brodie left, he tried to get back to work, but his concentration was once again lacking. A little before four, he closed his computer. He was eager to see Lizzie again. It had only been a couple of hours, but he found himself missing her, which was probably a better reason not to go back. He was playing with fire and it would be a lot safer if he put the matches away, as Lizzie wanted him to do. But he liked risk, and he liked her, so he was going to see what happened.

CHAPTER EIGHT

By four o'clock Wednesday afternoon, Lizzie thought she had everything under control. There was a repairman working on the furnace, and she'd managed to go at least an hour without thinking about Justin. It helped that she hadn't seen him all day. She had no idea where he'd spent his time, but it was probably somewhere cooler than the inn.

With the heat still raging, she'd decided to make her happy-hour cocktail party a margarita party. She'd set up a bar in the patio with three kinds of margaritas: plain, strawberry, and peach, thankful that the produce she'd picked up the day before had afforded her such a great offering of fresh fruit. They were also going to serve up lemon fizzes, thanks to the abundance of lemons. Naomi had made enough guacamole to feed an army, as well as homemade tortilla chips and a wide array of other appetizers.

While the outside temperature was only in the high sixties, she'd invited everyone to attend in shorts and flip-flops and, as perhaps the biggest irony of all, she had put her outdoor heaters on, so the patio temp would match the heat inside the inn.

Now, she was blowing up beach balls that could be batted

around among the guests, while listening to the set of summer beach songs she'd put on the sound system. Hopefully, everyone would get in the spirit of the event.

As she finished one beach ball, she gave it a pat to send it across the yard. It hit Justin square in the chest as he came out the door. Of course, it would hit him, because every time he showed up, something went wrong.

But he caught it with a smile, and she couldn't help but smile back. He wasn't in shorts but a pair of faded jeans and a navy-blue polo shirt that only enhanced the blue of his eyes. Her heart skipped a beat as an electrical current flowed between them. She really didn't want to like him, but she did. Although, it bothered her that she couldn't seem to stop talking about herself when he was around, while he managed to keep his own personal stories locked away. She was starting to get more and more curious about his life. If she couldn't get him to talk, she might have to try to squeeze some information out of his grandparents when they arrived.

Having Marie and Ben at the inn would probably also provide a good buffer between them, and they certainly needed that.

"I feel like I'm in Margaritaville," Justin said as he crossed the patio.

"Jimmy Buffett will be singing that song soon," she said lightly, her gaze running down his hard, masculine body with great appreciation.

"What's the status on the furnace?" he asked.

"Are you still hot?"

"Stupid question," he said with a grin.

"He's still working on it, but he thinks he has an answer. He had to run out and get a part. He just got back, so fingers crossed. In the meantime, I need to get everyone drunk so they don't think about how hot they are."

"I usually get hotter when I get drunk."

"It's the only plan I have." She couldn't believe he could get much hotter than he was, but she appreciated his easygoing tone. "You're being pretty chill about all this. I thought you'd be complaining that you couldn't work in the heat."

"I spent most of the day at Harvey's."

"Ah, good choice. He has the best coffee and pastries. I'm glad you could work."

"Do you need any help here?"

"I need a couple of more beach balls blown up." She handed him one.

"So, you think I'm full of hot air?" he joked.

"You said it, not me," she returned.

As they shared a flirty laugh, the air seemed to sparkle around them, and little shivers ran down her spine. Then his gaze darkened with a promise she still wasn't ready to accept.

"I want to kiss you again, Lizzie."

She sucked in a quick breath. "We already agreed we're not doing that."

"I don't think we agreed. Just one kiss."

"We had a kiss last night. That's enough." It actually wasn't nearly enough, and her lips were already tingling at the possibility of his mouth on hers.

As he leaned in, she felt an incredible pull toward him, and then a loud, female voice broke the tension between them.

"Here you are!" the woman said.

Lizzie whirled around to see Justin's grandparents, Benjamin and Marie Blackwood, walking toward them. Marie was a tall, thin woman wearing gray slacks and a white short-sleeve top, her hair a rich, dark brown. Benjamin was also tall, but stockier, with a square face, white hair, and cool gray eyes. He was in black jeans and a short-sleeve button-down shirt. She was more than a little happy now that she hadn't taken the kiss Justin was offering. His grandparents would have gotten the completely wrong idea.

"What happened to your head?" Marie asked Justin, concern in her voice as she gave him a hug.

"It's not a big deal. I had a fender bender on the way here, but I'm fine."

"Are you sure? Did you see a doctor?"

"I did. Lizzie insisted."

"Good," Marie said, sending her an appreciative look. "Thank you for that. I'm so sorry we had to cancel last night, Lizzie. Of course, we'll pay for the day."

"Don't worry about that," she said. "I'm just glad you're here."

"It's rather warm inside," Ben said, fanning his ruddy complexion. "The front desk clerk said there's a problem with the heater."

"I'm hoping it's almost fixed," she replied. "Can I get you a margarita? We have plain, strawberry, and peach, and the fruit is all from local farmers."

"Strawberry sounds wonderful," Marie said.

"I'll take it plain," Ben put in.

"And I'll get their drinks," Justin told her.

"It's no trouble."

"Exactly. It's no trouble for me," he said pointedly.

Since Marie and Ben were watching their exchange with some interest, she simply nodded. "Thanks. I appreciate that."

While Ben and Justin headed over to the margarita machines, Marie said, "I saw the flowers you put in our room, Lizzie. That was so kind and thoughtful."

"You're more than welcome. Are you excited for your vow renewal?"

"Now that we're here, and Justin is here, yes. I was getting a little concerned last night when our flight got canceled."

"You can relax now. You all made it."

"Maybe not all." Marie lowered her voice, as she gave her husband and grandson a quick look. Justin and Ben were engaged in conversation by the margarita machines and not paying them any attention. "There's a chance that Justin's father and mother might come in on Saturday."

"Really? I wish you'd told me. The inn is full for Friday and Saturday night."

"I know. They might stay in Denver and just come up for the day, but we'll see. No one has been willing to commit to coming."

"Why not?" she couldn't help asking.

"There are a lot of problems in our family," Marie said. "Justin doesn't get on well with his parents, nor they with him. Ben and I are caught in the middle. We understand all sides, but we're not getting any younger, and we'd like to get everyone back together, have some healing."

"Weddings can be good for reunions," she said, more than a little curious what they all needed to heal from.

"I hope so." Marie paused. "Don't say anything to Justin. I don't want him to leave because he thinks they might come, and then they don't show up."

"All right," she said, now even more curious as to what was going on between Justin and his parents, but Marie didn't seem inclined to say more.

"So, what do you think of my grandson?" Marie asked.

"He's great, very accomplished and driven."

"He is definitely driven. He never takes a vacation. It took a lot of persuasion to get him up here. I worry about him, because he needs to have some balance in his life, some fun."

"Well, this is the place for that," she said lightly.

"I think so, too," Marie said, as Justin and Benjamin returned with the drinks.

"What do you think, Grandma?" Justin asked, as he handed her a margarita.

"That Whisper Lake is the perfect place for you to have some fun for a change."

A grin spread across Justin's face as he glanced over at her. "Agreed. I've been thinking about what to do that might be fun. Any ideas, Lizzie?"

She could see the teasing gleam in his gaze. "Lots of ideas, starting with tonight's cocktail party. There will be more than a few single women attending. Maybe I can introduce you to some of them."

"That would be good," Marie interjected. "When's the last time you had a date, Justin?"

Now Justin was the one on the hot seat, and Lizzie loved it.

"That, Grandma, is none of your business," he returned.

"I don't want you to end up alone. Time goes faster than you think."

"I'm not worried about it."

"I know you're not; I am," Marie said. "I want you to experience all life has to offer and that includes marriage and children."

"Let's talk about your marriage," Justin said, changing the subject. "Are you changing any of your vows this time around? Will you mix things up since the first time you said I do?"

"We are going to make it more personal," Marie said, giving her husband a tender look. "Ben and I have been through so much together. We know a lot more than we did back then. We were a couple of crazy kids when we first tied the knot."

"Now we're still crazy, but not kids," Benjamin said with a laugh, as he put his arm around Marie's shoulders and gave her a squeeze.

"We're young at heart," Marie put in. "And we have lots of plans for this week, Justin."

"I'm sure you do," Justin said. "What's on the schedule?"

Marie glanced at her. "Were you able to set up tomorrow?"

"I was," she said, thinking Justin was not going to like the schedule at all. "You will set sail at nine a.m. on the Harbor Rose. Mike Olenski is the captain. He'll take all three of you out on the lake for an hour. I'll have snacks packed for the sail, but you can get a full breakfast when you return."

"Hold on—we're going sailing?" Justin quizzed.

"Yes, and after our sail and breakfast, we're going antiquing," Marie said with a happy smile.

"I can skip that part, right?" Justin asked.

"If I can't, you can't," his grandfather told him.

"It will be fun," Marie said. "Anyway, that's enough for you to know now."

"I do have to get some work done as well," Justin warned. "I want to spend time with you both, but I also have a company to run."

"And you have people who work for you. You promised me a no work week."

"I don't remember that."

Marie ignored him, her gaze moving to Lizzie. "And you and I will chat later about some other ideas I have."

"Of course," she said. "If you'll excuse me, I'm going to let our chef know that she can start bringing out the food."

As she left the Blackwoods, she ran into Keira and an older, silver-haired woman dressed in a slim-fitting navy-blue sheath dress.

"Hi, Lizzie," Keira said, giving her a quick hug. "This is Paula Wickmayer."

"Nice to meet you. Welcome to my margarita party."

"Thank you so much. You have a lovely inn. It's a bit warm tonight."

"We had a heating problem, but it's being fixed as we speak. In the meantime, we have cold, blended margaritas and plenty of food," she added as Naomi and Victor brought two large trays out to the patio.

"It looks good," Keira said. "But Paula wants to speak to you for a minute in private. Would that be all right?"

"Uh, sure." She was surprised by the question and by the way

Keira was avoiding her gaze. "We can just go around the corner into the garden. It's still a little too warm inside the building." She led them around the back of the inn and into the garden.

"This is beautiful," Paula said, her gaze sweeping the beautiful landscaped grounds that included an herb and vegetable garden as well as a colorful array of flowers.

"We grow our own herbs and vegetables," she said.

"That's a lot of work, but well worth it, I'm sure."

"Yes. We plan to open the inn for dinners in the upcoming months." She paused. "What did you want to talk to me about?"

"I work for Falcon Properties," Paula said. "I don't know if you've heard of the chain."

"Of course. Falcon is a luxury brand started by Maximo Corinthos, a Greek shipping billionaire, and his wife Athena. I studied the entire branding history in college."

Paula smiled. "The Corinthos family has built an amazing hotel chain, and we are now in the business of acquiring small, charming inns, and adding them to our very extensive portfolio."

"Really? But most of the Falcon hotels are huge properties with executive suites and five-star restaurants."

"We're expanding our portfolio. Our mission this year is to provide our guests with luxury and intimacy, a feeling of home away from home. From what I understand, you provide a very personal experience for your guests. I also read about your innovations in *Mountain West Magazine*. The photos didn't do it justice. Anyway, I happened to be speaking to Keira at a real-estate conference last week, and when I found out she knew you personally, I asked if she could introduce us."

"Why?" she asked, feeling a tightening in her gut. "I mean, I'm happy to meet you, but why did you want her to introduce us?"

"Because Falcon Properties is interested in buying the inn," Paula replied, quickly adding, "and before you say no, I'd ask that you hear me out. Most of the owners we've approached in the past are reluctant to give up ownership, but we've been able to show them how they can make money and also still be part of their inn's success. We have a great case study that you can review with an inn in Maine."

"I appreciate the offer, but I'm not interested in selling the inn. It's always been my dream to run a place like this."

"You'd still be running it, but you'd have someone to help with the background financials, the marketing and the repairs."

She frowned, knowing it would be difficult to argue that point with her heat on high. As her gaze moved to Keira, she saw the guilt in her friend's eyes and wondered why Keira hadn't given her the heads-up that this offer was coming. She felt blind-sided and a little betrayed. "I don't know what to say. I'm in the middle of a party."

"Would it be all right if I gave you some information?" Paula asked. "There's no pressure, Ms. Cole. You don't have to make any decisions immediately. It's just something to think about."

Paula pulled out a thick envelope and handed it to her. She reluctantly took it.

"I'll give it a look, but I wouldn't hold your breath," she said.

"I never do," Paula replied, with a confident smile. "But I also know the value of what we offer and the challenges facing small inns these days. I used to run one with my husband. We were innkeepers for ten years. We saw it all—the ups, the downs, the good times, the bad times, and while we loved every second of it, it took a toll on us. When we finally realized that we could have our dream in a slightly different way, it changed our world. We sold out. My husband retired, and I got a second career in real estate. Two years ago, I moved on to Falcon Properties, because it gave me the opportunity to get back into the business of hospitality. I have a lot of experience, Ms. Cole. I hope you'll give me a chance to talk to you about this offer once you've had a little time to think about it."

"I'm doing fine," she lied, wishing it were true. "But thanks for your interest. I will look through this. In the meantime, please feel free to have drinks, appetizers, mingle, and enjoy yourselves." She turned and headed through the side door of the inn, needing a minute to drop off the packet and take a breath.

She'd no sooner entered her office when Keira came through the door behind her.

"I'm sorry, Lizzie. Paula was supposed to come tomorrow. I was going to tell you last night, but then you left with Justin, and I thought I'd have a chance to speak to you today, but Paula arrived earlier than she said."

"You should have found a minute to warn me that you were bringing her by. And why did you even agree to introduce us? You know I don't want to sell the inn."

"I also know you're swimming in debt, and you look more and more tired every time I see you. I didn't think it was my decision to make. You don't have to do anything. I just felt like you should see all the opportunities available to you. Falcon Properties would keep you on as manager of the inn. It would still be your place."

"No, it wouldn't. It would be theirs. I would just be the hired help. I've done that." She was appalled that Keira thought she would even entertain the idea. But maybe she hadn't been hiding her problems as well as she thought. That was also disturbing. She didn't want her friends to think she couldn't handle her business. It felt like she was back in school, with classmates giving her doubtful looks and teachers wondering why she wasn't doing as well as her sister and brothers had done.

"Then don't do this," Keira said. "It's just an offer, nothing more. I'm not saying you should sell. I'm not pushing it, and I'm not taking a commission on anything. Paula is a nice woman. I heard her pitch, and it sounded interesting. I thought you should hear it."

"I just wish you'd told me, but you're right, it's just an offer, something to consider." She ran a hand through her hair. "It's been a difficult day with the furnace problems and the party planning. I don't want to talk about this right now. I need to get back to the party."

"I am sorry if I added to your stress."

"It's fine. We'll talk later."

"Lizzie—"

She put up her hand, seeing the concern in Keira's eyes. "Don't worry about it. Just go to the party and keep Paula entertained. I can't deal with her right now. I need to check on Naomi and make sure we're not running low on anything."

"All right. We'll talk later."

She walked out of her office and was immediately waylaid by Ted Robinson, the furnace repairman. As Keira headed to the patio, Lizzie steeled herself for what might be coming next.

"Good news," Ted said, although the look in his eyes didn't quite match his words.

"Really?"

"The heat is now working, or rather it's not working, but you know what I mean," he said. "If you want it on, it will be on, but at a normal temperature."

"I'm so relieved," she said, realizing it was already starting to feel cooler.

"And now for the bad news." He gave her an apologetic look as he handed her his bill—another piece of paper she didn't want to have in her hand. "I had to replace some rather expensive parts."

The bill was much higher than she'd expected, and her gut clenched as she wondered where she was going to find the money.

"Now, you don't need to pay it all right away. If you can do half or even a quarter today, that would work," Ted said, obviously reading her stricken expression.

"I can give you a check for a quarter now. And I'll get you the rest as soon as I can."

"I know you will."

She walked back into her office and wrote him a check.

He gave her an awkward look as he accepted it. "I wish I could have done it cheaper, Lizzie."

"I appreciate that, but you did a great job. Thank you for coming so quickly and working so hard."

"My wife loves seeing the inn thriving again," Ted said. "We're all rooting for you to do well."

"Thanks. I hope I don't let you down."

"I know you won't."

As Ted left the office, she let out a breath, wishing she was feeling as confident about her abilities as Ted was. The heating bill was a huge setback, and she'd already been running so tight on her budget. But there was nothing she could do about it now. Like the offer from Falcon, she'd put that problem off for another time.

CHAPTER NINE

JUSTIN WONDERED where Lizzie had disappeared to. The party was humming along. Victor, the bartender, was filling margarita glasses while a young woman made the rounds with trays of delicious appetizers. He grabbed a chicken empanada as it went by and popped it in his mouth as his gaze swept the patio once more. His grandparents were talking up a storm with their friends.

Vanessa and Roger Holt were in their seventies and were a somewhat reserved and quiet couple from Dallas. Roger and his grandfather had immediately gotten into a discussion on golf and were looking forward to a game they had lined up for Friday. Carlos and Gretchen Rodriguez were in their early sixties. They were gregarious and funny with lots of stories to tell, and Gretchen seemed to be entertaining the group with one of those stories.

Noah and Patty had also joined his grandparents' group. They appeared to be great friends now. Patty put her hand on Noah's arm and leaned in to whisper a secret. It was difficult to believe that only yesterday she'd thought he was a stalker and had had him arrested. But in Whisper Lake, even enemies became friends when there was a friendly innkeeper in the middle of the situation. Speaking of which…

Where was Lizzie? Her friends Gianna and Zach were already here. They were talking to Keira and an older woman he didn't recognize. Brodie and Chelsea had also just arrived and were talking to another young couple who he didn't recognize. They were probably more of Lizzie's friends.

He recognized a few other people he'd seen around the inn: a single woman in her forties, a couple of newlyweds who couldn't keep their hands off each other, and a man in his sixties, who always had his head buried in a book while the young male teenager with him was constantly engrossed on whatever was happening on his phone. Those two reminded him a little of his grandfather and himself. When they'd been in a room together, they'd always each been wrapped up in their own little world of a book or a TV show or a video game. But he had still liked having his grandfather there, even if they weren't talking. It had been a nice change from all the days he'd spent completely alone.

He was alone now, he realized. Although, he could easily join any group. He just wanted that group to include Lizzie. Since she wasn't here, maybe he'd check his phone, see if he had any emails or texts to answer. Before he could do so, Keira wandered over, a troubled, tired expression on her face, which was quite a contrast to the energized, fun-loving woman he'd met at the bar last night.

"Hi, Justin. How's it going?" she asked.

"Good. You?"

"So-so." She lifted the margarita glass in her hand. "I'm hoping this improves my mood. But it's my second one, and so far, I still feel shitty."

"I'm sorry to hear that," he said, wondering why he was surprised by her candor. The people in Whisper Lake seemed very comfortable with expressing their emotions to anyone who would listen. He wasn't used to so much sharing. On the other hand, it did make him feel like he was part of the group, and he kind of liked that.

"I blew it, Justin," she continued.

"What do you mean?"

"I hurt my friend and I didn't mean to, but I did. She told me not to worry about it, but I can't stop worrying about it. Because she's too nice. She probably hates me right now but can't bring herself to say that."

"Are you talking about Lizzie?" He wondered if whatever was bothering Keira was the reason for Lizzie's absence.

"Yes." She took a long sip of her margarita. "And now I'm starting to feel a buzz, but it's still not helping."

"What did you do?" he asked curiously.

"I brought a potential investor to the party." She tipped her head toward the silver-haired woman, who was still talking to Gianna and Zach. "Paula Wickmayer. She's a former realtor who now works for a large hotel chain, and they're interested in buying the inn. She thought I might know Lizzie, which, of course, I do. I heard her pitch, and Paula is a straight shooter, so I thought Lizzie should hear her out."

He was more than a little surprised that someone wanted to buy the inn. "What did Lizzie say to the offer?"

"She didn't hear the offer. She said she wasn't interested, but Paula insisted she take the packet of information, which she agreed to do."

He suspected she'd only done that under duress.

"I know Lizzie loves this inn and it's her dream, but I think she's drowning. She won't say that, but she's more exhausted every time I see her. I just thought she should know her options. But I could see the anger in her eyes and the hurt. She thinks I don't believe in her abilities, but I do." Keira took another long drink. "I don't know how to make it right."

"It sounds to me like you brought Lizzie an opportunity. That's not so bad."

Keira gave him a hopeful look. "You don't think it's terrible?"

"No. It's not like she has to accept it."

"That's what I said."

"I'm sure she was just surprised by the offer."

"I hope she can see that I'm just trying to help. Lizzie is just the sweetest person, you know? She's been so nice to me and to my mom. I don't know if she told you, but my mother was in a terrible car accident several years ago, and she has a lot of cognitive dysfunction."

"I'm sorry to hear that."

"Thank you. Anyway, I once told Lizzie how certain memories seem to bring my mom back into the world, and for some reason, the smell of oatmeal raisin cookies does that. The next Friday Lizzie sent over a plate of those cookies, and she's done that every week since then. They're always hot and fresh and smelling of happiness. My mom perks up when they arrive. That's just one example of how generous Lizzie is. But now I've probably wrecked our friendship."

"Lizzie doesn't seem like the kind of person who would let a friendship get wrecked over something like this, Keira."

"I'd like to believe that, Justin. And I'm sorry you had to listen to all that. I couldn't say anything to Gianna and Zach while Paula was there, and Chelsea and Brodie are wrapped up with Hunter and Cassidy and I can't say anything to them, because they're all related to Lizzie, and they're investors in the inn."

"Who are Hunter and Cassidy?"

"Hunter is Lizzie's cousin and Cassidy is his wife. They run a summer camp. They're really great people. Hunter used to be a firefighter and Cassidy is a landscape designer. They decided to start over with a new venture here at the lake."

"I heard about the camp from Zach last night," he said.

"Right. Zach was the architect." She drew in a breath and let it out. "Sometimes I meddle too much, Justin."

He smiled. "You don't seem to be alone in that, Keira. Lizzie is also a meddler."

Her face brightened. "That's true. Maybe she will understand." Keira finished her drink, then said, "I need another one of these. I think Victor watered them down. Do you want one?"

"No, I'm good."

As Keira left, he saw Lizzie come onto the patio. She had a smile on her face, but it didn't quite reach her eyes. As her gaze caught his, he gave her a nod. She tipped her head but then moved across the patio to talk to some of her other guests.

"Hello, Justin," Adam said, drawing his attention.

"Adam, I didn't see you come in."

"I just got here. I see your grandparents made it," Adam said, tipping his head in their direction.

"You also know my grandparents?"

"I met them the last time they were here," Adam said. "Ben must have talked to me for over an hour, but he's an interesting guy. He had a lot of stories from teaching overseas."

"That sounds like my grandfather. If you ask him one question, you'll be talking to him for a long time."

"Your job sounds interesting, too. We didn't get much of a chance to speak last night. I've had some experience with law enforcement robots, and I'm more than a little impressed with the future possibilities. I can't even imagine what will be coming next."

"The technology is constantly advancing," he said. "What we thought was impossible two years ago is now actually happening. Who knows where we'll be five years from now?"

"You're on the cutting edge."

"We are. It's an exciting time." He paused. "Your job must also be challenging. Did you always want to be a cop?"

"I did. The dream came early."

"Sounds like that is common in your family."

Adam grinned. "You're right. Lizzie wanted to run an inn since she was a little girl. We always had to play hotel with her. It was annoying. And Chelsea was singing her heart out before she was five. My brother Grayson wanted to be a doctor early on, too. Nathan was the only one who didn't have a grand plan. He still doesn't."

"What does he do now?"

"Honestly, I'm not sure. He's had a lot of different jobs, mostly in sales. He's our wanderer. Do you have any siblings?"

"No," he said shortly, not wanting to talk about Sean. "It must have been loud in your house growing up with so many kids around."

"I didn't know any different, but it was fun. There was always someone around if you were looking for something to do. Lizzie was game for anything. She was the baby of the family, and she hated to be left out, so if there was an invite, her answer was yes."

"That doesn't surprise me."

"What doesn't surprise you?" Lizzie asked, as she caught the tail end of their conversation.

"That you've always been up for anything."

"I do have a terrible fear of missing out," she admitted. Turning to her brother, she said, "Thanks for coming. And for bringing wine. Victor said you dropped off a case at the bar. You didn't have to do that, but I appreciate it."

"No problem. I was down at the Carmichael Winery last weekend and thought you might be able to use some bottles."

"I'm very appreciative. By the way, we should talk about Chloe some time."

"If you want to know what's going on with her, you should ask her, not me," Adam said, his tone sharpening. "I need a drink. Can I get anyone anything?"

"No thanks," he said.

Lizzie shook her head and then frowned as Adam hurried

away. "He can be so annoying," she said. "If he doesn't want to talk, he just shuts me down."

"Not everyone likes to talk as much as you do."

"I know that. But I'm worried about Chloe and I know Adam is, too."

"Yeah, he got rather heated about Kevin's behavior last night. He said a few things when you were on stage."

"Really?" She gave him a troubled look. "It's not like Adam to get in the middle of anyone's relationship, which is why I want to talk to him."

"Do you think he's in love with Chloe?"

"No," she said quickly. "I mean, I hope not. She's married."

"Maybe not happily."

"Adam and Chloe are friends. I know he would never hit on another man's wife. It's not who he is. He has a lot of integrity. He's probably the most ethical person I know."

Despite her words, he sensed she wasn't as convinced as she was saying.

"He just cares a lot about Chloe," she added.

"Maybe a little too much," he suggested.

"You can't care too much about your friends."

"Sure you can. You can care too much about a lot of things. Caring makes you weak, vulnerable, and sometimes it can bring you pain or distracts you from what else you want in life."

She gave him a thoughtful look. "You speak like someone who's been burned by love, but you said last night you don't have relationships. Is that why? Did you love someone too much?"

He stared back at her. "I did. Which is why I don't do love anymore."

"That seems like a sad and lonely way to live."

"I have a great life and a lot of fun. It's not sad at all."

"But at the end of the day, you're alone."

"You can be in a relationship and still be alone. That's why you have to be happy with yourself. There's no guarantee anyone else will stick around forever."

"What was her name?" she asked.

Before he could answer, Noah and Patty interrupted them.

"Lizzie," Patty said, giving her a tentative smile. "Sorry to interrupt, but we have a request."

"What's that?" Lizzie asked.

"Well, Noah and I are getting to know each other, and I realize that I was supposed to check out today, and Noah has been kind enough to wait for me to leave the room he needs to be in, but we've become friends, and…well, we're wondering if you have another room, or if I could switch into Noah's room, and he could take mine. Would that work?"

"Oh, no, I'm sorry. Noah's room is already spoken for. I have a couple arriving later tonight, who will be in that room."

Patty's face fell. "Of course, it's spoken for." She gave Noah a sad look. "We tried. I guess I should just get going then if I want to get on the road before dark."

"I wish there was something I could do," Lizzie said. "There is a room in the attic, but it's rather small."

"That's the room with the ghost?" Patty asked. "I don't know that I could stay there. I'd be nervous."

"That's just a rumor. I've slept there, and I've never seen a ghost," Lizzie said. "If you want to take that room, that's all I have to offer."

"I—I don't think so. I wouldn't sleep at all." Patty gave Noah an apologetic look. "I'm sorry, Noah."

"I could take the room," Noah said slowly.

"No, you need your room. It's your week, and it's important for you to be in room six. I understand that now," Patty said.

"I wish there was something else I could do," Lizzie began.

He wondered if she was about to offer up her own room, which she'd probably do if it meant keeping Patty and Noah happy. But she was looking tired and stressed, and he wasn't going to let her go that far.

"I'll take room ten," he said impulsively. "Patty can have my room. It's very nice. It has a view of the garden."

"That's so generous of you," Patty said, surprise in her eyes. "Are you sure?"

"Positive. You might have to have someone change my sheets. But I didn't mess anything else up."

"Does that work?" Noah asked Lizzie, hope in his gaze.

"Yes, but do you really want to move, Justin?"

"I saw the room earlier. It's fine. I have no problem with ghosts. I'll go put my stuff together and take it upstairs."

"Thank you so much," Noah said. "I'd be happy to pay for your room as a thank-you."

"I'm fine. It's not a big deal."

"You're a very nice man," Patty added.

"It's nothing." He headed into the inn, Lizzie on his heels.

"Justin," she said, when they got into the building. "You don't have to do this. I can give Patty my apartment."

"I knew you were about to make that offer, but you don't have to. This is a perfect solution."

"Not for you. I don't think your grandparents will be happy that you're stuck in the attic." She gave him an unhappy look. "I can take that room, and you can take my apartment, although, it's a little messy, but I could clean it."

"No. My grandparents won't know or care," he said, as he moved up the stairs and down the hall, opening the door to his room.

She followed him inside. "Why are you doing this, Justin? Why inconvenience yourself?"

"I couldn't stand to see you give away your apartment just to keep one of your guests happy."

"I've done it before."

"I'm sure you have, but not this time. I really don't have a problem doing this. I can sleep anywhere, and if I can't, I'll talk to the ghost."

"A ghost you don't believe in," she reminded him.

He smiled as he pulled out his suitcase and quickly repacked. "Maybe she'll change my mind. It's a she, right?"

"So the story goes. You know, Justin, when we first met, I wouldn't have pegged you for someone who would offer to give up their room to some lonely old couple. You were impatient and brisk and a little rude. Now you're being incredibly generous and kind. Who's the real Justin?"

"Guess you'll have to get to know me better if you want to find out. I can tell you one thing. When I want something or someone, I don't give up easily."

"This is about winning me over?"

"Maybe."

"You just want me because I said no. It's the chase you like. I've met men like you before."

"I don't think you have."

"You are so cocky, Justin."

He smiled. "I prefer confident."

"I'm going to get some clean sheets and change the bed."

Frowning, he said, "Don't you have someone to do that?"

"Not at the moment. My cleaners have gone home for the day. But I can handle it. You should get back to the party. Your grandparents are probably wondering where you are. I know they have dinner reservations set up for eight o'clock at La Ventana. It's right on the lake. I think you'll love it."

"They mentioned that."

"I'll get you the key for room ten so you can move your things." She moved toward the door. "Again, thank you. You made my life easier and two older people very happy."

"Speaking of your life getting easier, I was talking to Keira earlier. She mentioned that someone is interested in buying the inn."

Lizzie gave him a dark look. "I can't believe Keira told you that, and I am not interested in selling."

"She told me because she was upset. She thought she hurt you. Did she?" he asked curiously.

"She didn't hurt me, but I wasn't thrilled that she blindsided me."

"She's feeling bad about that."

"And she confided in you? She doesn't even know you."

"From what I've gathered so far, in Whisper Lake people feel very free to express their feelings to strangers," he said lightly. "I have to admit I'm more used to people who hide behind their carefully put-together masks. I usually have to dig deep to find out who someone really is and even then, I don't always figure it out."

"Do you really dig that deep?" she challenged.

"Good point. Not that often. It's easier to go with what people want to show me."

"And then you don't have to pull off your mask, either."

"That's true."

She folded her arms in front of her as she gave him a thoughtful look. "You said a few minutes ago that I should get to know you if I want to know who you are, but I'm not sure you would ever show me who you really are. It feels like you have secrets."

"Why would you say that?" he asked, feeling uncomfortable with her observation.

"I'm right, aren't I?"

"Everyone has secrets. I suspect you do, too."

"Maybe, but I doubt I guard them as well as you."

Her comments were hitting a little too close to home. "We should move along, so Patty can move her things."

"Ah, changing the subject. You really don't like losing control of a conversation, do you?"

"Do you want to get my room key?" he asked, not sure why

he was feeling so rattled. Maybe it was because there was a part of him that wanted to talk to Lizzie in a way he hadn't talked to anyone else, and that would be foolish.

"Yes, I will get your key, because I need to get this done so I can get back to the party. I'll meet you upstairs."

"Sure," he said. After she left, he quickly finished packing, and then headed up the stairs. Maybe Lizzie was right. Maybe they should keep their distance. He'd love to have sex with her, but tell her his secrets…not so much.

CHAPTER TEN

THURSDAY MORNING, Lizzie woke up to a cool chill in the air and felt relieved and happy that the heating was back to normal. She took a quick shower and put on leggings, a tank top, and her running shoes. Tucking her phone into a small pocket at her waist, and with her headphones over her ears, she jogged down the stairs, careful to be as quiet as she could. It was only six thirty and barely light out, but it was the best time for her to run. No one was up yet. No problems had come to surface, and she could enjoy the beauty of the day before it got started, before it became chaotic and busy. It was a good time for her to catch up on her thoughts and refocus her brain.

Unfortunately, as she ran out the front door, she saw Justin stretching his legs on the front lawn, and she realized her early morning sanctuary from the guests was not going to happen this morning. He wore running shorts and a T-shirt under a light-weight sweatshirt, and tingles ran down her spine at the sight of him. No wonder he was so fit; he was a runner.

He gave her a surprised look. "You're a runner, too?"

"Every day."

"Me, too."

Great, they had something in common. It worked better when she could tell herself they were completely different people and would never get along. "Are you coming back?" she asked hopefully.

"Nope. Just about to head out. Is there a good path?"

"There are a couple. One goes into the hills, one winds its way around the shore, and the other will take you through town."

"Which one are you running?"

"The hills," she said. "I like the challenge, but if you're concerned about altitude—"

"I'm not," he said, cutting her off. "Let's go."

"You seem like someone who would rather run alone," she said. "Don't feel you have to go with me."

He smiled. "I do like to run alone usually, but not today. And since I'm one of your guests, I'm sure you want to keep me happy."

"Of course. It will be awesome to run with you."

He laughed at her dry tone. "Great."

She bounced from side to side as she loosened up her legs. "But if I'm going too slow or too fast, you can run ahead or lag behind," she told him. "I want you to get a good workout."

"I think I can keep up with you. But you might not be able to keep up with me."

Her competitive spirit kicked in at his words. "I have three brothers, Justin. I've been keeping up with guys my whole life."

"Then let's see what you've got."

She took off on a medium pace jog, knowing the hills that were coming up. Justin fell into step alongside her. She wished the path was narrow, but there was plenty of room for them to run side by side. Maybe that was just as well. It would be distracting to have him behind her, and if he was in front of her, she probably wouldn't be able to take her eyes off him.

"How was your night?" she asked, wanting to distract herself from that thought. "Any ghostly encounters?"

"Not a one," he said, flinging her a smile. "I slept great."

"I'm glad to hear it. Did you enjoy dinner at La Ventana?"

"It was excellent. Incredible steak."

"And catching up with your grandparents was probably even better."

"It was," he admitted. "I don't see them or talk to them as much as I like. I travel so much. I'm always in a different time zone. It's hard to find a moment when we're all awake. So, is this our pace? Because it seems slow."

"I was just warming up, but I'm ready to go now. Are you?"

"Always ready," he said with his charmingly cocky smile. "Ladies first."

She doubled her speed, but Justin matched her stride for stride. With their new pace, the conversation ended, and she put her energy into her run, turning up the music in her ears. Her kick-ass mountain climbing music provided a nice backdrop for a run that had become a race, and she needed both the music and her competitive desire to win to keep up with Justin.

Up and down they went over rolling hills and through deeply forested areas, finally coming out along a path with an amazing view of the lake. When they reached the summit, she ran over to a low wall and gave it a tap. Justin hit the wall at the exact same time.

"Tie," he said with a grin.

Considering he didn't seem nearly as winded as she was, she had a feeling he could have gone faster. "You could have probably won," she said, as she pulled out her earphones.

"You think I let our race end in a tie?"

"Yes."

He laughed. "Does that score me any points?"

"No. I don't like it when people let me win or tie. I prefer to earn it. It means more."

"Then we'll have a rematch tomorrow."

Since making another date seemed like a bad idea, she turned her gaze to the lake and simply said, "We'll see."

"This is an amazing view," Justin said, pulling off his headphones and tucking them into his pocket.

"Worth the effort?"

"Definitely."

She wished she could find a way to stop smiling at him. But he was so damned attractive with sweat on his face, his brown hair mussed from the breeze, his cheeks red, his blue eyes as bright as the sunlight. "How do you fit daily runs into your busy schedule?"

"I get up early, like you."

"It is the best time of the day. Everything is possible. Nothing has gone wrong yet. It's all good."

He nodded in agreement. "I feel the same way. But I'm surprised you like to run. It's very solitary, and you seem like a people person."

"I am a people person, but I need time to myself, too. I actually started running with my brother, Nathan. He ran track and field in high school, and he'd let me come with him on his training runs. Since my siblings often left me out, I was thrilled to have someone who was fine with me tagging along."

He smiled. "Adam told me that you were always up for anything."

"Mostly because my brothers and sister were usually trying to ditch me," she said dryly. "Chelsea wasn't as bad as the boys, but then she got so into her music that that separated us a bit. Did you run with your brother?"

"No," he said shortly. "I always ran on my own. It was a good way to burn off my emotions."

"So, you do have emotions," she teased.

"Sometimes unwanted and unnecessary," he admitted.

"That's part of being human. Unless you'd rather be like one of your robots."

"That wouldn't be so bad. Robots are built on algorithms, logic, and math. No messy thoughts or feelings to wreck a perfectly executed program."

"But also no unexpected joy or surprise," she pointed out. "That's part of life, too. Unpredictability can be exciting."

"Or just bad."

"Why do you say that? You're a risk taker, aren't you?"

"I take risks, yes, but I'm usually in control of most of the variables."

"But I have to ask again, what about surprises? If you control everything, then there's no room for an unexpected beautiful moment."

"Most surprises aren't that good."

"But they can be. I love surprise parties, gifts, random acts of kindness, like the one you did yesterday when you gave up your room to Patty. That really surprised me, in a good way."

He acknowledged her point with a tip of his head. "Okay, once in a while there's a good surprise. But then there are also broken heaters, high interest rates, employees who slack off or quit, earthquakes, tornadoes. In my mind, the bad surprises usually outweigh the good."

"Well, I prefer to be optimistic."

"Big surprise," he said with a laugh. "Were you a cheerleader in high school?"

"I was the mascot, which happened to be a lion. I spent a lot of my time sweating in that lion costume. But I'd make the other kids laugh, and that was fun."

"So, you were still cheering, just not in a short little skirt. Too bad for the boys."

She grinned. "I wore short little skirts plenty of other times."

"Did you have a high school boyfriend?"

"I had one every year. Dave, when I was a freshman—he

lived on my block so we kind of grew up together. Once we got to high school, we started dating, but mostly because it was comfortable. Sophomore year, I was all about Brian. He was a soccer player and was super cute, but he never liked me as much as I liked him. We went to a dance together; that was about it. Junior year was lots of different guys but no one serious, and then senior year, it was Rick. We dated for almost the whole year. But he went out of state to college, and that was the end of that. What about you? Were you popular in high school?"

"Not even a little bit."

"I find that difficult to believe. Unless you turned into all this years later."

He grinned. "All this?"

"You know what you look like. Let's just say you're not ugly."

"Wow, high praise."

"So why no girlfriends in high school?"

He shrugged. "Who knows? I guess I wasn't a good date."

"This is why I think you have secrets. You get very vague when I ask about your past."

"And you get really chatty."

"I did tell you too much, didn't I?" She made a little face, then shrugged. "It's what I do. Unlike you, when people ask questions, I answer."

"Speaking of questions, I have another one for you."

"What's that?"

"Are you considering selling the inn?"

"I've been trying not to think about that. The inn is my dream."

"But?"

"There's no but."

"Isn't there? Isn't that why you got upset, Lizzie?"

She looked into his perceptive gaze and reluctantly nodded. "You're right. There's a part of me that wonders if I shouldn't look at the offer. The heating repair was quite high, and I was already in a bad spot. There have been a lot of unexpected expenses this year. I don't want to sell, but I also don't want to fail and have everyone who believed in me and trusted me with their money to lose, to be disappointed."

"Why not look at her offer?"

"I'm afraid it will tip the scales even more."

"If it's a good offer, you could end up making a lot of money, paying everyone off, and perhaps you could still run the place. Sometimes buyouts work that way."

"Paula said something about that. But it wouldn't be mine anymore. I couldn't just do whatever I wanted."

"Nope. But can you do whatever you want now?" he challenged. "With a new owner, you might have more funds to start your dinner service and other things you can't afford."

She gave him a thoughtful look. "Do you think I should sell?"

"I have no idea. I'd have to look at your financials before I could give an informed opinion."

The last thing she wanted to show anyone was her financial records. "I just wish the offer hadn't come now. I've only been open for two years. It takes time to build a business. Whisper Lake is also growing. There will be more opportunity down the road, if I can hang on."

"Would you consult your investors before making a decision?"

Another idea she didn't really want to consider. "Let's talk about something else. Actually, we should run back to the inn. You have a sail to get to."

"I almost forgot about that, which is unusual, because I rarely forget about anything. But since I've been in Whisper Lake, I'm a lot more distracted."

"Maybe because you're having fun."

"I could be having more fun," he said pointedly.

"You really don't give up easily."

"If I did, I wouldn't get what I want. And it doesn't sound like you give up easily, either."

"No. Sometimes I wonder if I hang on too long."

"If you ever do want to bounce off some ideas with me, I'm game. I might be able to help."

"You probably could, but I'm afraid your emotionless, robotic thinking will only look at the financials and not the feelings. And I have big feelings."

He gave her an understanding smile. "Believe it or not, I'm not unfamiliar with having feelings about a business you've created. I'm personally invested in mine as well. But you still have to be able to look at the numbers."

"Looking at numbers is not easy for me."

"You have to take the emotion out of it."

It wasn't just the emotion that made the numbers hard, but she didn't need to say anything more. She'd already shared far too much with Justin. "Shall we race back?" she asked as she put in her headphones and turned on her music. While he was fiddling with his earpiece, she took off, figuring she might as well grab a head start. He caught up with her in less than a quarter mile, giving her the cocky grin that made her heart flutter every time she saw it. And then she was looking at his back the rest of the way home.

Justin was stretching on the porch when she got back to the inn, feeling more breathless than she usually did. He had pushed her to her limit, and that felt both great and exhausting. As she reached the steps, her phone buzzed. Justin reached for his phone a second later.

She took it out and saw a group text from Justin's grand-mother to her and Justin. Marie wanted to let them know that Ben had had an allergy attack during the night, and they both wanted to sleep in. Since she'd already paid for the sail and didn't want Justin to go alone, Marie was hoping that Lizzie might go with him.

Justin lifted his gaze and met hers. "What do you think?"

"Mornings are busy," she said.

"But you like to keep your guests happy, and this is what my grandmother wants."

"And you keep telling me I can't make everyone happy."

"True. You can tell her no. I don't need to go on a sail. I can just do some work."

He would probably be just as happy working, but he would miss out on a great trip, and she'd be letting down one of the nicest women she'd ever met. It was just a ninety-minute sail, and Naomi and Victor could handle breakfast. Shay would be back by eleven. And they didn't have a lot going on today.

"Well?" Justin prodded. "What should I tell her?"

"It's really beautiful out on the water, and no trip to Whisper Lake is complete without a sail. You should go."

"By myself? That doesn't sound like fun."

She saw the gleam in his eyes. "You've told me more than once that you're happy on your own."

"True, but I'm also happy working, so if I'm going to be on my own, I might as well do that."

"You know your grandmother wants you to go."

"With you," he said pointedly.

"All right. I'll go. I'll take a quick shower and meet you back here."

"You really are dedicated to your guests' enjoyment."

"Happy guests usually lead to five-star reviews. I'll be expecting one from you."

"We'll see just how happy you make me," he teased.

She smiled back at him. "I'm only agreeing to a boat trip."

"For now."

She ignored that, heading to her first-floor apartment as Justin jogged up the stairs. She hoped she wasn't making a big mistake spending more time with Justin, but there was a good chance she was. But she wasn't going to worry about it. She actually loved going out on a boat on the lake, and it had been too long since she'd done that. Maybe a little time off would be good for her, too. She could use a little perspective on her life and being on the water might be just what she needed.

CHAPTER ELEVEN

BEING out on the water was more than a little fun, Justin thought, as they sailed around the lake. The captain, Mike Olenski, was a grizzled, weathered-looking man in his early fifties, who had a crooked grin and loved chewing on the toothpick hanging out of his mouth. Since they were the only two on board the fifteen-foot motorboat, Captain Mike, as he liked to be called, was happy to follow Lizzie's suggestion that they head north and then come back around the eastern shore.

Lizzie had brought along a picnic basket with bottled waters, orange juice, and some fresh scones, of which Justin had had several. They hadn't talked much but the quiet between them had been friendly and easygoing. Lizzie was a talker, but she seemed to be in a more reflective mood now, and he liked seeing that side of her, too. He was beginning to realize how much of her day was spent being on and ready to help someone else. He was also beginning to realize how long it had been since he'd taken even this much time off. It was a Thursday morning. He never just sat and did nothing for an hour and a half on a weekday. But he was having a good time. He was starting to feel like this obligation might be turning into a vacation.

As the boat took a fast turn, water splashed over the side, and Lizzie laughed in complete and utter abandon. No worry for her about getting her hair wet or her makeup washed off—if she even had any makeup on. She had a natural beauty. Her cheeks were warmed by the sun, her green eyes bright in the sunlight, her long hair flowing out behind her in silky waves. He found it impossible to look away from her. When she turned to him and met his gaze, his gut clenched with desire and another, more unwelcome emotion.

He was happy with the lust factor between them. He wanted to sleep with her. But he didn't want anything else coming into the picture. They lived in very different worlds, and while those worlds were intersecting for a short time now, that intersection would be gone soon. He didn't want to hurt her. Nor did he want to have any regrets himself. And while he'd always, always been able to walk away without regrets, he had this odd feeling that he'd never quite met anyone like Lizzie before.

"Are you enjoying yourself?" she asked.

"How could I not?"

"The lake is beautiful, isn't it?"

"So are you," he murmured, the words slipping out before he could stop them.

Her eyes sparkled. "Don't flirt with me, Justin."

"I'm just stating a fact. Whatever you might think about me, I never lie. In fact, I've been told I'm ruthlessly honest."

"I can believe that," she said dryly.

"I don't bury facts or look the other way. No good ever comes of that."

"Ah, another clue to the secrets of Justin Blackwood," she said. "Something happened. And it involved a lie."

"Or maybe just an avoidance of the truth."

"Care to explain?"

"No."

"Maybe another time."

"I don't think so."

"I can be just as persistent as you, Justin."

He smiled. "You like to compete, don't you?"

She was saved from answering, as the boat hit the wake from the Whisper Lake ferry and took a big bounce. Lizzie instinctively grabbed his arm as she practically fell into his lap. She laughed again as she smiled up at him.

His hands tightened on her arms, and he couldn't help but kiss her. She was too close. And he'd never been one to miss an opportunity.

She stiffened for a split second, but then gave into the attraction between him. He could taste the sugar from the scones on her lips. Or maybe that was just her sweetness. Whatever it was, he wanted to go on tasting her forever, but the boat bounced again, and she pulled out of his arms, looking quickly toward Captain Mike.

"He's not watching us," he assured her.

"I know." She tucked her wild hair behind her ears. "I just really wish you weren't such a good kisser."

"Right back at you. You're hard to resist, Lizzie."

"So are you." She cleared her throat. "But we need to keep trying."

"Do we?"

"Yes," she said firmly.

"Okay," he agreed, but he suspected they would end up in each other's arms before the week was done. "However, we may get thrown together again. You do realize that my grandparents set this up, right?"

Her gaze widened. "You and me? This is a setup? Are you sure your grandpa doesn't just have allergies?"

"I'm positive that that is not the reason they bailed on this trip."

"I can't imagine why they'd want to set us up."

"They like you. Hell, you might even be the reason they

decided to renew their vows here at the lake."

"I'm sure I'm not the reason. They love the lake, and they invited their friends here. This isn't about me and you." She frowned. "Although, it is kind of weird that she canceled and wanted me to come with you."

He smiled. "Face it, you were set up."

"Well, you were set up, too, and you don't seem too upset about it."

"I'm not. I'm having fun. You were right, Lizzie. This lake is changing me. Or maybe it's you."

"It's the lake and the mountains and the people. It all gets into your soul. You don't even realize it's happening. You just feel better, more alive, less stressed."

"Do you feel better being out here?"

"Yes, I think I needed the break as much as you did. It's been a busy two years. And the last two months have been especially hectic. I feel like I have so many balls in the air, and I have to keep juggling or they'll all come crashing down. Did you ever have that feeling with your company? Did you ever have any moments where you weren't sure you could do it?"

"In the very beginning, yes. I had a lot of big ideas, but not a lot of big money. It took a lot of creativity to figure out how to fund what I wanted to do and then do it. I'm sure there were moments I came close to the edge of failure, but I just didn't stop long enough to let the fear take hold."

"That's how I've been moving along, but I'm afraid I won't be able to outrun all my problems."

"Don't worry about that now," he advised. "The problems will be there when you get back."

"That's true. I just want to enjoy the lake. It is pretty perfect, isn't it?"

"Yes. I had no idea I'd like it this much." He'd also had no idea he would meet a woman at the lake who he liked this much.

"You should be careful, Justin. Once Whisper Lake gets in your heart, it's impossible to let go."

"But I will let go," he promised, knowing deep down he was talking about her as well as the lake. "Because my life can't happen here."

Her smile faded. "I know. But, hopefully, you'll have some lovely memories to carry with you."

"I'm sure I will," he said, wishing that wouldn't be the case. But he had a feeling that Lizzie would be a difficult woman to forget.

***

"This is going to be something I will always remember," his grandmother said, as he walked down Adams Street with her Thursday afternoon. After getting back from the lake, he'd worked for a couple of hours and then met his grandmother for lunch. She'd told him then that his grandfather wanted another nap after his sleepless night, so it would be just the two of them going antique hunting.

He'd really wanted to beg off, but he hadn't been able to crush the happy light in her eyes. So here he was window-shopping, probably one of his least favorite things in the world to do. He didn't even like shopping for his own clothes, much less trying to find treasure in what always appeared to be someone else's trash.

"We haven't found anything you've liked so far," he reminded her. "So don't get carried away."

"Oh, it's not about what we find; it's about you and me doing something together. I can't remember the last time. Can you?"

He wished he could. He wished he could say it hadn't been that long, but aside from a few dinners on various quick trips through Los Angeles in the past several years, he hadn't spent much time with her, and certainly not time like this.

Realizing she was still waiting for an answer, he said, "We can make up for some of the lost time today. I just hope Grandpa will feel better soon."

"Oh, he'll be fine. He just gets a little sneezy this time of year. How was your sail this morning? You haven't said anything about it."

He could see the gleam in her eyes, but he was not going to give her the satisfaction of thinking her little plan had worked. "It was fine. The lake was great."

"And Lizzie is wonderful, isn't she?"

"She's very nice," he agreed. "And very generous to step in for you."

"I hope she had a good time, too. She's always so busy when we come to stay at the inn, running around like a madwoman. She actually reminds me a little of you sometimes."

"I do not run around like a madwoman," he said lightly.

She grinned. "No, but you do work too much."

"I love working. It's what I do."

"It is what you do, but you're more than a job, Justin."

"It doesn't feel that way. I'm the company and the company is me. Eric is, of course, in there, too."

"But you're the driving force. I just want more for you, Justin." She paused on the sidewalk. "I know it's important for you to be successful, to have control over your life, to never have to worry where your next meal is coming from, but there is more to life than money."

"It's not just about money. I'm building a company that improves lives. That's what drives me."

"I do understand that. I just see the years flying by. You're thirty-two, almost thirty-three. You haven't introduced me to anyone in years. You never seem to have time for relationships. Do you really want to be alone?"

"I'm very comfortable being alone," he said, meeting her gaze. "You should know that."

"What I know is that having a partner, someone by your side, is what life is about. You can have all the success in the world, but if you don't have someone to share it with, then that success came with too big of a cost. When you're old like me, you'll appreciate the people in your life far more than anything else."

"Is that why you set me up with Lizzie?" he asked, enjoying the guilt that flashed through her eyes.

"Well, I worry about her, too. She also works too much. But she does make time for fun, and I think you should, too."

"I have fun, Grandma, but Lizzie is a small-town girl, and I am not a small-town guy."

"Oh, you can live anywhere. Isn't that what you always tell me? That technology makes the world a very small place?"

He frowned as she threw his words back in his face. "Still, it's not happening."

"That's too bad. I was hoping you would hit it off with her."

"She's great, but I'm leaving on Sunday."

"I know, and I wouldn't want you to hurt her, so maybe it's best you don't start anything. In fact, you're absolutely right. You and Lizzie would never work, but I hope you had a good time this morning anyway."

"I did have a good time, and I do like her, but she loves her work as much as I love mine."

"I understand. I just want you to be happy, Justin."

"I want you to be happy, too. That's why I'm here."

She gazed up at him, her expression serious and a bit conflicted. "I wish everyone could be here. Don't you sometimes wish that, too?"

"No. I stopped wishing for that a long time ago. You should give up on that dream, Grandma; it's not happening."

"Okay. Come on, let's go find something unusual and unique," she said, slipping her arm through his. "Maybe we'll find something for your apartment, too."

"I doubt it. My décor is modern."

"Well, you never know. Sometimes you find the perfect thing when you least expect it. You just have to open your eyes, so you don't miss it."

CHAPTER TWELVE

LIZZIE SPENT most of Thursday afternoon trying not to think about Justin. Fortunately, he'd gone antiques shopping with his grandmother, so he hadn't been around the inn to distract her, but he'd still come into her head. And now as she drove to her sister's house to meet up before the art and wine festival, she was back to thinking about him. She kept wondering why she was trying so hard to keep him at arm's length, when spending time in his arms was hot and exciting and pretty damned wonderful. She'd never thought she was a fling kind of girl, but when she was with Justin, she definitely wanted to be flung.

She smiled to herself at that crazy thought. Maybe she should stop fighting and just say yes. Maybe she should take what he had to offer now and forget about the future. If she ended up missing him later, would that be any worse than wondering if she'd missed out on something great?

She was no closer to an answer when she parked in Chelsea's driveway. It was good she was meeting the girls and going to the festival with them. She could have fun with her friends and forget about Justin, at least for a little while. She had a feeling he'd probably show up at the festival with his grandparents, but if he did, at least they'd have chaperones around them. Maybe that would keep the wild feelings at bay, although she doubted it.

Getting out of the car, she walked up to Chelsea's front door and rang the bell. Checking her watch, she saw she was five minutes early. Not bad considering how many small tasks she'd tried to accomplish before leaving the inn. Since Chelsea lived the closest to the art and wine festival, they'd all decided to meet here and then walk into town together.

A moment later, Chelsea threw open the door with a smile. She wore a flowing dress set off by a pair of heeled sandals, always managing to pull off a bohemian, free-spirited look. Lizzie wished she'd found something a bit more stylish to wear than her white jeans and teal-colored tank top. But she should really just be happy she'd made it at all.

"Hi, Lizzie," Chelsea said, giving her a hug. "I'm glad you came. I thought you might not be able to get away from the inn."

"I'm here. Shay is manning the desk tonight."

"How was her trip to Denver to meet her future in-laws?" Chelsea asked, waving her into the house.

"It was good. They liked her."

"Why wouldn't they? She's very likeable."

"Is Brodie coming with us?" she asked, seeing no sign of her sister's fiancé.

"No. He got called in to work. It will be just the girls. Chloe and Kevin are spending the evening celebrating his parents' wedding anniversary and neither Hannah nor Keira are bringing dates."

"That's fine. We haven't gotten together just the girls in a while. What about Gianna?"

"She said they were going to skip the festival and just barbecue at home."

"She and Zach and Hailey are a little family now," she said, as she followed Chelsea into the living room. She sat down on the couch while Chelsea took the chair across from her.

"It's sweet," Chelsea said. "They're very happy together. I'm sure it isn't easy being a stepmom, but Gianna seems to get along great with Hailey."

"Everyone is coupling up. First Gianna, then you."

"Maybe you'll be next, Lizzie."

She uttered a short, doubtful laugh. "I don't think so. I'm already in a very demanding relationship with a hundred-year-old inn. And, yes, it does keep me warm at night and make me happy."

Chelsea gave her a mischievous smile. "It doesn't do everything you need."

She grinned. "It does enough."

"Seriously, Lizzie, you need to get out and date, kiss someone."

She flushed at that comment.

Chelsea's gaze narrowed. "Wait a second. I've seen this look before. You have kissed someone. Who?"

"I don't want to talk about it."

"You have to tell me. I'm your sister. We share everything."

"You didn't tell me when you first kissed Brodie," she pointed out.

"Well, I told you pretty soon after the first time. Come on. Who was it?"

"It was an impulsive, spur-of-the-moment thing."

"With…" Chelsea's gaze grew speculative. "Wait a second. I think I can guess. It was Justin Blackwood. You two walked home together after Adam's party. Did you kiss him then?"

"We might have had a kiss at the lake," she conceded.

"The lake? You took a detour on the way back to the inn."

"Justin hadn't really seen it yet."

"Sounds like he was looking at you and not the lake," Chelsea teased. "How was it?"

"Really great," she admitted. "Probably because the kiss

made me feel reckless and sexy, and I haven't been either of those things in a while."

"Well, good for you. What happened after that?"

"Nothing. We walked back to the inn and decided we would not kiss again."

"That's disappointing."

"It's not, Chelsea," she said. "Justin is a guest. He's leaving on Sunday. Starting something with him would be stupid."

"Or fun."

"Now you sound like Justin. And believe me, I'm tempted. I'm just afraid I'll like him too much. I'm not very good at casual. I know that about myself."

Chelsea nodded. "Then you're being smart. You should trust yourself. Don't listen to me. What do I know? I've made a lot of mistakes in my life."

"But you're on the right track now. You have a great guy in Brodie. And you have your music back."

"It's sometimes difficult to believe now that I gave it up for as long as I did. I was really in a bad place." Chelsea paused. "But you were there for me, and you were very patient."

"You're my big sister. And you've always been there for me, too."

"Maybe not so much the last two years."

She waved off her apology. "We're not keeping score. Sometimes you're up and I'm down and vice versa. It all evens out."

"You're right. I am a little worried about you, Lizzie. And I'm not just talking about dating. You look stressed every time I see you. Are there problems at the inn that you're not sharing?"

She debated how to answer that question. Chelsea was one of her investors, and she deserved the truth. "There have been some financial setbacks that I wasn't expecting. It's an old building and everything seems to be breaking at once. Our bookings are up and down. Some months have been better than others. The winter was good, but now we're in between snow and hot days and there aren't as many tourists in town."

"There's a lot this week. Everyone wants to see the eclipse."

"Which is great for me. I have a full house and I'm thrilled. But next week doesn't look so good."

"Can I do anything to help?"

"No. I'm going to figure it out."

Chelsea met her gaze with an encouraging smile. "You always do. I have no doubt that you'll make the inn a success. But if you do need some cash…"

"No. You've given me enough. Plus, you're building your studio and planning your wedding. Don't worry about this."

"I can still help."

"I will let you know if I need you."

Chelsea gave her a doubtful look. "You never like to need anyone. You've always been stubbornly independent."

"I think that runs in our family."

The bell rang, and Chelsea jumped to her feet. Lizzie stood up, following her to the door.

Hannah and Keira came in together, a contrast in color and style. Hannah with her red hair and pale skin wore skinny jeans and a falling-off-the shoulder peasant blouse. Keira was dressed in a red and white sheath dress, her dark hair swept back in a messy but stylish ponytail.

She hugged each of them, but Keira's embrace was a little stiff.

"Are you still pissed at me?" Keira asked, her brown gaze worried.

"Why would she be angry with you?" Chelsea asked before Lizzie could respond.

"Yeah, what did you do?" Hannah put in.

"I'm not angry, and she didn't do anything," she said.

"She must have done something," Hannah said.

Judging by the curiosity on both Hannah and Chelsea's faces, she didn't think either one was going to let her get away with that vague response. "Keira brought an opportunity to me," she said. "To sell the inn."

"What?" Chelsea exclaimed in surprise. "You want to sell?"

"She doesn't," Keira said quickly. "But someone I knew came to me and wanted an introduction and I thought Lizzie might want to hear her out. But I should have given her a heads-up, and I didn't. That's why she's mad at me."

"I'm not angry, but you should have told me, Keira. The reason you didn't find the time was because you knew I'd say no, right?"

"Maybe that was part of it," Keira conceded. "If it helps, I did tell Paula to back off and let you come to her if you were interested. I said you wouldn't respond well to pressure."

"That's fine, but I'm perfectly capable of saying no if she does reach out."

"You can't sell the inn," Hannah said, giving her a confused look. "It's your dream job."

"I don't want to sell it, and hopefully it won't come to that."

"It won't come to that," Chelsea said. "I will help you keep it."

"So will I," Hannah said. "I don't have a lot, but I can invest if that will help."

"Me, too," Keira said.

She sighed, hating that everyone was looking at her like she was in trouble. Maybe she was, but she didn't want the whole world to know that. "Look, it's all fine. It's good for me to have options. But right now, nothing has changed, and we don't need to talk about this anymore. What's going on with everyone else? Someone must have something fun to share."

"Well, I do have a little news," Keira said slowly, her gaze moving to Chelsea. "Should I tell them?"

Lizzie looked over at her sister, who had a gleam in her eyes. "What are you two up to?"

"I asked Keira to design my wedding dress," Chelsea said.

"What? Wow, that's amazing," she said.

"You haven't sketched in years, have you?" Hannah asked Keira.

"No, I haven't, not until lately. I ran across my old sketch-book a couple of months ago, and I found myself going through it. When I left New York and my job in fashion to take care of my mom and run her real-estate business, I didn't think I would ever get back to designing. But I've missed it. Chelsea came by one day and saw some of my sketches, and we started talking, and she had the crazy idea that I should design her wedding dress. But she still has the right to say no if she wants to buy something else."

"I already love the first couple of sketches you showed me," Chelsea put in. "You really understand my style and my vibe, and that's important. I'm counting on you."

"I hope I don't let you down," Keira said. "I did pull out my sewing machine the other day, and I'm going to make some patterns and run everything by you before we go any further."

"What about our bridesmaids' dresses?" Hannah asked. "Are you designing those, too?"

"I don't know if I'll have time," Keira said with a nervous laugh.

"I want her to," Chelsea said. "But she wants to do the wedding dress first and then we'll see."

"This is great," Hannah declared. "I always felt bad that you had to give up on being a fashion designer."

"Designing this dress isn't going to change my career path. I still have the real-estate company to run, and it's important that it continue to be successful."

"Maybe you can have a side business," Hannah suggested.

"We'll see. So, are we waiting for anyone else?" Keira asked.

"No, it's just us," Chelsea said. "Let's go."

As they left the house, Chelsea and Hannah took the lead

while Lizzie and Keira walked behind them. "I'm excited for you," Lizzie said. "I can't wait to see your sketches."

"I'm pretty rusty. There's a good chance Chelsea will want to find another designer, and I'm sure there are tons of really good designers who would want to dress her. She's a celebrity."

"Sometimes I forget that."

"That's easy, because she's down to earth." Keira paused. "Lizzie—"

"Don't apologize again," she warned.

"All right. I just hate when I mess up."

"So do I," she said, relating to that feeling. "But you didn't mess up. You were looking out for me. That's what we do as friends."

"Speaking of looking out for each other—I'm worried about Chloe. I was talking to a friend of mine who works at Hogan's Bar, and she said that Kevin has been hanging out there late at night, all by himself. Well, actually, he's not always by himself."

She frowned at that piece of news, which seemed to back up Chloe's fear that Kevin was having an affair. "Do you know who he's been hanging out with?"

"Not any particular woman, from what I understand, but he's apparently very friendly." Keira paused. "Since I've already made one blunder this week, what do you think? Should I tell Chloe?"

"I don't know."

"I'm leaning toward keeping quiet. I mean, Chloe must know he's somewhere when he's not at home. And I don't want to cause them trouble. On the other hand, it feels like I should try to protect her."

"It's a tough call," she admitted, feeling torn herself. "Maybe we should go to the bar one night and see what's going on."

"That's not a bad idea. If Kevin sees us, maybe he'll come clean to Chloe so that we don't have to."

"That would be a better scenario."

"I can't believe he's acting like such a jerk," Keira continued. "All these years she waited for him to come back, and he always said how much he missed her, and now they're at odds, and they have a new baby. How is this happening?"

"I wish I knew."

"Chloe has been holding down the home fort for a long time. When does she get a break? When is it her turn?" Keira demanded. "Maybe I should tell her what Kevin is doing. I hate that she's being taken advantage of."

She smiled. Keira was always fiercely protective of people. She was the kind of friend who would always have your back, and the lingering resentment she'd had toward her bringing Paula's proposal to her disappeared. Keira hadn't been trying to hurt her, but to help her. She was just being too sensitive.

"What do you think, Lizzie?" Keira continued.

She focused back on Chloe. "Well, we can't do anything tonight. They're having dinner with Kevin's parents, who are celebrating their anniversary."

"Hopefully, he spends the entire night at home with his parents and his wife and his child."

"Hopefully," she echoed, as the art and wine fair came into view.

Wicker Avenue had been closed down to traffic, and a dozen or more tents had been set up along several blocks, offering wine, art, and appetizers. There was quite a large crowd filling the street, and she hoped all of the guests at the inn were here. She'd made a point of encouraging everyone to attend. She wanted them to not only fall in love with her inn but also with Whisper Lake, so they would continue to come back as often as possible.

They stopped at the first booth to grab plastic glasses of wine and then meandered through the art in the booth next door. As she paused to study a landscape of the lake, Hannah moved up next to her.

"I heard you've been hanging out with the very sexy Justin Blackwood," Hannah said. "What have I missed the last two days?"

She smiled. "Not much. I'm just being a good host."

"And what is he being?" she asked, with a mischievous smile.

"He's being a good guest."

"Hey, I want the juicy stuff, not the stuff you'd tell your parents," Hannah complained.

She hesitated. "We might have kissed."

"Really? Okay. Now we're getting to the good part. It was good, wasn't it?"

"Oh, yeah, the man can kiss."

"What else can he do?"

"I'm not going to find out."

Hannah groaned. "Why not? He's one of the hottest guys I've seen in a long time. Why wouldn't you find out? It sounds like you're both interested. Is he married or something?"

"No, he's single. But he's just passing through."

"Good. Then if he's bad in bed, you won't have to see him again."

"Unfortunately, I don't think that will be my problem."

"You're afraid you're going to fall in love with him."

She was actually afraid that was already happening, but she didn't want to say that. "I think it's better that Justin and I keep a professional relationship. I don't want to complicate things, and his grandparents are two of my best repeating guests. They've also sent several friends my way. I don't want to ruin that relationship by messing around with their grandson."

Hannah grinned. "If anyone understands love, it's probably Marie and Ben. Look how long they've been married."

"They are great role models for love," she admitted. "And Justin is very sweet to them. He took his grandmother antique shopping today. She was over the moon about it."

"It says something about him if he's willing to shop with his grandmother."

"Yeah, it does," she said. "So, are you dating anyone?"

"No. I just haven't connected with anyone in a while. I've had a couple of dates, but they've just been boring. And I feel like I keep saying that." Hannah frowned. "Maybe I'm the one who's boring. Do you think it could be me?"

She laughed. "You are not boring, Hannah. You just haven't met the right person."

"Sometimes I think I need to move to a bigger city."

"Really? I'd hate to see you leave."

"I love living here, but maybe it's too small for me."

"It's growing every day and the new medical center is nice."

Hannah smiled. "Don't worry. I'm just having an off day. I'll probably never go anywhere, except to the next booth. I want to try a different wine." She finished off what was left in her glass as they headed next door.

For the next hour, they looked at art, drank wine, and ate mini quiches, veggie sticks and too many cheese squares to count. It was nice to be with her sister and her friends. Lizzie felt more relaxed than she had in a long time. But that ease evaporated when she saw Justin. He was standing next to his grandmother, who was trying on an embroidered sun hat. He smiled at his grandmother with great affection, and it touched Lizzie's heart.

Justin said he didn't do love, but she could see love in his gaze now. He had a relationship with his grandparents, but he didn't seem to want any other kind of relationship, and she couldn't help but wonder why. He didn't want to talk about his parents, and Marie had implied that there were problems between Justin and his parents, but she'd never said what the problem was. It felt like it was something deep, something dark, that affected the way he looked at love. Or maybe she was making too much of their estrangement.

Justin could just be a man who didn't want to commit to a woman. It wasn't like she hadn't met that kind of man before. He didn't have to have a secret, although she still thought that he did. She wondered if they got closer if he would tell her.

But getting closer was a bad idea, she reminded herself.

On the other hand...

Justin suddenly turned his head and caught her eye. A smile slowly curved his lips, and her heart flipped over in her chest.

She gave him a brief smile, then turned away, pretending to join the conversation between her sister and Keira, but she had no idea what they were talking about. Her entire body was humming with excitement and a feeling of recklessness. She couldn't look back at Justin. She couldn't let him see what he was doing to her.

"Are you all right, Lizzie?" her sister asked, giving her an odd look.

"Yes," she said. "But I have to get back to the inn. I just remembered something I need to take care of."

"Now?" Chelsea quizzed, a speculative look in her gaze.

"I thought we were getting dinner after this," Keira put in.

"Sorry. You guys have fun. I'll catch up to you tomorrow." She tossed her empty plastic glass into the recycle bin and left before they could ask her any more questions.

But it wasn't really their questions she was running away from; it was Justin.

CHAPTER THIRTEEN

JUSTIN GOT BACK to the inn around nine after having dinner with his grandparents. When they headed upstairs to their room, he moved toward Lizzie's office. There was no one at the front desk, and her office was empty as well. He walked down the hall to her apartment and knocked on her door, but no one answered. As he returned to the lobby, he ran into Noah.

Noah gave him a smile and said, "Hello."

"How's it going?" he asked.

"It's all right," Noah said.

"Have you seen Lizzie by any chance?" Considering how often Noah walked the grounds, he was probably the best person to know where Lizzie might be.

"I have," Noah said. "She's up on the roof deck. It's one of her favorite places. I often see her up there late at night when she finds a little time for herself."

"Thanks. I'll check that out."

"Be careful," Noah said.

At Noah's unexpected words, he paused and glanced back at him. "Why would you say that?"

"Because I know how easy it is to fall in love in this place."

"I just want to talk to her." Actually, he wanted to do a lot more than talk.

"That's what I said to myself when I went to find Alice the night after we met. I knew she was married, but I told myself I just wanted to talk. It was a lie. I wanted Alice with every breath that I took."

He didn't know what to say to that. "I'm sorry she hasn't come back," he said quietly, seeing the pain in Noah's eyes. "Lizzie told me your story."

"You must think I'm a fool to keep coming back for Alice, waiting, hoping…"

"I don't think you're a fool," he said carefully. "Maybe a bit too optimistic."

Noah gave him a tired smile. "That's diplomatic."

"I just hope you don't miss what's right in front of you because you're looking for someone else."

Noah stared back at him. "Are you talking about Patty?"

"Or anyone."

"Have you ever had a dream, Justin?"

"Sure. I'm running my dream company right now."

"Did you ever let anyone talk you out of chasing that dream?" Noah asked.

He smiled. "No. And I see your point. It's none of my business."

"You were very kind to give Patty your room, so it is your business. I know my actions don't make sense to anyone else, but I'm doing what I have to do. Alice and I had a connection that was deep, personal, and so very honest. I'd been married before and thought I loved my wife beyond belief, but with Alice, it was different. It was all-consuming."

"Perhaps because it just lasted a short time," he couldn't help saying. "You didn't have time to fall out of love, to be bored, to get annoyed with each other."

"You think I'm romanticizing her. You might be right. Or you might be wrong."

"That about covers it," he said dryly. "Why didn't you ever go look for Alice? Why just wait?"

"Because she asked me to. Because she said she'd return when she could."

"How do you know if she's even…" His voice drifted away as he realized he was getting far too involved in Noah's life.

"Alive?" Noah finished. "I don't know if she's alive. I hope so. I hope she's happy, even if she's not with me."

"What about you? Are you happy? Can you be happy if you can't let go of her, of the possibility of her?"

"Patty asked me the same thing earlier. We've gotten very close, very fast. Patty lost her husband; she understands grief and longing and the hope for a second chance."

"Where is Patty now?"

"She's waiting for me in my room. I had to take a walk around the gardens one last time. We're going to play some cards now."

"That's good. Enjoy yourself."

"I will. You, too."

He started to turn, then paused. "Just for the record, you don't have to worry about Lizzie. I'm not going to hurt her."

"I hope not. She hides behind her smile, but she has a fragile heart."

"I think she's tougher than you might believe."

"Or maybe you just want her to be," Noah said with a gleam in his eyes. "Have a good night."

As the old man ambled away, Justin headed toward the stairs, Noah's words ringing through his head. Maybe he shouldn't go up to the roof. Maybe he should just go to his room and leave Lizzie alone.

But as he hit the fourth-floor landing and felt a breeze

coming through the French doors leading onto the roof, he could not turn away.

Lizzie was sitting on a couch, her feet propped up on the coffee table next to a bottle of wine and an empty glass. She hadn't yet become aware of his presence, and for a moment, he just watched her. She was looking out at the view, her hair blowing gently in the breeze. It was another starry night. There seemed to be no lack of them in Whisper Lake.

As he stepped forward, she turned her head, giving him a startled look as he came around the couch.

"I found you," he said, sitting down next to her.

"I wasn't missing."

"Perhaps not, but I was missing you."

"I thought you'd be with your grandparents all evening."

"We spent a lot of time together today. We just had dinner at the Three Pigs."

"Did you get the pork chops?"

"I did. They were amazing."

"Your grandmother is going to make sure you eat well this week. Are they having a good time? Has your grandfather recovered from this morning's allergy attack?"

He gave her a dry smile. "He was apparently too sniffly to go antiquing, but he felt fine when it was time to drink wine and have dinner out."

She smiled. "Your grandfather is no fool. How was shopping? Did you buy anything?"

"My grandmother bought a jewelry box and an old desktop clock, both of which seemed old and boring to me, but she was quite excited about her finds. And they're small enough to fit in her luggage, which was apparently part of her criteria for purchasing."

"That's good. Did you carry her bags while being a good sport?" she asked with a teasing smile. "Or were you checking your phone for texts and emails the whole time?"

"I managed to keep up with some messages while also being an attentive grandson." He paused. "I saw you at the festival, but you disappeared before I could say hello."

"I had work to do."

"But no work now?"

"I just finished up. I often come up here in the late evening. It's usually empty. Most of the guests use the patio and the garden if they want to go outside. How did you find me?"

"Noah said he saw you out here."

"Right. I waved to him as he was making his nightly walk."

"I talked to him for a few minutes. He told me about Alice."

"Did you tell him to stop waiting for a woman who is never coming back?"

"I didn't say it exactly like that, but I did mention that he might miss what's right in front of him because he keeps looking to the future. He said Patty told him the same thing. But then he challenged me by asking if I'd ever let anyone talk me out of my dream, and I had to say no."

"He turned the tables on you."

"Yes, he did."

"I looked up your website earlier," she said, surprising him with her words. "It's very cool. I liked the original logo that you displayed in the origin story of your company."

"Robbie the Robot," he said with a laugh. "I actually drew that figure when I was eleven years old."

"And from that robot in your imagination, you built a huge global company. But I'm curious. It also said in the story that you named the company after someone who inspired the dream. You didn't say who."

"It's not important to the outside world who my inspiration was."

"Then why did you mention it at all?"

"Because he was important to me, but his identity is private."

"He doesn't want you to say who he is?"

He hesitated, knowing that the simple answer was yes. But with Lizzie's compelling gaze upon him, he felt it difficult to lie or even to dodge. "It's not that. He doesn't know anything about the company."

"How is that possible? From what I saw, you're pretty well known in the industry."

"He died long before I built the business."

Her smile dimmed. "Oh, I'm sorry, Justin. I didn't know. I was being pushy again. You should have just told me to shut up."

"You weren't being pushy, just curious."

"Well, I'm still sorry, and whoever he is, I think he'd be proud of what you built based on his inspiration."

"I'd like to think so." He wanted to tell her more. He felt like the words were on the tip of his tongue, but by force of habit, he held back. Opening up that locked door would only bring pain, and he wasn't looking for that tonight or any night. So, he changed the subject. "Who were you at the festival with? I thought I saw Chelsea and Hannah."

"Keira was there, too. It was just the girls tonight. It was fun to catch up."

"Catch up? It seems like you see each other all the time."

"This week, maybe, but we are all pretty busy these days." She lifted her gaze to the sky. "It's another starry night. But tomorrow, we'll have the eclipse, and the sky will go dark."

"I don't understand why that is so exciting to everyone."

"It's out of the ordinary, a special time. A lunar eclipse can only happen when the moon is directly opposite the sun. The earth's shadow blocks the sun's light, which otherwise reflects off the moon. And it has to happen during a full moon."

"I suppose that's kind of interesting."

"And there's also a legend, you know."

He grinned. "I'm not surprised. Want to tell me what it is?"

"There are several different stories, but there's one I particularly like. I have to warn you, it's romantic."

"Lay it on me," he said with a laugh.

"Once upon a time," she began with a sparkle in her gaze, "there was a love story between the sun and the moon, and they traveled the world together. And then the moon betrayed the sun and slept with the morning star. They were punished by the universe. From then on, the moon and the sun could never meet. The moon had to travel by night, the sun by day. But during an eclipse, for that brief time when the world goes dark, they can kiss, until they are forced to part ways. The eclipse is supposed to be a time for second chances. Which is why Noah is so excited that this particular week is also the week of an eclipse, which is when he met Alice."

"That's quite a tale, but not all that romantic since the moon cheated on the sun. Maybe they don't deserve a second chance."

"That is true, but you're kind of missing the romance of it all."

He grinned. "That's me. I do tend to miss the romance." He paused. "And I don't really believe in waiting for rare events like eclipses to kiss a woman I want to kiss."

His words brought more light to her eyes.

"Justin, you're making it hard to say no."

"Then don't say no."

She stared back at him. "I do want to kiss you. I've been thinking about it since this morning, which seems like a very long time ago now."

His gut clenched at her unexpected admission. "Well, stop thinking about it and take what you want. I'm right here."

"It's risky."

"You're not afraid to take risks, Lizzie. You did it with this inn."

"That's different."

"Is it?"

At his challenging question, she sat up and framed his face with her hands. She took her time, her gaze moving across his face, dropping to his mouth, and damned if his body didn't grow harder with each passing second. She was a spectacularly pretty woman and every nerve on his body was tensing with anticipation. If she wanted to kill him slowly, she could probably do it.

Finally, she moved forward, touching her lips against his. She started out tentative, gentle, and exploring. Then desire took over and they moved into each other's arms, kissing with a hunger that couldn't be denied. The connection between them deepened with each kiss. He felt like he was addicted to her. Every taste made him want more. His heart was pounding, his body humming, and as his hands roamed over her sweet curves, he couldn't even conceive of stopping. He wanted to take her into his room. He wanted to get rid of the clothes between them. He wanted to lose himself in her and for her to lose herself in him.

"Bed," he murmured, as they came up for air. "Yours… mine…doesn't matter." She stared back at him with her beautiful green eyes that were filled with emotion. "Don't say no." The words slipped past his lips before he could stop them. He didn't like sounding so desperate. Even worse, he didn't like feeling so desperate. But he needed her. And he had to have her.

"There are a thousand reasons why I should say no," she said.

"But at least one good reason why you shouldn't. I want you, Lizzie. And if you want me, too…"

"Then we should go to your room, because it's closer."

A relieved smile lifted the corners of his mouth. "Good choice." He kissed her again and then jumped to his feet, pulling her up along with him. They'd only taken one step away from the couch when a scream lit up the air.

They froze for a split second and then ran toward the door. They heard someone scream again, and they dashed down the stairs. There, on the third-floor hallway, they found Noah passed out on the floor. Patty was on her knees next to him, trying to shake him back to consciousness, and a dark-haired woman wearing a dress and heels, a suitcase on the floor stood next to her.

"What's going on?" Lizzie demanded as she reached the group first.

The woman turned her face into the light. "He saw me, and he passed out," she said.

Lizzie sucked in a breath. "Oh, my God! Alice? Is it you?"

CHAPTER FOURTEEN

JUSTIN COULD NOT BELIEVE that Noah's long-lost love had just appeared, the way Noah had always thought she would. It had been ten years, and now she'd come back. No wonder Noah had passed out cold. Hopefully he hadn't had a heart attack. "Should I call 911?" he asked, pulling out his phone.

"What's going on?" Carlos Rodriguez asked, as he came out of the adjoining room. "Is he all right?"

"He's waking up," Patty said, as Noah opened his eyes.

Noah gave Patty a bemused look. "What happened?"

"You don't remember?" Patty asked. "There was a knock on the door, and you opened it."

Noah's gaze moved past Patty and connected with Alice. His eyes widened, and he struggled to sit up. "Am I dreaming?" he asked. "Is it you?"

"It's me, Noah. I came back." Alice's gaze took in the couple in front of her. "Maybe I shouldn't have. You're with someone else now. I should have guessed you would be. I should go."

"Hold on." Noah struggled to his feet. "You can't leave, Alice. I've been coming here every year for ten years."

"I didn't really believe you'd be here," she said. "It has been so long. I thought you would have forgotten about me."

"Never. How could I?"

"This is crazy, isn't it?" she murmured, as the two locked eyes.

Justin didn't think they were even aware of anyone but each other. He could not believe Alice had come back to find Noah, that the old man hadn't been as crazy as he'd thought.

"I've thought about you many times over the years," Alice said. "But I wasn't free."

"Are you now?" Noah asked.

"Yes. At last."

"At last," Noah echoed.

As they went into each other's arms, Patty cleared her throat. "I'm going back to my room, not that anyone cares."

He could see the pain in her eyes before she walked away.

Lizzie gave him a helpless look. "I need to go after her. I know she's just my guest, but—"

"She's in pain," he finished. "Go."

"I'm sorry, Justin."

"Don't be."

As Lizzie hurried down the hall, he saw Noah and Alice exchange a kiss. Noah had waited over a decade for Alice. He could wait a little while longer for Lizzie.

On his way back to his room, he was stopped by several guests, who wanted to know what was going on. He reassured them all, including his grandparents, who had come up from their room on the second floor after having heard a loud thud. Most were excited for Noah, having heard his story or at least parts of it. The incredibly romantic reunion got everyone talking.

It took him almost an hour to extricate himself from the other guests, plenty of time for his blood to cool and his pulse to slow down. But when he got back to his room and flopped down on the bed, thoughts of what had almost happened with Lizzie brought his temperature right back up. She was clearly taking her time with Patty, and he doubted she'd come back to him when she was done.

For better or worse, the moment between them had passed, and he doubted he was going to get another such moment.

Unless he went to her. There was nothing stopping him from doing that. But he felt a little like Noah now, like it was up to Lizzie to come back to him.

That was crazy. He didn't wait for what he wanted.

Maybe he was waiting, because he wasn't sure that what he wanted was what he should have. There was incredible chemistry between him and Lizzie. And he wanted to take her to bed more than he wanted to do anything else. *But what about after?*

Damn! He never thought about after, not when it came to sex. *What was happening to him?*

An odd creaking sound brought him into a sitting position. The rocking chair in the corner moved back and forth, a gentle rocking motion. He frowned. The window was closed. He didn't feel a breeze. But there it went again, rocking back and forth. It had to be a vibration from the floor or the wall or the heating system—something.

He got up and walked around the room, searching for some breezy spot that would make the chair move, but he couldn't feel a thing. The chair was no longer rocking, but he couldn't stop staring at it. He looked at it so long that his eyes began to blur. He felt like he was seeing the shadow of someone.

He was losing his mind. There was no ghost in his room. He didn't believe in ghosts. Not anymore.

That caveat reminded him that a long time ago, he'd desperately wanted to believe. He'd wanted a sign. He'd wanted to know there was more out there, that there was a life beyond this one. But he'd never ever gotten a sign. And he'd stopped looking for one.

He walked into the bathroom and brushed his teeth, then took off his clothes and got into bed. He snapped off the bedside lamp and slid under the covers. The sheets felt cold. He closed his eyes and tried to sleep, but fifteen minutes later, he knew that wasn't going to happen. The rocking chair had started rocking again, and the creak was making him crazy.

Turning on the light, he grabbed his computer off the nightstand. He wouldn't sleep; he'd work. That was the one constant in his life. And he almost immediately felt better when he started digging into the latest testing report on their newest robotics device. Numbers and charts always helped him focus on what mattered. He concentrated on that instead of the rocking chair, instead of the woman he'd almost taken to bed, instead of the reunion going on downstairs.

***

"You must think I'm crazy to be so upset," Patty told Lizzie as they sat at a small table in Patty's room.

"Not at all," Lizzie said, as Patty blew her nose again. The tears had finally stopped, but now Patty just looked miserable.

"I barely know Noah. And I've been aware from the first minute we met that he was in love with someone else. It's not like this was a surprise. I knew he was waiting for Alice, desperate to have her show up. I just didn't think it would happen."

"I don't think any of us did, not even Noah," she said. "I still can't believe it."

"It's a good thing," Patty said, trying to sound positive. "Noah has been waiting a long time. I've never met anyone so devoted to someone who they weren't married to, who they'd only spent a week with. But Noah just kept telling me that love isn't defined by time. It just is. It's there when it's there. You can't force it. You can't fight it. You just have to decide whether you want to accept it or not."

Patty's words made her think about Justin, about the decision she'd made to sleep with him. If not for Alice's sudden appearance, they'd be in bed together now. She would have taken a step she couldn't take back. And she probably would have loved every second of it. But now that they weren't kissing, she could see how fast she'd been running toward the edge of a cliff. Maybe it was good she'd had a chance to rethink. Or maybe it wouldn't matter, because she could still feel a tingle run down her spine every time she thought of Justin. Whether she slept with him or not, she didn't believe she was ever going to forget him.

"What do you think, Lizzie?"

She suddenly realized that she'd lost track of the conversation. "I'm sorry, Patty. What did you say?"

"Should I leave now or in the morning?"

"Definitely not now. It's late, and you don't want to drive through the mountains in the dark."

"That's true. It's just difficult to sit in this room and think about what's going on two doors down." She paused. "Noah kissed me earlier. It was really nice. I was feeling very close to him. But he's not mine. He belongs to Alice, and I need to go back to my life and stop pretending otherwise."

"I wish I could help" Her heart went out to Patty, who had clearly fallen for Noah.

"You are helping. You're sitting here listening to me when I'm sure you have lots of other things to do. Or maybe you'd just like to go to bed."

"I'll get there. I don't mind hanging out with you."

"Really? You wouldn't rather be spending time with Justin? You two seem to be together whenever I see you."

"We've become friends."

"Perhaps more than friends?"

"Haven't gotten there yet."

"But you like him."

"I wish I didn't."

Patty gave her a weak smile. "We can't choose who we love, and Justin is very handsome."

"I don't love him, but he is handsome. I get that nervous feeling every time I see him."

Patty gave her a knowing smile. "I feel the same way when I see Noah. But I think his heart only flutters for Alice. What about Justin? Is he available?"

"He's single. I don't know that he's really available, though. He's very guarded when it comes to his feelings. I think maybe he's been hurt by someone, but I don't know. He hasn't opened up. I hit a wall every time I get close. Clearly, he doesn't trust me enough to share his truth. How can I like someone who can't really talk to me?"

"Because you see the shadows in his eyes. You know there's pain somewhere."

"I believe that's true. He said he loves to run, and I can't help think he's running away from something. Maybe that's also why he buries himself in work."

"He doesn't want time to think."

"No, he likes to move fast."

"Do you bury yourself in work because you're running from something?" Patty asked.

She frowned at the question. "I'm just busy. I'm building a business."

"Is that all it is?"

She thought for a moment. "Maybe I am trying to outrun my insecurities." She shrugged. "Justin and I are two workaholics, for whatever reason. That's also probably a recipe for disaster."

"You're both passionate. Nothing wrong with that," Patty said. "My husband and I were both passionate about what we did, too. Rick was a musician, and I was a baker. We met when he came into my bakery to buy chocolate eclairs for someone in the band who was having a birthday." Patty's voice softened. "He said he saw me with flour on my nose and the heat of the oven on my cheeks, and he fell hard."

"What did you think of him?"

"I was a bit intimidated by his tattoos, but he was the sexiest man I'd ever met. I was twenty-two years old and he was only six months older. My parents didn't like him at all. And he was traveling a lot. It shouldn't have worked, but it did. We made it work. We were too in love not to. We got married five years after we first met, and we were together for twenty-six years after that until he passed away. That was eight years ago." Patty took a breath. "I didn't think I'd ever meet anyone who could make me feel love again. But Noah did that. I don't know how, but he did. I guess I should be grateful for that. Now I know that I have the capacity to love someone else. If it's not Noah, maybe there will be another man."

"I think there will be," she said, with a reassuring smile.

"But my point for you, Lizzie—if you like Justin, don't let him get away. Break down his walls, be a little pushy, don't take no for an answer. Give love a chance."

"It's not love. It's probably just lust."

Patty smiled. "That's not so bad, either."

She grinned. "Thanks, Patty. I came here to make you feel better, and you turned the tables on me."

"I always wanted a daughter, but kids were not in the cards for me. It's nice to give someone younger a little advice, even if you don't take it."

"It was good advice. I think you would have made a great mom."

"Thanks. I'm going to go to bed and try to get some sleep before I leave in the morning."

Lizzie got to her feet. "Can I offer you one piece of advice?"

"I think that's only fair."

"Don't leave without talking to Noah. Whatever happens with him and Alice, you need to say good-bye, and I think he does, too."

"I'll consider it. I just feel a bit foolish."

"If you were being a fool, so was he."

She left Patty's room and walked down the hall, pausing by Noah's door. She could hear the murmur of voices, but she couldn't hear exactly what they were saying. It was sad that Noah's dream coming true had hurt Patty, but she had to admit there was something incredibly moving about his reunion with Alice. Ten years had passed but neither one had forgotten the promise they had made to each other. That was something.

When she got to the stairs, she hesitated once more. She could go to Justin's room, or she could return to her apartment. Before she could question her decision, she jogged up the stairs and knocked on Justin's door. Her heart was beating out of her chest. She hoped she was making the right choice. A minute ticked by. She couldn't hear any sound coming from within the room. She knocked once more. No answer.

It was only eleven, but maybe he was asleep. He probably hadn't thought she'd come back. It had been almost two hours since she'd left him. She waited one more moment and then walked away, telling herself it was just as well. She'd probably just avoided a huge mistake, but she couldn't shake the disappointment that followed her down the stairs.

Justin had just turned off the light when he heard her knock. He knew it was her, even though she didn't say anything. And there was a very big part of him that wanted to answer that door, but he'd spent the last hour convincing himself that he should stay away from her.

Sitting up, he stared at the door, heard the second knock. Dammit. He really wasn't good at being noble, at trying to protect someone's heart. But Lizzie was different.

And then he heard her footsteps as she moved down the hall.

His heart was racing, but she was gone. He'd let her go because he didn't want to have regrets or for her to have any, but right now that's all he was feeling.

He laid back down, staring once more at the ceiling, at the slight beams of moonlight creeping through the parted curtains.

Lizzie had looked so pretty in the moonlight when they'd been at the lake, when they'd been on the roof. But she'd also looked pretty in the daylight, running up the hills with him, sailing across the lake, the wind in her hair, the sun on her face.

He closed his eyes, wishing he could forget her, but her image still floated through his brain. He stopped fighting it and just let himself remember her smile, her laugh, the way she played with the end of her hair when she was thinking, the kindness in her eyes when she'd dealt with Patty, the laughter and joy she had with her friends, the sexy, sultry look she'd given him right before they kissed.

The images flew around in his head. He couldn't stop them from coming so he didn't even try. If he couldn't have her, maybe he could just dream about her. Perhaps that would be enough.

Fifteen minutes later, it wasn't enough.

He got out of bed, turned on the light, threw on his clothes, and headed down to the first floor.

He knocked on her door, and a moment later, she answered.

They stared at each other for a long minute, and then she took his hand and pulled him into her apartment, where the passion between them exploded. He backed her up against the wall as he kissed her, his hands sliding down her body to her hips.

She slipped her hands under his shirt, and he sucked in a

breath as her touch on his back made him shiver. But he wasn't cold. There was nothing but heat between them.

He moved away from her mouth to kiss her neck. A whisper of delight came from her lips as his tongue slid along her collarbone. She was so sweet. Her scent surrounded him. Every breath he took was her. He went back in for another kiss and then pulled her away from the wall, so he could lift the hem of her top and pull it over her head.

She shook out her hair as her top fell to the ground and gave him a sultry look as his gaze shifted to her breasts, delightfully spilling out of her lacy pink bra. He cupped her breasts with his hands as their mouths came together once more. Her soft curves drove him mad. He loved the lace, but he wanted to feel nothing but skin.

When she reached for the back clasp of her bra, he took a quick second to pull off his own shirt, while she slipped the straps down her shoulders, and they moved together in a delicious friction of heat. Their jeans and underwear came off next and then Lizzie grabbed his hand and pulled him into her bedroom, making a stop in the bathroom to grab a condom.

He'd almost forgotten, and he never forgot something as important as protection, but this woman was making him more than a little crazy.

They kissed their way to the bed, falling onto the soft mattress in passionate abandon. He wanted to go slow, but he couldn't, especially not with Lizzie's mouth and hands on his body. She might have been reluctant to take this step, but now that they were here, she was all in. She made love with the same passion, energy, and generosity that she brought to everything else in her life. She was beautiful and sexy as hell, and it had never felt this right before.

He tried to hang on to some kind of control, but that was a battle he couldn't win, because he was quickly losing himself in her, and what an amazing feeling that was. She encouraged him to let go, and he did. They flew together, so high, so fast, so deep, so...everything.

It was a long while before he came back down to earth...

But she was there, and so was he. They wrapped their arms around each other and held on.

CHAPTER FIFTEEN

LIZZIE HAD NO WORDS.

Her heart was still pounding, her body tingling, every nerve ending on fire. Muscles she hadn't known she had were aching in such a delicious way, and she didn't want the feelings to end. She wanted to stay right here in Justin's arms, in this moment, forever. Or as long as possible, she quickly amended, knowing forever was probably out of the question. But she wasn't going to think about that now.

How could she worry about the future with the most perfect male body next to hers? And why would she want to?

Justin's arms tightened around her back, and she lifted her gaze to his. His blue eyes were dark and shadowy, his sexy mouth full and inviting, and she couldn't help but kiss him again. There wasn't a desperate passion to this kiss, but rather an intimate affection.

He smiled. "That was nice."

"I thought you didn't like it when I described our first kiss as nice."

"Good point. Amazing. Spectacular. Mind-blowing. How are those adjectives?"

"Much better." She rolled onto her side so she could get a better look at him. "What made you change your mind?"

"What do you mean?"

"I knocked on your door. You didn't answer." She paused. "I thought maybe you were asleep, but you weren't, were you?"

"No, I wasn't."

"So, why did you come here?"

"Because I realized how stupid I'd been not to answer the door."

"Why didn't you, Justin?"

"I don't know. I thought the moment had passed. You were gone a long time."

"Patty needed to talk." She took a breath. "And I wasn't sure if the moment had passed either, but when I got to the stairs, I found myself going up instead of down. When you didn't answer, I didn't know if I should feel relieved or disappointed."

"Well, I felt like an idiot for worrying about the future instead of enjoying what's happening right now."

"I didn't think you were worrying about the future," she said, surprised by his statement.

"I saw how upset Patty was when Alice showed up. Clearly, she'd developed feelings for Noah in a very short time. I couldn't help wondering if we weren't heading for the same kind of bad ending. I don't want to hurt you, Lizzie."

"Are you just worrying about me? Or also yourself?"

"Both. I have to admit you've turned my very well-controlled life upside down. I've been off-balance since the first moment we met. You have gotten under my skin in a way that no one else has."

She liked that. "It goes both ways, you know. I wasn't expecting anything like this." She licked her lips, choosing her next words carefully. "I realized tonight that I didn't want to miss out on something great just because it had an end date. Patty said that life is made up of moments, and she didn't regret falling for

Noah, because the time they'd spent together had woken her back up. He'd made her feel alive again. I started thinking that you kind of woke me up, too. I didn't want to miss our moment. We have some time before Sunday. We should enjoy it."

"That sounds good to me," he said with a warm smile.

"I'm glad. So, are you a snuggler, or are you counting the seconds right now as to when you can make a quick exit?"

"If I'd had to answer that question yesterday, I'd have said I'm not a snuggler, as you call it. But right now, I have no intention of letting you go any time soon. This feels too good."

"Agreed, and I'm okay with that."

"You better be, because it's happening."

Even though she liked to be in charge as much as Justin did, it was nice to have him call the shots. She'd felt so overwhelmed with decisions lately that not having to make one more felt great. "Good," she said. "I like to snuggle. I also like to talk."

"That's no surprise. You've been talking since we met. But since we're in bed together, are we going to talk dirty?" he asked with a hopeful expression.

She laughed. "Maybe later, but I was thinking maybe we talk… secrets." She could feel him stiffen, and she almost regretted her suggestion, but then her curiosity took over. And she remembered Patty telling her to push a little. "You shut down every time I get close to your personal life. What don't I know about you, Justin?"

"A lot."

"Can you tell me anything?" Silence followed her question, and she could see the conflict in his gaze. "When we were talking earlier about your friend who died, the one who inspired your company, I got the feeling there was more to that story."

"I don't talk about Sean."

"Sean? Wait? Isn't that your brother?" she asked in confusion. "Was he the inspiration for the company?" More facts slid into place. "Sean is dead?"

He let out a breath. "Yes."

She had not been expecting anything as tragic as the loss of a sibling. "I'm sorry. I didn't know. Marie and Ben never said anything about your brother or his death."

"No. They just told you there were tensions in the family."

"That was really an understatement, wasn't it?"

"Big-time. But that's the way my family is. They like to sweep things under the rug."

"I'm surprised you let them. You're very direct."

"Now I am—probably because of the way I grew up." He paused, his gaze reflective, as he stroked her arm.

"You don't have to talk if you don't want to."

"I want to tell you about Sean, Lizzie. I just don't know where to start. Or if I should start. I've been holding him behind a big wall, a dam, you might say. If I pull a brick out, the whole thing might collapse. It's a huge risk."

She was touched by his emotional words. They hadn't come easy for him. She was beginning to understand why he'd built a robot company. He'd surrounded himself with objects that could never die, never cause him pain, and he could never hurt them. There was more than pain in his eyes; there was also guilt. She wanted to know so much more, but it had to be on Justin's terms. She didn't want to push him into revealing something he wasn't ready to share.

"We don't have to do this, Justin. You don't have to say anything. You don't owe me your confidences. I just want to know you as much as I can. But that's because I'm rather fascinated by you."

His expression lightened. "Even though I'm leaving?"

"I've accepted that your departure is going to sting no matter what else we say or do, but I'm not going to regret being with you. I know that."

"Good." He paused once more, then said, "Let's see how far I can get." He drew in a breath and blew it out. "I told you that Sean was my half brother, my mom's son."

"Yes. And he was a lot older than you, but you were close."

"Very close. Sean looked after me from the day I was born, and in some ways, he became a surrogate parent to me."

"Why?" she asked curiously.

"My father is an infectious disease scientist. My mother is a nurse. The first several years they were together, my mom stayed home with me and Sean. We had a normal childhood. At least, that's what I'm told. I don't really remember that time. What I do remember is all the years that came after normal. When I was six and Sean was twelve, my parents got involved with a global medical team that went into poverty-stricken third-world countries to provide medical care. They hired a nanny to take care of us when they were gone. She was nice enough, but she wasn't our mother, so Sean and I turned to each other for support."

"That makes sense, but you must have missed your parents."

"Very much—in the beginning. It was never supposed to be more than two or three weeks every couple of months, but the assignments got longer with less time between them. They were missing big holidays. I remember one Christmas when they couldn't get back. We spent it with the nanny's family, and it was weird, but I actually liked that Christmas better than the others. It felt like a family should feel. But then Gloria, the nanny, she got another job. She wanted to take care of little kids, and I think Sean was pissing her off. He was fifteen by then and he did not want a nanny asking him questions. The next few people my parents hired stayed for a few months at a time. And sometimes Sean took care of me in between, which was fine. We ate pizza and played robot wars."

She could hear the depth of affection in his voice for his brother. Justin had told her he didn't do relationships, and she'd thought that meant he'd never felt love for anyone, but he'd loved his brother. He'd gone all in on that relationship, and then his heart had been broken. She felt a wave of anger toward his parents. "I don't understand how your mom and dad could just abandon you like that."

"They had a higher purpose. They were working for the greater good. And it was always supposed to be ending. They'd be back in a few weeks or next month or next year. There were so many excuses. I finally stopped asking when they'd be home. I couldn't believe whatever promise they gave me. I couldn't count on them to be there if I needed them. I had to take care of myself and Sean and I looked out for each other."

"What about your grandparents? Where were they? It seems like Marie and Benjamin would have stepped in."

"They were living in Europe during that time. My grandfather was a professor at Durham in the UK. My grandmother worked in a tea shop," he added, with a small smile. "I don't think they had any idea how much my parents were gone. I believe my father lied to them. I heard him on the phone once saying they would only be gone two weeks, but that trip turned into two months. Anyway…we're getting to the hard part."

"Do you want to stop?"

"I don't think I can stop."

She moved in closer to him, putting her arm around his waist. "I'm here—if the dam breaks."

"You think you can catch me?"

His question was meant to be light, but she could feel the weight behind his words. "I know I can," she said.

"Sometimes you're as overconfident as I am, Lizzie."

"That might be true, but I'll give it my best shot."

He met her gaze. "You're a very kind person. You have a big heart, for friends and for strangers."

"We're hardly strangers now."

"That's true. And at some point, we need to discuss that tattoo you have on your hip. That was an interesting surprise."

"And to think you don't like surprises," she teased.

"I liked that one," he admitted. "I hate to turn this night into a downer."

"We can talk about something else. I can tell you about my guilty TV pleasures, the fact I spend a little too much time watching the below-deck crew on a sailing yacht."

"I've never heard of that show."

"It's really fun. I think it appeals to me when I'm feeling a bit overwhelmed with work and an old house that needs constant care. Sailing off the coast of Greece in a luxury yacht feels like a good escape, not that I'd want to be the crew on that yacht. I'd have to be a guest."

"I've actually been on one of those yachts."

"Really? How was it?"

"As amazing as anything I've ever done."

"And here I thought a little cruise around Whisper Lake would be the highlight of your boating career," she teased.

"That wasn't bad, either, but mostly because you were there. I can't seem to stop smiling when I'm around you."

"That's a good thing."

"Which is why I should stop talking."

Despite his words, she sensed he felt a need to let out the pain. "It's your call."

"And I'm stalling, but I've come this far." He paused, gathering his thoughts. "When Sean was a junior in high school, he really got into partying. His grades plummeted. He was always cutting class. His friends were losers. I could see the downward spiral, even though he tried to keep it away from me. Somehow, he graduated from high school, I'm not sure how. After that, he went to the community college, but he wasn't into school. I think he was rebelling against our super-intelligent parents, and by then, he didn't want to be anything like them. My parents finally realized how bad things had gotten when he was arrested for a DUI. He was nineteen then, and they put him in rehab. My grandparents also came back to the States around that time. I felt like my family was finally rallying together. But it was too late. We had several decent months and then Sean OD'd. I was fourteen. He was almost twenty-one."

Pain came off Justin in waves of emotional heat. She wrapped her arms around him and held him as tightly as she could, feeling like maybe she did need to catch him, because while he wasn't crying or talking, it felt like the dam was breaking. "I'm so sorry," she whispered.

He didn't say anything more for several minutes. He just held onto her with a fierce need.

The connection between them now felt even more powerful than before. They weren't just physically connected now but also emotionally. They were bound together by Justin's secret, by his trust in her, and she was deeply touched. She couldn't really understand what he'd gone through, the world he'd grown up in. It was so very, very different from her own, and she couldn't help but think how lucky she'd been to have her parents, her siblings, her big extended family. She'd won the lottery when it came to family and Justin had not.

Finally, Justin's grip on her eased and he let out a breath. When his gaze met hers, she could see that the painful shadows had receded. He shifted slightly. "Thanks. You were right. You were strong enough to catch me."

"And you were strong enough to let go. Sometimes, that's even more difficult."

He nodded. "I'm okay. Better than I thought I would be. No one in the family talks about Sean. And I haven't spoken about him to anyone in years. Only my business partner knows the story, because I met him when I was eighteen."

"And you've never told anyone else?"

He shook his head. "No. I was never even tempted. I'm actually good at hiding my feelings. That seemed to change when I got here. Somehow when you're around, I want to bare my soul. Actually, I think that's the magic of this town. Every person I've met felt free to confide in me, and it just kept blowing me away how open everyone was. But now I'm doing the same thing, spilling my guts."

She smiled. "There is magic here."

He smiled back at her. "Maybe you're the magic, Lizzie."

"I wish I had that power. What happened with you and your parents after Sean died?"

"We were so angry with each other. I blamed my parents and also my grandparents. They blamed each other and also me."

"Wait, no way. You weren't to blame. You were a kid."

"But I knew better than anyone what Sean was doing. They might have been fooled by his funny, charming, loud, gregarious behavior. He was the life of the party, and everyone thought he was happy, but I saw him when he wasn't putting on a show. I knew he was partying too hard. I should have said more. I tried to tell him I was worried about him, but he always said he had it under control."

"He was young. Everyone thinks they have it under control when they're a teenager. And you were even younger, Justin. His death was not your fault. Your parents are another story. Your grandparents, too. I'm a little disappointed in Marie and Ben."

"To their credit, when they realized there was a problem, they moved back. After Sean's stint in rehab, they insisted that both of us live with them. Of course, Sean wouldn't do it. He said he needed to be on his own, but I moved into their house. My parents were still in and out, although they were around more then, but you could tell their heart wasn't in LA or in the family. They were adrenaline junkies and hunting for cures was their drug of choice. We need people like that in the world, because they do amazing things, but they probably shouldn't have kids."

"Probably not," she agreed.

"Anyway, my grandparents saved me. After Sean died, they overwhelmed me with attention and love and caring. They were constantly watching me, constantly trying to make sure I was all right. I think they were trying to make up for all the years they weren't there. And it helped. I couldn't connect with my parents, but I had them to lean on."

"Well, that's good. I would have expected that from them."

"They definitely kept me on track, not that I wanted to follow in my brother's footsteps. He loved feeling out of control and wild. I didn't like that at all. I wanted to feel the solid ground under my feet. I wanted to know who was around me and what I was doing. I wanted to remember every second of my life."

"That's where the need for control and predictability came in."

"Yes. I didn't want any more horrible surprises. I controlled everything I could, except my parents. That would have been an impossible task, so I didn't bother. And they didn't seem to care. Whatever relationship we'd had before Sean died was shattered. It was irreparably broken. It was almost better knowing that we were done. I didn't have to keep wishing for them to be the parents they were never going to be. The worst had happened. And there was no going back or moving forward with them."

"I can't believe they didn't want to be in your life after losing Sean. It seems like it would have become more important to them, not less."

"They'd tell you they tried. They'd tell you they did their best. They'd tell you they only left again because I didn't want anything to do with them." He paused. "Maybe some of that is true, but it's still not good."

"No, it's not. I have to say, Justin, after everything you went through as a kid, you got it together as an adult. You built an amazing company. That's an accomplishment that you should be so proud of."

"I am proud of my company. It started out as a tribute to Sean. It was his dream as well as mine, and I wanted to make it happen for him."

"You did that and then some."

"I just wish he could have seen it all," he said, his voice heavy with grief.

"He would have been very impressed with his little brother. I'm sure your parents must be proud of you, too."

"They don't have a right to be proud. They contributed nothing to my success."

"When's the last time you saw them?"

"Three years ago. We didn't make it more than ten minutes without a screaming match. I blame them for everything, and they blame themselves for nothing, so we are a billion miles apart. But I don't care about them anymore. It's not like I lost anything. You can't lose something you never had." He drew in a breath and let it out. "So, that's my story. That's my secret. Now, let's talk about you and more of those guilty pleasures."

She stiffened at his words, not because she was afraid of revealing her secrets, but because she realized she was holding a secret that belonged to his grandmother, one that could affect him. Marie had asked her not to tell Justin that his parents might come to the ceremony on Saturday. *But after what she'd just heard, could she keep that secret?*

"Justin, there is something I should tell you," she began.

He frowned. "You sound suddenly serious."

"It's not that big of a deal. Actually, it might not even be a deal at all." *Was she making a mistake to create drama and anger with his grandparents for something that might not even happen?* Maybe she should talk to Marie first and let her know that she needed to come clean to her grandson. It was really her secret to tell.

"You know what? I think we've talked enough for one night," Justin said.

He was letting her off the hook, and while she knew she shouldn't take the reprieve, she really wanted to. If she told Justin his parents might show up on Saturday, he would probably leave immediately, and she wasn't ready to say good-bye to him yet.

"Hey," Justin said, running his fingers down the side of her face. "No more frowns. Let's get back to fun. Whatever you have to say can wait. I have other ideas for the next few minutes."

"Only minutes?" she asked lightly.

He smiled. "How about hours?"

"We should sleep at some point."

"At some point," he agreed, as his hand slipped between her legs.

A wave of desire drove every thought out of her mind but one—she wanted him. And he wanted her. Sometimes, she just needed to keep it simple. There was always tomorrow.

CHAPTER SIXTEEN

JUSTIN WOKE up a little before seven to a buzzing text alert coming from his phone, which was still in the pocket of his jeans. It was probably Anthony. The London meeting would just be ending.

Lizzie was still fast asleep and so very pretty with her cheeks pink, her lips soft, and her hair flowing in silky waves down her bare shoulders. He did not want to get out of bed. He did not want to leave her. For the first time in he couldn't remember when, he actually wanted to say to hell with business and focus on making her say his name with a sexy little gasp of pleasure at the end of it.

But as his phone buzzed once more, he rolled out of bed, grabbed his jeans off the floor, and moved into the bathroom.

He was right. Anthony needed to talk. He sent him back a quick text, then dressed and returned to the bedroom. He gave Lizzie one last wishful look and then left.

Upon entering his room, he immediately fired up the computer on the desk, starting a video call with Anthony. He wished he'd had time for coffee, but Anthony sounded rather desperate. A moment later Anthony's face filled the screen. He looked tired and his brown eyes were worried. This was not the face of the young, cocky guy he was used to seeing around the office.

"What's wrong? What happened?" he asked.

"Everything was going well, but then Maxwell started asking me questions about the latest version of the R720 and suggested that Vinton Industries had a better prototype."

"They don't. I gave you all the competitive specs."

"I know. I told him that. I just didn't quite have the facts right in front of me. I had trouble refuting some of the points of his argument. I was juggling a lot of balls."

He drew in a tight breath, knowing that it wasn't completely Anthony's fault, because he'd been thrown into the meeting last minute, but still... He'd expected him to know the most important information as well as he could. "All right. What else?"

"They liked the rest of the presentation, but they're hesitant on the R720."

"Which is a big part of this deal."

"Maxwell is open to taking a call from you tonight. He'll be available after a dinner meeting, so after nine, our time. I figured you'd say yes, so I told him you'd call him."

"Good." He checked his watch. He had about ninety minutes to prepare to make his case.

"Just so you know," Anthony continued. "Maxwell's dinner meeting is with Vinton's VP, Carl Kramer."

"Damn. Carl is in London?"

"Yes."

"I should have known he'd make a bigger play. All right. I better get to work."

"Sorry I wasn't able to close the deal."

"I appreciate your effort. I'll touch base with you after I talk to Maxwell."

"I'll be here."

Justin ended the call and then got to work. He had to save

this deal, and he was at a huge disadvantage, with Vinton in London and him in Whisper Lake. But he needed to find a way to show Maxwell that they had the best product at the best price, with the best service and support systems in place. And he would have to do that after Maxwell had been wined and dined by his biggest competitor. Well, he'd always liked a challenge, and he definitely had one now.

A knock came at his door, and his head jerked up. He should ignore the knock. He couldn't see Lizzie now. He couldn't get distracted by her pretty face. He had to concentrate. He had to focus. He had a lot on the line.

But it wasn't Lizzie's voice that rang out; it was his grand-mother's.

He got up and opened the door.

"Good morning," she said with a bright smile. "Are you ready for breakfast?"

"No, sorry." He'd completely forgotten he'd promised to have breakfast with his grandmother. "I can't do breakfast. I have a small crisis with a deal in progress. I'm going to be tied up for a few hours."

Disappointment filled her eyes. "This was supposed to be a no-work week, Justin."

"I'm trying to balance everything. But you have to trust me when I say this can't be avoided."

"All right. We'll meet up later. You will make the beach picnic, right? We'll be heading down to the lake around four. Lizzie is making up picnic boxes and it's a whole big thing before the eclipse. I don't want you to miss it."

He nodded. "I'll be there. I just have to take care of this now."

"All right. I'll let you go. I just want you to know how appre-ciative I am that you came, being as busy as you are. This week, tomorrow especially, is really important to me. The older I get, the more I realize that family is everything."

He couldn't quite agree with that statement, but he didn't want to upset her. "You and Grandpa saved me when I was a teenager. I'll never forget that."

Her eyes grew a little misty at his words. "I wish we'd done more sooner."

"You did what you could. I wasn't your responsibility."

"I know you still have a lot of anger—"

He put up a hand. "I really can't talk about anything now. I'm sorry."

"Of course. Do your work. We'll get together later."

He nodded, then shut the door before she could say anything else. He didn't want to be rude, but he had a deadline, and the clock was ticking.

Lizzie wandered through the dining room around nine o'clock, checking on her guests, making sure that everyone had everything they needed for breakfast, but her mind wasn't really on her job. It kept drifting back to Justin and the incredible night they'd spent together. She'd been disappointed to find him gone when she woke up. She would have liked waking up in his arms, next to the heat of his body, instead of putting her hand on a cold sheet that had only reminded her whatever they had was over. Although, they could have two more nights together before he left on Sunday. It didn't have to be over yet.

Unless Justin was backing off. Maybe he regretted telling her his personal story. He wasn't one to naturally share, which made her wonder why he'd confided in her.

She wanted to believe it was because he trusted her, because he liked her, because they'd shared more than a physical connection. And maybe all that was true. *But what did it mean? Or did it mean anything?*

This was the problem with hookups, and why she didn't

engage in them very often. She thought too much. She dissected every word, instead of just taking it all at face value.

They'd had great chemistry together and incredible sex and they'd laughed and talked, too. It had been a perfect night, and if that's all it ever was, then she was going to be happy about it.

"Lizzie?"

She looked at Shay, suddenly realizing she'd ended up at the front desk. "Did you ask me something?"

"You look like you're in a daze."

"Just tired."

Shay gave her a thoughtful look. "I heard about what went on last night. I can't believe Alice made her fated reappearance."

At Shay's words, she realized she'd forgotten all about Alice and Noah and Patty. And she hadn't seen any of them in the dining room. "Yes, she showed up late last night. How did you hear? Have you seen them?"

"Yes. Alice and Noah had breakfast in the dining room about an hour ago. I couldn't believe it was her when Noah introduced me. Alice is a very attractive woman. And they seemed to be having a good conversation. It was hard to believe they hadn't seen each other in ten years."

"I know. It's the craziest thing. Have you seen Patty this morning?"

"No. I was just going to ask about her."

"I wonder if she already left."

"She didn't check out or leave her key. But she must be upset. She and Noah were getting really close."

"She was shaken last night. She was with Noah when Alice knocked on the door. Noah opened it and passed out."

"Wow," Shay said, amazement in her eyes. "What a story. It's so romantic. They finally found each other again, and right here at the inn where it all started. We should call the travel magazines. We should pitch the story, Lizzie. It could bring in some great press."

"Maybe. I'd have to ask Noah and Alice first, get their permission."

"I'm sure they'll agree. Noah has been haunting the inn for ten years, waiting for his lost love to return." Shay's eyes sparkled with enthusiasm. "We could get a lot of mileage out of this, Lizzie. People will come just to see the room where they reunited. It could even be a movie."

Shay had always had creative marketing ideas, and while Lizzie liked her energy, she felt a little unsure about this one. "I'll talk to them, but I want to give them some space right now. I don't want to do anything to ruin whatever is happening between them."

"I suppose that's best. I guess we should make sure they do end up together for good before we pitch the story. But I'm telling you, Lizzie, it could be a great marketing ploy."

"I'll think about it. I'm going to do some work in my office this morning. If you see Patty, will you have her stop in to see me before she leaves?"

"Sure." Shay paused, grabbing her notepad. "One more thing. You had a call from a Paula Wickmayer. She said she'd like to speak to you and hoped you would get back to her today." She ripped off the piece of paper and handed it to Lizzie. "I asked what she wanted, but she just said you'd know."

"I do. Thanks." She took the paper and walked into her office, closing the door behind her. Sitting down at her desk, she set the phone message aside and picked up the stack of bills in her inbox. She still had the remainder of the furnace bill to pay. Utilities were going up with the increase in guests, but since she'd had to comp some of this week's guests, she would still be in the hole despite having a full inn. Landscaping and gardening services were the same, but she hadn't yet paid for the current month. And then there were the food bills. They offered a first-rate breakfast, but that meal probably cost more than they could afford.

With a sigh, she opened her computer to check out her bank account. The balance was even more depressing. *Was she fighting a losing battle?* She'd been trying to make the inn profitable for almost two years now, and she wasn't gaining any ground. In fact, she was losing more ground each month.

Her phone buzzed, and she reached for it like a lifeline. Anything to take her mind off her bills. It was her mother, and she smiled as she answered her phone. "Hi, Mom."

"How are you doing, Lizzie? I was thinking about you and the lunar eclipse this evening. Is the inn packed?"

"Every room."

"That's great. Your dad and I are so proud of you, honey."

"Thanks," she said, feeling a little guilty. *Was she doing enough to be deserving of that pride? Or was she going to lose all their money and end up with nothing to give back to them or any of her investors?*

"We'd like to come up next month for a visit."

"I thought you were going to Florida next month."

"We decided to put that off. The plane tickets are so expensive right now."

She hated the idea that her parents were scrimping on vacations and plane tickets when they'd invested a chunk of money in her business.

"We'd rather just drive up and see you," her mom continued. "Maybe around Mother's Day. Do you think you'll have any rooms open?"

She pulled up the calendar on her computer. She wished she could say she didn't, but the inn was only half-full that weekend. The real rush to the lake would come June through August, when the summer heat was a big draw. "I have rooms available."

"Great. I'm trying to talk Grayson into coming as well."

"What about Nathan?"

"Who knows where he'll be. Adam told me about his accident. It doesn't sound too serious. Have you talked to him?"

"No," she said, realizing she'd meant to send Nathan a text, but she hadn't. "I'll see if I can get a hold of him."

"I hope you can. I've texted him. But other than sending me back a thumbs-up emoji, he had nothing else to say. I hope he's having fun, but I worry about him. It doesn't seem smart for him to take so much time in between jobs. But I can't really complain, because he's self-supporting and seems to enjoy his life."

"He does seem to have a good time," she agreed.

"I just hope you stay in touch with him, Lizzie. Even though he's not the best at calling or texting back, I think he needs to hear from us. He needs the connection to his family."

"Why would you say that?" she asked curiously. "He's always been so independent."

"True, but he's also the middle child. Adam and Grayson were tight. You and Chelsea were close, and Nathan got lost sometimes. I think that's why he likes to pretend he doesn't need anyone."

"I never thought about it like that," she said slowly. "Nathan was always the funny guy in the family. He never seemed to have a care in the world."

"That's what he wanted everyone to think, but I suspect his constant wanderlust is because he's looking for a place to belong. That makes me a little sad, like I didn't do enough."

"You did great. All your kids know you love them," she assured her mom, reminded once again how lucky she was to have not just one parent but two who cared deeply about her and her siblings and their family unit. Justin's parents might be brilliant medical professionals who had saved countless lives, but they hadn't been aware of what was going on in their own family, especially when their kids were young. Her mom was still worrying about her brother, and Nathan was in his thirties.

"You always make me feel better, Lizzie," her mom said. "How is everything with you? Are you seeing anyone? Or is that a silly question? I'm beginning to think that inn will be the closest thing I get to a son-in-law."

"You're getting Brodie. Focus on that."

"I love Brodie. But I want all my kids to find their special someone, including you. I know you're busy with the inn, and it makes you happy, but work isn't everything. Oh, why am I wasting my breath? I know where your priorities are right now, and that's on building your incredible business. Dad and I can't wait to see what else you've done with the place."

"I can't wait to show you," she said, hoping by the time they came in May some of her problems would be behind her. Because the last thing she wanted to show her parents and her investors were the stack of bills in front of her. "But, Mom, I have to ask…"

"What's that, honey?"

"You were looking forward to Florida, to seeing your friend Linda. Is it a money thing? Do you need some of your investment back?"

"Oh, no. We're fine. We'll go to Florida another time. Don't worry about us. We'd rather come to the inn and see you."

"If you're sure."

"We are. Now, have fun tonight."

"I will. Bye." As she ended the call, her gaze moved from the bills to the packet from Falcon Properties. She really didn't want to think about selling the inn. But if she failed at keeping the inn running, there were a lot of people she loved who were going to suffer a loss right along with her. Her mom had told her not to worry, but she couldn't help but be concerned. It wasn't just that her parents weren't going to Florida, but that she found herself wondering what else they were putting off because their money was tied up.

She stared at the folder for another long minute. She wasn't ready to look at their offer yet. *Was she?*

Justin didn't get done talking to Maxwell until after eleven. After two hours of intense discussion, he'd finally won him over, and the deal was done. With that verbal agreement, he'd checked in with Anthony to fill him in on next steps. By the time he ended all that, it was after one, and he was starving. The beach picnic for the eclipse wasn't starting until four, and he needed some food. He also needed to see Lizzie. He wasn't sure which hunger was bigger.

He grabbed his key and headed downstairs. Shay was at the front desk. She gave him a friendly smile.

"I heard you've been working all morning," she said. "Your grandparents were disappointed you couldn't join them for breakfast."

"It was unavoidable. Is Lizzie around?"

"She's in her office."

"Thanks."

He moved past her to knock on the office door.

"Come in," Lizzie said.

When he entered, she gave him a conflicted look. "Hi," she said, her gaze filled with memories of the intimacy they'd shared. But there was also wariness in her eyes as she got to her feet. "How has your morning been?"

He frowned at the cool note in her voice. "Seriously? You're going to talk to me like I'm a guest after the night we had?"

"What do you want from me, Justin?"

"I want you to act like you, not like a stranger."

"I'm sorry. No. I'm not sorry," she amended. "You left without saying good-bye. It was a weird way to end things."

"I got an emergency text from my colleague in London. I had to take his call, and I didn't want to wake you up. There was a big problem with our deal, and I had to jump into the middle of it. I just finished, and I came to find you before I did anything else."

She looked slightly mollified by his explanation, although she still had her arms folded across her chest. "Okay, I understand. I just missed you. And that terrible feeling reminded me of why I'm not good at hookups. I have a hard time separating the emotional from the physical."

"It wasn't just a hookup, Lizzie. You know that. We talked a lot."

"We did." She sighed. "I'm afraid I just like you a little too much, Justin. It's what I do. I get involved. I care too much."

Her candid admission touched his heart. "I like you, too, Lizzie. And I care about you as well."

"That's nice."

"We're back to nice?" he teased.

She gave him a smile that melted the ice between them. "I guess we are back to where we started."

"No, we're not. We can't go back. We move forward and we don't have regrets."

"I don't have regrets about last night. I'm not sorry we were together. I'm just very aware of time passing."

"Our time isn't up yet."

"That's true."

"Then we don't need to end things now."

"No, we don't."

"Good." He walked around the desk, pulled her into his arms, and gave her a long kiss that filled him with lust. When they broke apart, he said, "Are you really busy right now? Any chance you could take a break upstairs, in your bedroom, or in mine?"

She gave him a breathless smile that unfortunately came with a negative shake of her head. "I wish I could. But I can't, Justin. I have to figure out where to find some money."

"What's going on?" he asked.

"Too much debt, not enough income." She sat down behind her desk. "I keep looking at the numbers, but I can't figure out a way to make things work." She rubbed her eyes. "Also, some of this just doesn't make sense. So, I need to go over it again and again until it does."

His gaze narrowed as he took in her troubled expression. He pulled a chair around the corner of her desk and sat down next to her. "Let me help."

"You just got done working. You don't need to do this."

"I want to do it." His gaze moved to the open brochure on the desk. "Is that the offer from the company that wants to buy your inn?"

"Yes. I started reading it, but I haven't gotten through it. Some of it is confusing. And there's still a part of me that doesn't even want to consider it, but maybe I should. I'm not just going to take myself down; I'm going to take everyone down. I have really tried so hard not to fail, but maybe I'm just not up to this."

"Whoa. Where is this defeatist attitude coming from?" he asked in surprise. "What happened to my cheerleader?"

"Reality happened. I've been running away from the truth. I've worked really hard to overcome my weaknesses, to play to my strengths, but this inn, this hundred-year-old building, keeps falling apart. And the choices I've been making are probably wrong. You said yourself I give too much stuff away."

"That's true, but you're just having a bad day."

"A lot of bad days."

"And you're tired, which is partly my fault. But you can do this. You're smart. If the ship is going in the wrong direction, you can turn it around."

"Or it might just go down."

"Lizzie. What aren't you telling me?"

She gave him a weak, emotional look. "I'm not that smart, Justin. I have some issues…"

Her words surprised him once more. "What kind of issues?"

"I don't like to talk about them."

"Well, tough. I told you all my secrets. Let's hear something from you."

She hesitated, then said, "I have dyslexia, which means I sometimes have trouble reading or comprehending things without spending a lot of time on them. I can mix up numbers if I'm not careful. I can usually work around it, but sometimes I still make a mistake. And when I'm tired, it gets more difficult."

"I'm sure it does, which means you should not be working on any of this now."

"I can't avoid my problems. I've been putting bills aside for a while, and they're all due or past due."

"You can take a few more hours, maybe a day or two?" he suggested, growing more concerned at the weary look in her eyes. She wasn't just exhausted from their night together. This weariness came from a much deeper place.

"Maybe," she said. "I just feel so stupid sometimes, and I hate that feeling."

He was beginning to understand that Lizzie's relentless optimism was a cover for insecurities she'd very cleverly hidden away. "When did you find out you had issues with learning?"

"Middle school. I faked my way through elementary school, but when I got into sixth grade, I started falling behind. It was awful. I'm the youngest of five kids, who are all super smart, and almost every teacher I had compared me to one of my siblings who had gone before me. They always thought I wasn't applying myself, because clearly I should be as smart as they were."

"How did your parents react?"

"They were disappointed with my grades, but they didn't understand the severity of my issues for a long time. I would just pretend that I was distracted or that I didn't do my homework. I thought it was better if they thought I was lazy or impulsive. My siblings would call me Dizzy Lizzie, because I was always spinning around, going from one thing to the next."

"You were trying to outrun your problems."

"Both literally and figuratively. Running helped me calm down so I could think. But all I could think about was that I was stupid. Finally, a teacher figured it out and called my parents in, and I had some testing, and then we all got on the same page. I received a lot of help after that, but it's not something you can fix, and it doesn't just go away." She paused. "My parents blamed themselves for not realizing I wasn't just being lazy, and they have done everything they could since then to get me whatever help I need. When they decided to invest in the inn...when my siblings did as well...it felt like everyone really believed in me. There are so many reasons why I can't fail." She tapped her finger against the Falcon Properties folder. "And I can't help thinking that maybe I should take this offer, because then everyone will get their money back and then some. I'll have achieved something."

Now he understood where she was coming from. "I get it. If you quit now, you don't fail. But you also don't win. You're not a quitter; you're a fighter, Lizzie. You've fought to get this far."

"Maybe this is as far as I can go. This morning when I took a shower, I heard a banging in the pipes, and I've had a plumber tell me that I might need to replace a lot of the pipes. I can't afford that. And if one breaks before I do the repairs, I could have a disaster on my hands."

"You could," he agreed. "But maybe you need to narrow down which pipes have to be replaced now and which ones can wait. Let me take a look at your books. Let me help."

"You don't need to do that. You should spend the afternoon with your grandparents."

"They're having tea in some Victorian house downtown. I'm going to meet them at the beach barbecue, so I'm free now, and I want to help."

"You're just going to tell me what I already know, that I should sell."

"Maybe it's not as bad as you think. You might just need to get creative."

She gave him a look of disbelief. "I thought I was the optimistic one."

"You are. So, let's get back to your let's make lemonade out of lemons attitude. Come on, babe. Snap out of it."

"Snap out of it?" she echoed.

"That's not going to work?" he teased.

"I don't think so," she said, but a reluctant smile parted her lips.

"Then let's work through all your options together. Maybe I can be the one to make lemonade this time."

"Are you sure you want to do this?"

"Positive. But I might need to get a sandwich first. I haven't eaten all day."

"I can take care of that." She got to her feet. "I know you hate the word, but you are nice, Justin."

"So are you. And, for the record, I think you're one of the smartest people I've ever met."

Her eyes watered. "And just for that, I'm going to bring you some cookies, too."

He laughed. "Good. Now get out of here and let me get started squeezing those lemons."

CHAPTER SEVENTEEN

JUSTIN'S OPTIMISM faded as he studied Lizzie's financials. The inn was bleeding money, and even though bookings were up, it would take her a while to dig out of the hole she was in. He could see that the bulk of the money had gone into repairs. He wondered how many of those problems had been or should have been disclosed at the time of purchase, but that was in the past. He needed to figure out how she could move forward from where she was.

The first thing she needed to do was stop comping people for minor complaints. But beyond that, she might need to take a hard look at breakfast. It wasn't just the food, but also the chef's salary that was putting a dent in the profit margin.

He sat back in the office chair, taking a moment to think. After making him lunch and watching him work for a half hour, Lizzie had disappeared, asking him to let her know when he was ready to chat, but until then she couldn't handle watching him go through her books. He didn't blame her. He probably hadn't been hiding his emotions very well.

His gaze drifted to the offer from Falcon Properties. He'd also taken a good look at their proposal. It was generous. It would allow Lizzie to pay back her investors with a small percentage return on their investments. She would also bank some cash and receive a good salary that would be over and above what she was taking home now, which was next to nothing. But then, everything she had was invested in the inn.

However, what the offer didn't spell out was exactly how much autonomy she would have in decision making. *Would she truly be running the inn or just be another employee, a cog in the wheel of a huge corporation?*

The office door opened as he was pondering that question, and Lizzie entered with a look of trepidation in her beautiful eyes. He hated seeing the worry. He much preferred her laughing eyes or the delighted look that entered her gaze when he was touching her in just the right spot. He'd learned a lot of her favorite spots last night, and his body hardened at the thought of making love to her again. In fact, he couldn't really understand why they were doing this instead of that...

"Well?" she asked.

It took a minute to realize she was referring to her financial statements and nothing else.

He cleared his throat. "You have a complicated situation."

"Please don't sugarcoat it. I need to hear from the ruthlessly honest Justin Blackwood."

"Okay. You're hemorrhaging money and you'll have to make some big changes if you want to survive."

His words took the energy right out of her, and she sank onto the hard-back chair in front of the desk.

"I knew you were going to say that," she said heavily. "But bookings are up starting in June. The summer looks good."

"That is a bright spot," he agreed. "But the rest of April and May will be rough. You need to rethink breakfast and your chef."

"She does more than breakfast. She does the happy hours and the cookies..." Her voice trailed away. "Which you don't like, either."

"I love them, but they're costing you too much. And this beach picnic tonight—why are you paying for everyone's dinner? That should have been a separate event fee."

"It's because of the eclipse. It's a special event."

"You have too many of those. The most important thing for you is to sell rooms. Until your bookings are consistent on a year-round basis, you're not bringing in enough income to cover the extras. You probably need to cut the hours of some of your workers as well. Do you need someone at the front desk in the evenings? Can you cut Victor's hours back?"

"His girlfriend is pregnant. He needs the hours."

"That's not your problem."

"He's my employee. I can't be heartless."

"He's not even that good of an employee. I've seen your notes."

"He's getting better. He's young."

"And the cook's daughter? Why did you pay her top dollar for taking a tray around a cocktail party? You could have set the appetizers on a buffet."

"She's saving for college."

"And you're not running a charity, Lizzie. These people are your employees, not your family."

"They can be both."

"You need to get to profitability first, then worry about family and friends and helping everyone else out."

"And?" she asked hopefully. "Do you have a plan?"

He wished he did. "Honestly, I'm not sure there is another option besides selling out. This offer is good. You'd still want to negotiate, see if you could get more, but you'd end up in the black and so would your investors."

"But I wouldn't be running the inn anymore."

"Well, you would be, but it wouldn't be yours."

"I've worked for a lot of chains, Justin. I know what it's like to be an employee. I've put in so much time and effort…to end up being another staff member. I don't want to do it. But…" She drew in a breath. "I might have to do it, because it's not just my money or my time on the line."

"Is anyone asking for their investment back?"

"No, but when I first asked for money, I told everyone I'd try to at least get them their initial investment back within four years. I have another year to go on that promise."

"That buys you some time."

"The things you want to cut are why the inn is popular. Guests don't just come here for a cute, charming bedroom. They want the beautiful breakfast, the happy hour on the patio, the people who make them feel like they're at their home away from home. Just ask your grandmother. She's my customer. And she keeps coming back because of what I offer."

"You need more guests like my grandmother every day of the year. Which brings us to marketing. You need to rethink your advertising and your marketing plans."

"I don't spend that much."

"Exactly. But what you are spending might not be targeted appropriately."

"Shay thinks we should sell Noah and Alice's story to some travel magazines. Their romantic reunion might create new interest in the inn."

"That's a great idea. And your ghost should be more prominently featured. Find out more about the girl who is allegedly haunting my room and talk her story up."

"Everything you say makes sense. I just need to find a way to make an objective decision and not an emotional one."

"Good luck with that," he said dryly.

"Thanks for working on all this. I need to think about everything you said."

"No problem. I like business problems and challenges, puzzles to figure out."

"I guess I'm happy that I've given you a puzzle to work."

He grinned. "How about giving me something else that's fun —maybe a kiss?"

"You have probably earned it." She got up from her chair, leaned across the desk and met him in what should have been a lighthearted kiss, but as soon as their mouths touched, the desire flared.

He grabbed her shoulders and held her in place as their kiss got deep and hot.

She broke away a second later, her eyes sparkling. "You're like a fire. Every time I get too close, I feel like you're going to consume me."

"That's how you make me feel, too," he said, wondering how he was going to walk away from her in a few days.

The door opened behind Lizzie, and she jumped, stepping away from the desk as Shay walked in.

Shay gave them a surprised look. "Oh, sorry. I didn't mean to interrupt."

"It's fine," Lizzie said, tucking her hair behind her ears. "What's up?"

"Naomi is almost done packing up picnic boxes. Ramon will take them down to the beach in the truck. The guests will be meeting in the foyer in thirty minutes."

"Great."

"I'm going to head down to the beach now, to set up our table. I'm assuming you're coming with the guests."

"Yes, I'll make sure everyone has a ride. Thanks, Shay."

"No problem. And no hurry. We still have an hour. You can finish up whatever you were doing..." She gave them both a smile and then left.

"So, we have a little time," he said.

"No, we don't," Lizzie said quickly. "I need to get ready for the picnic. I didn't realize it was so late. Time seems to fly when we're together."

He was becoming acutely aware of just how fast time was

flying. But he couldn't think about the end, not yet. They still had a couple of days…a couple of nights.

"Are you coming to the beach?"

"I'll come down with my grandparents. But later tonight… you and me?"

"I should say no, because it feels like every minute we're together is just going to make it harder to say good-bye," she said.

"Or we could take advantage of the time we have."

"I'll think about it."

As he got to his feet and followed her out of the office, he knew he should think about it, too. On the other hand, while their affair might have an end date, that date didn't have to be today. Hopefully, she'd agree. Because he wanted at least one more night with her.

CHAPTER EIGHTEEN

AN HOUR LATER, Lizzie had sent all the guests, except for two, down to the beach. Now, she was waiting for Noah and Alice to come downstairs. She'd volunteered to drive them to the lake, and she was looking forward to finding out more about their reunion story. She was also happy to have a little more space from Justin. She didn't know what she was going to do about him, but she didn't think she'd have much success in saying no to anything he asked. She was too caught up in him. He lit her up every time he kissed her, and she wanted to hang on to that feeling as long as she could.

Her heart twisted at the thought of never seeing him again and she mentally scolded herself for getting so emotionally involved. But it was too late now. It was what it was.

Thankfully, her distracting and depressing thoughts were interrupted by the arrival of Noah and Alice. They both looked happy and relaxed, dressed in casual beach wear. Noah wore tan slacks and a cream-colored shirt. Alice had on a sundress with sandals. The smiles on their faces were as bright and sunny as the day outside.

"We're ready," Noah said. "Thanks for waiting."

"Of course. I'm glad we'll get a chance to talk before the big picnic."

"You have some questions," Noah said, meeting her gaze. "You want to know if our reunion will last."

"Now that you mention it, I am curious. Last night was rather dramatic."

"That's my fault," Alice said. "I didn't really expect Noah to answer that door. I thought it would be a stranger. I would apologize for disturbing him and then I would go downstairs and get a cab. But there he was."

"And then I was on the ground," Noah said dryly. "I've never passed out before."

"It was scary," Alice said. "Not just for me, but also for your friend."

Noah's gaze sobered. "I feel bad about Patty. She said she understood, that she'd always known I was waiting for Alice, but I fear I might have hurt her."

"I feel badly about that, too," Alice said. "I should have just tried to find you, to call you, but I just had this crazy idea that the eclipse this week was the moment we would reconnect."

"You were right."

"Because you were here," she said, meeting his gaze. "I didn't deserve your loyalty, but I'm so grateful. I feel so blessed." Alice turned to Lizzie. "Did Noah tell you why I disappeared all those years ago?"

"He said you had a family emergency and that you'd come back when you could. He just didn't expect it to be this long."

"My husband had a car accident while I was in Whisper Lake. When I got back to Paris, I found out that it had occurred on his way to the airport," Alice explained. "He'd been rushing to make a plane to the US, to Denver, actually. He had realized I was slipping away from him, and he wanted to get me back. But it was a terrible accident. He was in a coma for weeks and then he had damage to his brain and his spine. I couldn't leave him like that. I felt partly responsible, because if I hadn't stayed in Whisper Lake, if I hadn't had the affair with Noah, maybe he wouldn't have been hurt. I nursed him for almost eight years. When he passed away, I thought it was too late." She paused. "But when I heard about the eclipse last month, when I realized it could be seen from Whisper Lake, I thought it was a sign. Maybe it wasn't too late."

"I told you I'd be waiting when the time was right," Noah reminded her.

"I hoped you would be, but I didn't expect it. You should have moved on. You should have loved someone else. Perhaps you were starting to this week, when I arrived."

Lizzie watched their exchange with complete and utter fascination, not really sure what she thought. She felt badly for Patty, who had fallen for Noah. But this reunion was too romantic for words. Their love had lasted a decade without contact, without knowledge of each other, only a certainty that one day, someday, they'd be together.

"I liked Patty, and we had a good time talking together. I was thinking I might need to let go of you and move on," Noah admitted. "That's me being as honest as I can be, Alice."

"I understand. You can still go after Patty."

"No. The second I saw you, I knew you were the only one for me, Alice."

Alice's lip trembled. "Oh, Noah, I don't deserve you."

"Sure you do. Most people think I'm nuts," he said lightly.

Alice smiled. "I can't believe you would wander the inn, looking for me every time you came."

"I can attest to that being true," Lizzie cut in. "He was unwavering in his certainty that you'd come back, Alice."

"I'm sorry it took so long."

"We have no more time to waste on being sorry," Noah said. "We have now. That's all we need. The past and the future don't matter. Just this moment."

Noah's words made Lizzie think about Justin, about the now that they were having or could be having, and suddenly, she was very eager to get to the lake.

"Let's go," she said. "I don't want you to miss the picnic."

Lizzie's beach picnic was a big hit, Justin thought. He just wondered where she was and why she wasn't enjoying it with her guests. They had two long picnic tables tucked under some tall trees about twenty-five yards from the water's edge. The guests were mingling happily, as if they'd been friends for years and not just random people staying at the same inn. He had to admit that Lizzie had a talent for making her guests feel like they were family.

But she was the head of that family, and she should be here. It seemed to be taking forever for her to arrive with Noah and Alice. Hopefully, there was nothing wrong with that duo. He'd thought the man was a fool for hanging on to his dream woman for so long, but Noah had proved him wrong. He'd believed in Alice, and she'd come through. It had taken ten years, but they had a second chance.

He saw a group coming through the trees, but he frowned when he realized it wasn't Lizzie.

"She'll be here," his grandfather said, as he walked over to him and handed him a soda.

"I don't know who you're talking about," he lied, as he opened the can.

His grandfather laughed. "I'm talking about the very pretty innkeeper who you can't stop looking for."

"I am curious as to where she is," he admitted.

"I guess your grandmother's plan is working."

He gave his grandfather a wry smile. "Yeah, I figured that the boat trip was a setup. I can't believe you went along with her. I thought you were on my side."

"I'm always on your grandmother's side, Justin. But I thought it was a good idea, too, and my allergies were acting up."

"They seemed to recover after the antiquing day was over."

"I thought you might enjoy spending some quality time with Marie."

"I did. But I like hanging with you, too. And I thought we'd all agreed to no more setups like five years ago."

"Right. After that disastrous dinner with that fitness trainer who your grandmother brought home from the gym," Ben said with a laugh. "I didn't know what Marie was thinking with that woman. But Lizzie is a sweetheart, and she has your same drive for business."

"She does."

"So…"

"So, I'm leaving on Sunday. I live in San Francisco. She lives here."

"People move all the time."

"Lizzie won't leave Whisper Lake. This is her dream job. And my work is everywhere but here."

"Jobs come and go. Relationships are what matter. Having people in your life you love and care about, people who you trust to have your back."

Lizzie was probably the first woman he'd ever really trusted. *Why else would he have told her about Sean?* He'd never told any woman about his brother. He realized now he'd never really wanted to open up like that. But he'd wanted to tell Lizzie. He'd wanted to share that part of himself, and he still wasn't entirely sure why.

"But you'll make your own decisions; you always do," his grandfather continued. "I just wish sometimes you weren't so damned stubborn and laser focused. You get tunnel vision."

"I'm not that narrow-minded."

"I hope not. Marie and I want you to be happy, Justin."

"I am happy. I have everything I ever wanted."

"Everything?" his grandfather challenged. "Because the very best thing in my life has always been your grandmother and our marriage."

"You two are an exception to the rule."

"Maybe. Although, your parents are still happily married."

"Yes, they've always been happy with each other. They make great spouses. Parents—not so much." He heard the edge of bitterness in his voice, but he couldn't do anything about that.

His grandfather's gaze narrowed. "You're still so angry."

"Actually, I don't feel much of anything anymore, not for them anyway. But let's not discuss my parents. Are you ready for the vow renewal tomorrow?"

"I think so," his grandfather said, but he suddenly appeared distracted. "We should find your grandmother, talk about tomorrow."

"Sure. Is there something special you want me to do?"

"She had some ideas. She said she was going to talk to you about them tonight."

"Well, I'm happy to hear her thoughts. Whatever she wants."

"The ceremony, having her family there, it means a lot to her," Ben said.

"I know. That's why I came."

"And we appreciate that so much."

"You were there for me after Sean died. If it hadn't been for you and Grandma, I would have lost it. But you kept me grounded. I'll never forget that."

His grandfather gave him a tense smile. "It sometimes felt like too little too late, but we can't change that."

"No, we can't."

"I think Sean would have liked this place," his grandfather said, then quickly added, "Sorry, I know you don't like to talk about him."

CAN'T FIGHT THE MOONLIGHT

"Actually, he's been on my mind a lot this week. And you're right. He would have liked this town. He would have been the center of the action, the life of the party. Right about now, we'd be hearing his big, booming laugh."

His grandfather gave him a sad look. "Wish I'd known that laugh covered up so much pain and emotional problems. I didn't realize until it was too late."

"I was the one who should have rung the alarm louder and longer."

"You can't keep blaming yourself, Justin. Sean's choices were his own."

"I don't just blame myself," he said.

"I know," his grandfather said heavily. "We need to find Marie and talk."

Justin gave him a vague nod, distracted by Lizzie's arrival. Her arms were full with grocery bags, and Noah and Alice were also carrying in more goodies. "Later," he told his grandfather. "I'm going to help Lizzie."

"Of course you are," his grandfather said with a knowing smile.

He shrugged. "You don't know everything."

"I know enough."

He let his grandfather have the last word, because he needed to get to Lizzie, and that need was a little shocking, but he wasn't going to waste time analyzing it. Not when her smiling gaze met his, and his heart flipped over in his chest.

"Let me help you," he said, taking a bag out of her arms. "What is all this?"

"Dessert and some goodie bags for the eclipse."

"Really? What's in the bag?"

"Some fun facts about lunar eclipses, glasses with the date etched in glitter, that kind of thing."

He shook his head.

"I know. I know," she said. "It's an expense I probably couldn't afford, but here we are."

He grinned. "I'm sure they're great. I was wondering where you were," he added, as he set the bag down on the end of the picnic table.

"I had to wait for Noah and Alice, and we got to talking."

"So, are they together now?" he asked, his gaze moving to the couple, who had settled in at the table. Noah had his arm around Alice's shoulders, as Victor poured them each a glass of wine.

"Now and forever, according to them. It's a miracle."

"I must admit, I'm surprised it happened. The old man wasn't crazy after all."

"He believed in love, and it paid off." She cleared her throat. "How are things going here?"

"Great. Everyone is having fun. The food is amazing as always. Brodie came by earlier. He said he's on duty but will check back in a while. I haven't seen your other friends yet."

"Adam took a bunch of people out on his boat. He invited me, but I wanted to do something for my guests."

"I didn't realize Adam had a boat."

"He's a big boater. He likes to fish and ski and tube—all that."

"You, too?"

"Yes. I've never been one to just lay around. I have too many ideas for that, and I love being on the lake, in the lake, by the lake."

"I get it—you like the lake," he teased.

She smiled. "I really do. I think you do, too. You look so much more relaxed now than when we first met."

"I am more relaxed. It has been a good break for me. I'd been running so hard and so fast for so long, I didn't know how to stop. Until a truck braked in front of me, and I hit a fence and killed all my electronics. I guess I needed a wake-up call, and I got one."

"Sometimes we all need that. The furnace breaking might have been my wake-up call, and then another call came with Keira's friend. But I'm still not sure how to answer all those calls."

"You'll figure it out."

"I will. And I don't want to talk about it anymore today or tonight," she murmured.

He saw the spark of fire in her eyes and his body stiffened. "So, later..."

"Yes. Later," she promised. "But now I need to make sure everyone is having a good time."

"They look happy to me."

"But they can get happier," she said with a laugh. Then she moved over to the table. "Who wants to play cornhole?"

As the group enthusiastically responded yes, Victor set up the cornhole boards a short distance away and Lizzie divided the group into teams. His grandparents would start by facing off against Noah and Alice.

While Lizzie took charge of the game, he grabbed a beer out of the cooler.

"That looks good," Chelsea said.

He smiled at Lizzie's sister, then handed her the beer and grabbed another one for himself. "I thought you were out on your brother's boat."

"I was going to be, but I got caught up in songwriting, and I decided I'd just come down to the beach and check out Lizzie's party. It looks like everyone is having fun."

"I don't think your sister would allow for anything else," he said dryly.

She grinned. "Good point. How about you? Are you having fun?"

"More than I would have expected," he admitted.

"This town grows on you. I never thought I'd settle here, but the lake healed me and gave me a new start and then, of course, I met Brodie."

"Why did you stop singing?" he asked curiously.

"Lizzie didn't tell you?"

He shook his head. "Nope. But if it's private—"

"I can tell you this much. I had an experience with a fan that shook me up, made me question whether I wanted to be a public figure, whether I could keep on singing. In the end, I was able to find my voice again. Brodie helped a lot with that. Lizzie, too. Music is important to me, and I came to realize that I couldn't let one person stop me from doing what I was meant to do."

Her cryptic story made him even more curious than if she'd told him nothing, but he wanted to respect her privacy. "Well, I'm glad you found your way back to what you love."

"Lizzie told me a little about your business. It sounds very cool and on the cutting edge."

"I've always liked to lead from the front, even if I sometimes make mistakes. I'd rather be the first one to try something than the last."

"You must not be afraid to fail."

"I usually learn something when I do."

"Does that go for love, too?"

He frowned. "Are we talking about love?"

"I don't want my sister to get hurt. And I saw you talking earlier. The way you looked at her…the way she looked at you…there's something going on."

"You should talk to her if you're concerned."

"Oh, she'll just tell me she knows what she's doing. She always says that. She hates to ask anyone for help. She thinks it makes her look weak."

Knowing now about Lizzie's learning disabilities, he understood better why she would worry about looking weak or dumb or any of the bad labels she used to put on herself.

"But I'm her big sis," Chelsea continued. "And I'm putting you on notice—don't hurt her. She's not as tough as she looks."

"Got it." He actually appreciated her sisterly protectiveness. In some ways, she reminded him of his brother. In fact, he could see Sean now, standing up to Rex Hillerman, the bully in Justin's fifth-grade class. Sean had taken Rex by the arm and given him a shake and told him to stay the hell away from his little brother, or he'd answer to him. Rex had been so scared he'd practically peed his pants in his hurry to get away. Justin had never had any trouble with him again. *God, he missed Sean.*

The pain hit him hard and unexpectedly. He'd thought he'd gotten past those shocking waves, but somehow being here in Whisper Lake was making his absence feel so much stronger, the loss so much more recent.

"What are you two talking about?" Lizzie asked, as she joined them with a curious smile.

"How we're going to take you on in cornhole," Chelsea lied.

"Really? You two are going to pair up? Then I need a partner," Lizzie returned. "And guess who just arrived?" She waved her hand toward the man approaching.

Justin frowned at the brown-haired, good-looking, muscled guy in jeans and a T-shirt, and a pair of aviator glasses over his eyes. He disliked him even more when Lizzie gave the guy a hug.

Then she turned to him. "Justin, I want you to meet Jake MacKenzie. He's the owner of Adventure Sports. Jake, this is Justin Blackwood, one of my guests."

He was a hell of a lot more than one of her guests, but he managed to refrain from saying that. "Nice to meet you," he muttered, as Jake gave him a friendly smile.

"You, too."

"So, what do you say?" Chelsea asked. "You two want to engage in a little friendly cornhole competition?"

"Always game," Jake said.

"I'll take Justin," Chelsea said. "You and Lizzie can partner up."

"Sounds good," Jake said.

Justin didn't think it sounded good at all. He would have preferred to be partnering with Lizzie, but she and Jake were already walking away.

Chelsea gave him a grin. "They're just friends."

"I don't care."

"Good, because I like to win, so I'd prefer if you weren't distracted."

He saw the glint in her eyes. "You Coles are very competitive."

"We are."

"Okay, then. Let's beat them." He'd enjoy taking a win from Jake MacKenzie. He might be a great guy, but right now, Jake was way too close to Lizzie. Not that Justin had any right to think that way. He was leaving on Sunday. And Jake lived here. Jake and Lizzie would be together, in whatever way they wanted to be together long after he was gone. But he didn't want to think about that.

While Chelsea and Lizzie headed for one board, he and Jake wound up next to each other.

"Gotta warn you," Jake said. "The Cole sisters like to win."

"Chelsea mentioned something about that," he said. "You first."

"All right." Jake took aim and then tossed his bag onto the opposing board. He came very close to the center hole, but didn't make it in.

Justin was up next, landing his bag a few inches from Jake's. They were tied.

Jake's next bag sailed through the center hole and Jake gave him a proud smile. "I just raised the bar."

He took an extra second and then tossed, feeling an immense

sense of joy when his bag also landed in the hole. "And I just met your bar," he said.

And then it was up to Chelsea and Lizzie.

Both were good, but Lizzie managed to sink the bag on her second time for three points, while Chelsea was just short.

He had to smile as Lizzie did a little happy dance around her sister, while Chelsea gave her a disgusted look.

As the game went on, they stayed very close in points. Jake had clearly played a lot of cornhole in his life, hitting the hole two times more than Justin. Lizzie was also able to best her sister, and Justin and Chelsea ended up losing.

"Good game," Jake said.

"You, too." He stepped back as the next two teams lined up.

"Sorry, Justin," Chelsea said. "I was definitely the weakest player in that round."

"I was right there with you."

"Whereas I was great," Lizzie said with a laugh, and then exchanged a high-five with Jake. "You weren't bad, either," she told her partner.

"That was fun. Who needs another beer?" Jake asked.

"I do," Chelsea said.

As they wandered away, Lizzie gave him a happy look. "Did you have fun?"

"I would have had more fun if I won."

"Jake is one of the best cornhole players in Whisper Lake."

"I got that feeling. And I'm more than a little out of practice."

"You held your own."

As she looked up at him, he had to fight the urge to put his arms around her and kiss her. But it wasn't easy.

"What's wrong?" she asked.

"It's been too long since I kissed you."

Her eyes lit up. "We said later…"

"I'm thinking later could be now."

"I can't leave my guests."

"I know."

"But…"

"There's a but?" he asked hopefully.

She checked her watch. "It's almost time for the eclipse. When it goes dark, anything could happen if you're in the right place at the right time."

"Good point. Then you better get used to me being glued to your side."

"I'm okay with that," she said, sliding a little closer to him.

He wanted to throw his arm around her, but Chelsea and Jake had returned.

"How's business going?" Jake asked Lizzie.

"It's good this week," she replied. "What about you?"

"A little slow. Waiting for the heat to kick up a notch, so we can get more people on the water. But that probably won't be for another month. I have been running some kayaking tours this week. I got two new boats. You guys should try them out—on me, of course."

"Not me. I'm not a lover of boats that require me to work at moving them," Chelsea said with a laugh. "But I'm sure Lizzie will take you up on it."

"Maybe next week if things slow down," she said. "I do like getting out on the water."

"What about you, Justin?"

"I'm leaving Sunday."

"Where are you from?"

"San Francisco."

"Love that city," Jake said. "Well, if you're free tomorrow, let me know. I have some open slots in the afternoon."

"Tomorrow I will be going to my grandparents' vow renewal ceremony."

"Oh, you're Marie's grandson," Jake said. "I didn't know that."

"You know my grandmother?"

"Sure. I took her and Ben on a guided hike last summer when they were here. Those two have more energy than people half their age."

"That's true." His gaze drifted to his grandparents, who were surrounded by their new friends. He'd never had the same ease at fitting into a group. He'd never been all that interested in meeting new people, but his grandparents were perpetually curious about everyone who came into their presence. Sean had been like that, too. He was sadly probably more like his parents, who were only extroverts when it involved their work. He frowned, not wanting to ruin this day by thinking about them at all.

"There's Brodie," Chelsea said, drawing his attention away from his grandparents.

"I want to talk to him, too," Jake said. "I'll catch up with you two later. Nice to meet you, Justin."

"You, too," he said, having a hard time disliking such a friendly guy. But as they left, he heard himself say something he'd never expected to say. "Have you and Jake ever gone out?"

Lizzie looked at him in surprise. "No. We're friends."

"Is he single?"

"Yes. He's very popular with the ladies."

"Not with you?"

"Why do you care?"

"Just curious. You seemed friendly."

"Because he's my friend. He's also a fellow business owner. We help each other out when we can. He's been great at showing my guests a wonderful time on the water or in the mountains, whatever they want to do."

"Okay. Whatever."

She smiled. "I like that you're jealous."

"I'm not jealous. If I want something, I just get it for myself."

"Does that mean you don't want me, or you do?"

"You are a little more complicated than I'm used to," he admitted.

"So are you. I really didn't want to like you, but I couldn't stop myself."

"I'm glad you didn't."

"I just wish we had more time. The days are passing so quickly. But we still have later…"

He smiled back at her. "Which may not be too long from now. It's getting darker."

"You're right," she said, turning her gaze toward the sky.

The crowd around them seemed to hush as the light began to dim.

It was a bit of an eerie feeling to have the daylight vanish so quickly—to have no moon, no sun.

And in the following darkness, Lizzie's hand slipped into his, and he found her mouth with unerring accuracy. They didn't need light, not when they had each other. He kissed her with the longing that had been building within him all day. He kissed her with a feeling of urgency, a desire to slow down time, to keep them together as long as he possibly could.

And she matched him kiss for kiss, her desire as palpable as his own. He could feel her heart beating against his chest as their bodies pressed together. And his own pulse raced in return as they clung together, sharing a passion that seemed almost over-whelming. And then the light began to seep back into the day.

She pulled away, giving him a breathless look, her lips pink and puffy from the onslaught of his mouth, her eyes bright and sparkling, and full of promise, a promise he wanted to take advantage of. But the sun was coming back out, and they were no longer alone in the intimate darkness. The party was back on.

"Lizzie," Shay called, waving to her from the other side of the picnic table.

"I'll be back," she said.

He nodded, thinking maybe it was just as well she was moving away. He needed a minute to get his head together.

But he wasn't going to get that minute, he realized, as his grandparents approached.

"That was so fun," his grandmother said. "Wasn't it?"

"Very cool. I've never been outside during an eclipse."

"It wasn't night or day, it was just in between," his grandmother added.

"He gets it," his grandfather put in. "And you're stalling, Marie."

Justin got curious at his grandfather's words. "Stalling about what?"

"There's something I need to tell you," his grandmother said. "I should have said something before now, in fact."

"Is something wrong?"

She exchanged a quick look with his grandfather. "I wasn't completely honest with you, Justin, and the reason I wasn't was because I didn't know if it was going to happen. I didn't think it was worth upsetting you. But now." She frowned as her phone buzzed.

"What?" he prodded, as she read the text.

"Oh, dear," she said. "They're already here. I didn't think they were coming until tomorrow."

"Who's here?" he asked, his heart sinking. He could see the answer in their faces. And then he heard footsteps behind him. He did not want to look. And then he heard her voice, followed by his.

"Justin?"

CHAPTER NINETEEN

JUSTIN STILL DIDN'T TURN around. Instead, he glared at his grandparents, feeling incredibly betrayed. "You said my parents weren't coming."

His grandmother gave him a look of apology, but it didn't begin to dent the rage growing within him. Finally, he turned his head, seeing the two people he had loved and hated for most of his life.

His mother was a tall, slim woman with short, dark hair and blue eyes. His father was also tall, but broader and stockier. His once brown hair had turned to silver, and his blue eyes were closer to gray today. In his mind, they were monsters. They were cold. They were uncaring. They were dismissive. He hadn't seen them in three years and their last meeting had lasted about fifteen minutes before he'd taken off.

Today, he didn't think it would last that long.

The tension between them drew the attention of the group from the inn. The friendly chatter dimmed. He saw Lizzie out of the corner of his eye walking toward them.

He didn't want to ruin her party. So, he wouldn't.

"This isn't happening," he told his parents and grandparents. "I'm leaving."

"You can't go," Marie pleaded. "We need to talk—all of us."

"There's nothing to talk about. You told me they weren't coming."

"I didn't know if they would," she said. "I wasn't sure until today. And I didn't think they were coming until tomorrow. I told them there weren't any rooms at the inn. Lizzie, did you give them a room?"

At his grandmother's question, his gaze swung to Lizzie, and the bottom dropped out of his world as he saw the guilty look in her eyes.

"You knew they were coming?" he asked her, shocked by that realization.

"I wasn't sure," she said. "And I didn't give them a room."

He didn't care about the room. But he did care that she'd kept their arrival a secret. Even after he'd told her about Sean, about his parents, about how they'd let him down, she'd kept silent. "You should have told me," he said, hearing the icy cold tone in his voice.

"Justin—"

"No."

He cut her off by turning his back and walking away. He stormed through the trees, hearing footsteps behind him.

Lizzie caught up to him in the parking lot. "Justin, wait," she begged.

"How could you keep that a secret?" he demanded.

"I honestly didn't know if they were coming. Your grandmother mentioned it a couple of days ago, but she asked me not to tell you. At the time, I didn't know anything about your past."

"But you knew last night, and you still didn't say anything."

"I was going to, remember? I said I had something to tell you."

He shook his head. "Here's the thing, Lizzie. This is why you shouldn't get so involved with your guests. Why did you promise my grandmother anything? Why are you in the middle of my personal family life?"

"I was just trying to keep everyone happy."

"You can't do that. You can't please everyone. You need to start running your business like a business instead of like a family. It's no wonder you're in such financial trouble. If you spent more time paying off your bills than making up goodie bags you can't afford and getting involved in the personal lives of your guests, you might not be drowning. Why are you even involved in my grandmother's secrets? It's ridiculous. It's not a learning disability that's making you fail, it's your inability to be professional, to just run your damn business and not mess up other people's lives."

She paled at his harsh words, and he felt a momentary regret, but there was so much anger burning within him, he couldn't stop it from coming out.

"I trusted you," he added. "I told you things…" He shook his head, his lips too tight with rage to say any more."

"I know, and I'm so sorry."

"I need to get out of here. I drove my grandparents here in their rental car. Can you get them back to the inn?"

"Yes. But can we talk—after this is over?"

"We don't have anything to talk about. Good-bye, Lizzie."

"You can't disappoint your grandmother. She needs you at the ceremony tomorrow."

"She has her son and her daughter-in-law. They'll have to do."

He walked away, not interested in hearing anything else she had to say. He felt like the very few people in his life who he trusted had all betrayed him. And he hadn't felt this shockingly alone in a very long time.

He got in the car, slammed the door, and then drove to the inn. He ran up the stairs to his room and started throwing his things in his suitcase. But when he finished packing, he didn't quite know what to do.

His grandparents would be forever hurt by his departure. And even after this stunt, he still didn't want to cause them pain. Maybe his parents would leave now that they knew he wasn't interested in talking to them. Why they'd come all this way, he couldn't even understand. It wasn't like they'd ever made family occasions. *Why this one? Why now?*

He looked down at his packed suitcase. He should leave. But he didn't have his own rental car. If he took his grandparents' vehicle, he'd leave them stranded. Not that they didn't deserve it. And his parents could give them a ride back to the airport when they left.

Glancing at his watch, he realized it was past six. He doubted he could get to Denver and get on a plane back to San Francisco tonight. However, he could spend the night at a hotel by the airport. He could put Whisper Lake in the rearview mirror.

But he wasn't just leaving his parents and his grandparents; he'd also be leaving Lizzie.

Anger ran through him again at her betrayal. He shouldn't care that he was leaving her, that he'd never see her again, but he did…

Lizzie took a few minutes before returning to the beach. She was still shaken by what Justin had said to her. A part of her knew he'd lashed out at her because he felt like she'd betrayed him. But his words had cut deep. He'd taken the things she was most insecure about and thrown them in her face. She was in financial trouble and maybe if she had spent more time looking at cold hard facts instead of making up picnic boxes and goodie bags that she couldn't afford, she wouldn't be on the edge of disaster. She also couldn't refute the other facts he'd thrown at her. She had gotten too involved with his grandparents. She had made a promise she shouldn't have kept. And she had broken his trust.

Of course, she hadn't realized his parents would show up early or even at all, but she'd had a chance to tell him the night before, and she hadn't. She'd selfishly wanted to hang on to him for as long as possible. But now he'd been blindsided, and he was as angry with her as he was with his family.

When she finally walked back through the trees, she saw that Justin's parents and grandparents had moved away from the rest of the group and were having a private conversation at another picnic table. She didn't want to interrupt. She could see emotions were flowing. But there was also a part of her that wanted to walk over there and yell at each and every one of them. *Didn't they realize their secret plan had hurt Justin?*

"Lizzie," Chelsea said, walking over to her, concern in her gaze. "Are you all right?"

"I'm not the one who was hurt."

"I don't really understand what's going on, but I'm guessing it has something to do with Justin's parents."

She nodded. "I can't tell you the story, but there's a lot of anger between them. Marie wanted to heal the family by forcing them all together, but that was a bad idea. And the worst thing is that I knew about it. Marie told me it might happen and asked me not to tell Justin. I went along with it, but I should have told him."

"It wasn't your secret or your responsibility."

"He confided in me last night. I had a chance to tell him. I didn't take it. I thought he would leave immediately, and I didn't want him to. How selfish is that?"

Chelsea gave her a sympathetic look. "You really like him, don't you?"

"I wish I didn't. Now, he hates me." She felt like her heart was breaking.

"He might be angry, but he does not hate you. In fact, I think he's quite fond of you. He couldn't take his eyes off you earlier."

"That was before this." She let out a breath. "I was stupid to get involved with him. Even putting all this aside, he was going to be leaving on Sunday. His life could never be here. And mine can't be anywhere else."

"I feel like we had a similar conversation last year when I thought Brodie might be moving to LA or I might be going to Nashville, and my very wise sister told me not to let geography get in the way."

"This is different."

"Is it? If you want to be together, one of you has to compromise."

"There's no compromise to be made now. There's nothing. Justin is furious. And I understand, because he really opened up to me, and I let him down. I'm sure he's already on his way to the airport. He's gone, Chelsea, and I have to accept that."

"What can I do?"

"Nothing." She squared her shoulders and lifted her chin. "This is still a party, and I am still the host, so I need to mingle and make sure everyone is having a good time."

"Can you really do that?"

"I have to do it. This is business, and I shouldn't be mixing business and personal."

"But you always mix business and personal. That's why the inn is so special."

"Well, I might need to change that."

Her sister frowned. "I don't like what I'm hearing."

"I can't help that. And I can't talk about this now."

"All right. I'm going to take off then. But call me later—anytime. Or come by. You can always spend the night at our place, if you want to get away from the inn."

"I'll be fine." She gave Chelsea a hug and then walked over

to the picnic table, forcing a smile onto her face. "Who's ready for dessert?"

At the chorus of ayes, she got Victor and Shay to help her pass out angel food cake topped with strawberries and cream. She took a tray holding the last four plates over to Marie and Ben and Justin's parents.

"Thank you, Lizzie," Marie said, as she handed out the dessert. "I'm sorry about earlier. I shouldn't have involved you."

She gave her a tense smile. "Justin took your car back to the inn. If you need a ride, I can take you in my SUV."

"We'll go with Grant," Marie said, waving her hand toward her son. "You all didn't officially meet. Katherine, Grant, this is Lizzie Cole. She runs the inn."

"Hello," she said, trying not to let her feelings show. She hadn't had a great impression of Justin's parents last night, and she had even less of one now.

"We didn't mean to make a scene," Katherine said. "But with Justin, everything gets very dramatic very quickly."

"Justin is probably the least dramatic person I've ever met," she couldn't help saying. "But when he's cornered and blind-sided, he's going to come out swinging." His parents seemed taken aback by her comment. She turned to Marie. "I'm sorry I promised to keep your secret. I didn't know anything about the situation with Justin and his parents and his brother. But he filled me in on the family history last night. I thought about telling him then, but I didn't. I made a mistake. So did you. This wasn't the way to handle this."

"I wanted to bring the family together. But I knew Justin wouldn't come if I told him his parents would be here."

"We actually weren't that happy with the surprise visit, either," Grant put in. "I told you, Mom, that Justin wouldn't like it. Dad said the same thing, but you wouldn't listen."

"I'm getting old, and I'm tired of all the anger and unspoken words," Marie said passionately. "It has to stop. We have to talk to each other." She paused, her gaze moving back to Lizzie. "I'm surprised Justin told you about Sean. He never talks about him."

"Did he tell you that he blames us for not being there for Sean, for not seeing what was happening to his brother?" Katherine asked. "Did he even explain at all that we were both working and traveling, and it wasn't just about being selfish? We were working for the greater good."

"He did say that you were both involved in medicine and charities."

"Well, I guess it's something that he can admit that," Katherine said. "We loved both our boys, Lizzie. It broke my heart when Sean died. He was my child. Of course I had guilt. Of course I blamed myself. I just can't believe that I had to lose Justin, too."

"Lizzie doesn't need to be in the middle of this," Grant said wearily.

"I just want her to understand. She seems to be close to Justin."

"It doesn't matter," Grant said. "Justin is gone. Maybe we should go, too."

"No," Ben said. "You both need to stay for the ceremony. It's important to Marie that we do this with at least some of the family present."

"Yes, please stay," Marie said. "I know you and Katherine are hurting just as Justin is, and Ben and I have been caught in the middle. But we can't go on like this. We can't keep blaming each other, because it doesn't change anything. Will you stay for tomorrow's ceremony?"

Grant exchanged a look with his wife and then they both slowly nodded. "All right," he said. "We'll stay."

"Thank you," Marie said, then turned to Lizzie. "I am sorry I involved you. I think you and Justin were hitting it off, and now this secret has ruined that."

She shrugged. "He was always going to be leaving on Sunday.

It just happened a few days earlier. For what it's worth, I think Justin wants to find a way to make peace, but he can't be the one who has to fight for it." Her gaze moved to his parents. "This is none of my business, but I'm going to say it anyway. Justin has needed both of you to show up for him. He's needed that his entire life. You should go after him now, and if you can't catch up to him, then after this weekend is over, go to San Francisco and stand in front of his door until he lets you in. Call him until he blocks your number. But don't give up on him. You say you love him—show him. He needs you to fight for him, to put him first in a way that you never did before." His parents looked at her with surprise in their eyes, but they didn't say a word. "That's all. Excuse me."

As she walked away, she let out a breath, hoping she hadn't made things worse, but that didn't seem possible. She had no idea if Justin would ever let his parents in even if they did stalk him, but she did know one thing for certain: he would never come back to them.

She knew one other thing, too. He would probably never come back to her, either.

Justin knew he should have left the inn, but he hadn't. He'd gone up on the roof and thought about his life and Lizzie and his grandparents, and even his parents, and then he'd seen the cars coming back from the beach, so he'd hightailed it back to his room. He didn't want to go downstairs and risk running into Lizzie or anyone in his family, so he'd stayed in his room, thinking he'd take off early in the morning, before anyone was up.

He tried to work, but he was constantly distracted by sounds. He'd hear footsteps and wonder if Lizzie was coming to his door. At one point, those footsteps seemed to stop right outside his door, and his heart had started beating hard and fast. But then they'd faded away. No knock tonight.

He'd gotten several texts from his grandmother, his father, and his mother, but he hadn't looked at any of them and had turned off his phone so he wouldn't be tempted to read what they had to say. But then that had seemed rather silly. *What was he afraid of? And why was he hiding?* They were the ones in the wrong. He'd turned his phone back on but left it facedown on the nightstand.

After forcing himself to read through pages of research data, his pulse finally began to slow down. At eleven, he turned off the light. He needed to sleep. He needed to get to tomorrow. And then he needed to leave.

Because he'd gotten so little sleep the night before, he actually felt tired, and he thought he might drift off. But as soon as he closed his eyes, he could see Lizzie's pretty face, and it woke him right back up.

He fought to get her out of his head. After tossing and turning for what seemed like hours, he started to feel a different kind of tension. He was cold. And there was an odd noise—click, click, click.

He struggled to open his eyes, but his lids felt so heavy.

Panic ran through him. It was the same panic he'd felt as a kid when he woke up alone, when he didn't know where anyone was. He'd cry out, but his parents wouldn't come. They were somewhere else. But then the light in his room would go on, and Sean would be there.

A light went on now.

But it wasn't coming from the lamp by his bed. It was the moon beaming through the curtains.

And that sound…it was the rocking chair. It was moving back and forth. There was someone there.

The ghost of room ten? Was he going crazy?

The person shifted, moving into the light. And his heart stopped.

He sat up to get a better look. It was Sean. His green eyes were smiling. His brown hair fell over his brow, the way it always had. And there was a reassuring gleam in his gaze as he rocked back and forth.

"You're here," he said, suddenly realizing how clear Sean was. He could see him for the first time in a very long time. "I've wanted to see you for so long. I wanted to know you were all right."

"I'm more concerned about you, Justin."

"What do you mean?"

"What are you doing? Why are you in here alone? Why are you hiding?"

"Because Mom and Dad showed up. They want me to forgive them, to forget how shitty they were as parents, how they let you down. They let us both down."

"I let them down, too. It wasn't their fault, Justin. I'm not dead because of them."

"Yes, you are, and it was their fault. They were more concerned about saving the world than saving you, and it wasn't even about the world. We both know that. They're adrenaline junkies. They live for the thrill, the excitement, and the danger. If they save people along the way, that's fine, but that's not why they do it."

"It's not that simple. They do care about the people they're trying to save. Maybe it gives them a rush to be heroes. But that's better than taking a drug to get a rush, right? How can I blame them without blaming myself?" Sean paused. "Don't you blame me, too, Justin?"

"Yes, I blame you. Why did you have to do everything to the extreme? Why did you have to keep wanting more?"

"I could ask you the same question. You're doing fantastically well, but you keep pushing, keep driving yourself hard, and at what cost? What are you going to miss out on?"

"We're talking about you. About why you're not here when you should be."

"It was an accident, Justin. I didn't want to die. I just didn't have enough sense to be more careful. I thought I was invincible. It was my fault what happened. It wasn't on Mom and Dad. Sure, they were gone a lot, and maybe if they'd been around, I wouldn't have had the opportunity to be as free as I was. But it might not have mattered, because I liked pushing the envelope. You have to find a way to forgive them."

"I can't."

"Yes, you can. You know why I never gave you a sign before?"

"Why?"

"Because you weren't ready. You couldn't hear me. Your heart was frozen shut."

"I was in pain," he admitted. "I missed you so much, Sean. You were the only one who was there for me. You practically raised me."

"I think you've forgotten that Mom and Dad were around at least some of the time."

"I don't remember that; I just remember you being there, and then you weren't."

"But I taught you well. You're doing good. You took my robot and turned it into an incredible company. I'm proud of you."

"I did it for you."

Sean shook his head. "If you want to do something for me, stop using me as an excuse."

"I don't use you as an excuse."

"Yes, you do. You're not a kid anymore. You need to talk to Mom and Dad. You need to look at them, see them for who they are. They're human. They made mistakes. But they aren't all bad. And they do love you."

"It's hard to let go of the anger," he admitted.

"It's getting easier, isn't it, since you met Lizzie? She's really something. Grandma did a good job setting you two up."

He frowned. "I don't want to talk about her."

"Because you hurt her tonight."

"She deserved it. She betrayed me."

"Now she's the villain, too?"

"You don't know what she did."

"I know she cares about you, and you care about her. Are you really that angry about what she did, or is it that you're looking for a reason to push her away?"

"I wasn't looking for her to betray me."

"But now you're using your anger to end what could be great."

"It was going to end anyway. It's just happening a day earlier than it would have."

Sean gave him a disappointed look. "You're so brave in other parts of your life. You take risks. You put yourself out there, but when it comes to love, you're a coward."

"I'm not a coward; I'm a realist. Love sucks. There's always disappointment and pain. Why go through that?"

"Because of all the good shit that comes with it. Don't live such a narrow life, Justin. Be better than me, than Mom, than Dad. We all had tunnel vision, and it cost us. You're going down the same road. But you can open your eyes and your heart. Do it before it's too late. The one thing in your life you've always wanted is love. If someone wants to give it to you, don't you think you should take it?"

"I can't have Lizzie and my job."

"You can find a way to have everything you want. If I know anything about you, Justin, I know that."

"I wish you were here—really here," he said, feeling the pain down deep in his soul. "There's so much I want to talk to you about. But you're just a dream."

"I'll always be with you, kid. But you don't need me. You just need to stop being angry and take a chance with your heart. If you don't want to let this woman go, then find a way to keep her. Or find someone else who makes you happy. But don't go through life alone. You deserve more than a ghost in a rocking chair."

His brother laughed, and the sound warmed him from the inside out. In fact, he felt so hot, the room began to spin. And when his vision cleared, he threw off the covers in confusion. He looked at the rocking chair. It wasn't moving. And there was no one there. Sean was gone. It had just been a dream, but it had been a good dream.

His lids felt heavy, and he slid back down on the bed, closing his eyes once more. Sean's image floated through his head. "I heard you," he murmured, feeling a remarkable sense of calm as he slipped into oblivion.

CHAPTER TWENTY

JUSTIN WASN'T GONE. Lizzie's heart beat faster as he came down the stairs and into the lobby just after ten on Saturday morning. He was dressed in dark jeans and a blue polo shirt, and he looked as handsome as always, but he also looked tired, like he'd had a long night.

As his gaze met hers, she mentally steeled herself for another round of attack, because he didn't look happy to see her.

"I thought you'd left," she said, as he paused in front of the desk.

"I was going to, but I didn't."

She stared back at him, not knowing what to say.

"Did you come by my room last night?" he asked.

"I did," she admitted. "I saw your grandparents' car in the lot, and I figured you might still be in your room, but the light was out, so I left."

"Because the light was out, or…"

"Because I wasn't sure you'd want to see me. You were really angry with me. I am sorry I didn't tell you that your parents might show up, Justin. I should have."

"But you'd made a promise to my grandmother. You already explained."

"The promise wasn't really what stopped me."

Surprise flickered in his eyes. "Then what stopped you?"

"Fear. I thought you'd leave the second you found out, and I didn't want you to go. I had another day before they'd show up. I thought we could have one more night together. It was selfish."

"You should have said something, Lizzie. You didn't like it when Keira blindsided you, and that was nothing compared to this. How do you think I felt being confronted by the two people who hurt me the most?"

She sucked in a quick breath, his words cutting her to the quick. "Really bad. But if I had told you, you would have left, right?"

"Probably right away. But that should have been my choice. You took that away."

She realized that was a big part of his issue with her. She'd taken away his control, and after the way he'd grown up, he needed to be able to control his life as much as he needed to breathe.

"You're right. I should have been honest." She paused. "Why didn't you leave last night?"

"Because my grandparents asked me to be here for them, and I made a promise, so I'm going to keep it. I'll stay through the ceremony and leave tonight."

She was more than a little surprised. "They'll be happy to hear that. They were very upset last night."

"Good. They deserve to be upset. But I don't want to ruin their anniversary or their big day."

"That's generous of you." She was happy that he'd managed to work through his anger with his grandparents, even if he couldn't do the same with her. Marie and Benjamin needed to have him at their vow renewal.

"Is it too late for breakfast?" he asked.

"No. There's a buffet out this morning. Probably way more food than we need."

He shrugged, then started to turn toward the dining room.

"Justin, wait. I have to apologize for something else," she said.

He gave her a wary look. "What did you do now?"

"Last night after you left, I spoke to your parents, and I kind of told them off."

"What did you say?"

"They started explaining to me how they weren't to blame and how you won't forgive them or talk to them, and I said that it was on them to make things right. That they needed to show you that they want you in their lives. It wasn't on you to fight for them; it was on them to fight for you. I suggested that they stalk you, text you, and stand outside your apartment in San Francisco until you opened the door."

He looked at her in astonishment. "What did they say?"

"Nothing." She licked her lips. "But they're in the dining room right now, and they told me they weren't leaving until they spoke to you. I know that I butted into your personal business again. I just couldn't stand hearing them excuse themselves, acting like they had done everything they could when in reality they've done next to nothing to heal their family. Anyway, now you know."

He gave her a long, thoughtful look. "I can't believe you said that to them."

"You know I talk too much," she said with a shrug. "And I meddle. And I'm pushy. All the things you pointed out last night."

For a split second, his gaze softened. "I was probably harsher than I needed to be."

"But you weren't wrong." As his gaze moved toward the doorway to the dining room, she said, "Are you going to give them a chance?"

He glanced back at her. "It seems almost unimaginable that I'm actually considering that. Do you think they deserve a second chance?"

"Only you can decide that."

"I don't really know why they've decided they want to change things now. It's too late."

"Is it?" she challenged.

"I don't need them in my life now."

"Maybe they need you."

"They never did before," he snapped back.

"I'm going to shut up now," she said.

For some reason, her words brought a reluctant smile to his face. "I doubt that will last long."

For a split second, she felt like they were back on solid ground again, but then his expression hardened, and the very first Justin she'd met—the cold, angry stranger—was facing her. She just didn't know if he'd put on the mask for her or because he was getting ready to speak to his parents.

"If you'd rather have breakfast in your room…" she began.

"No. I'm done running. I'm done hiding. They want to talk, we'll talk."

As he walked away, she let out a breath, thinking that conversation could go either way. But she wasn't going to get in the middle of it. She left the desk and moved into her office. Justin was taking care of his problems, and she needed to deal with hers. It was time for her to stop running away, too. She had to face the debt and figure out a plan.

She sat down, picked up her phone, and punched in a number before she could change her mind. When the woman answered, she said, "Hello, Paula, it's Lizzie Cole. I'd like to talk to you about your offer."

His parents were sitting in the dining room. They were completely alone. Apparently, the breakfast rush was over. His mother had a half-eaten grapefruit in front of her and was sipping her coffee. His father was finishing up the last of his French toast. The familiarity of the scene hit him like a truck, bringing all kinds of unwanted memories and emotions. In his dream, Sean had told him it was time to face his parents, to really look at them, and he was finally doing that.

They were older, he realized. His dad was thinner. His mom looked tired. They weren't talking. They just seemed sad.

That was different. When he was a kid and he'd come upon them having a meal, they'd been talking a mile a minute, each one fighting for airtime. Their passion for their conversation had been palpable, and he'd always felt outside of whatever they were discussing. They'd had their lives, and he'd had his, but it hadn't felt like they were living in the same world or even the same family.

Now, it actually felt like they were in the same space. They were all uncertain, unhappy, not sure what to say or do. But it was happening. This reluctant reunion was going to take place, and they were all going to have to deal with the repercussions. He crossed the room and pulled out an empty chair at their table and sat down.

Both of his parents gave him surprised and worried looks.

"Justin," his mom said. "I'm glad you didn't run when you saw us."

"I'm done with that."

"Good," his father said. "We need to talk."

"So, talk," he said harshly. Lizzie was right. This was on them. If they wanted forgiveness, if they wanted him in their lives, that it was on them to try to make that happen.

"We're sorry that we didn't tell you we were coming," his mother said.

"Fine, but that's not what we need to talk about, is it?"

"No," his dad replied. "We need to talk about Sean. You blame us for his death."

"I do. I did," he amended.

At that correction, his mom's face brightened. "You don't anymore?"

"Let's just say I think there's plenty of blame to go around. And some of that blame is on Sean."

His father's jaw dropped. "I can't believe you'd admit that. Sean was your hero."

"Sean was also my brother. But he had faults and weaknesses, and I probably knew that better than anyone. I should have made sure that you knew as well."

"You were a kid. You weren't to blame, Justin," his father said.

"I saw how much Sean was partying. I could have told you more. I could have asked you to come home."

"You did ask us," his mom said. "More than once. And we knew that Sean was out of control when he got that DUI. We tried to get him help, but it wasn't enough. He was too old for us to control. He was too far into his substance abuse. We let you both down. We know that, Justin. Believe me, we know that."

"You never said that before."

"We were in shock and pain, and we got defensive when you blamed us, when your grandparents blamed us," she said. "Then we tried to shift that blame to everyone else, which didn't help. There was so much anger in the family. And then things got worse, because we lost you, too."

"Lost me?" he echoed, picking out those two particular words. "How could you lose someone you never had?"

"Justin—" his dad began. "We can't change what happened."

"Let him talk," his mom said. "Say whatever you need to say."

"Why did you have kids?" he asked. "Why did you have me? Sean was already in the picture when you two got together. Why have another child when you wanted to travel and work on health missions around the world?" He hadn't thought he'd ask the questions that had plagued him for so long, but they came out before he could stop them.

"We didn't know when we had you that we would get so involved overseas," his dad said. "And we were in love. We wanted a baby to be a part of that love."

"We always wanted you, Justin," his mom put in. "You weren't a mistake or an accident. We chose to have you."

"And you chose to leave me—a lot. By the time I was nine, you were gone for at least a third of the year, and then it was half the year. I spent more time with the nanny and with Sean than I did with either of you."

"We couldn't take you with us. It was too dangerous. But we thought we'd provided a good home for you. Gloria was a wonderful nanny. You loved her. And you and Sean were so tight. You had each other."

"Gloria was great, but she wasn't my mother, and she left, too. Then there were just random people taking care of us. Sean was more of a parent to me than anyone else. Even after he died, you only stayed home for six months before you left again."

"You weren't even talking to us," his mom said. "And you were living with your grandparents. You were happy there."

"Because they gave me a family, which is something you two couldn't give me." He paused. "Why did you stay here after I left last night? You don't usually stick around when things get tense."

His mom gave him a helpless smile. "Your friend, Lizzie, said some pointed things to us, and they were hard to hear, but she was right. She said we needed to show you that we cared enough to fight, and we do. Maybe it's too late. I hope it's not. But we want a chance to know you now. We can't go back, but maybe we can go forward."

"I wanted you to care enough to know me for most of my

life, but it doesn't really matter to me anymore. I don't need you."

"Maybe we need you now."

"Why should I care what you need?" he asked harshly.

"You shouldn't. I just want you to understand that we're coming from a place of love. We made a lot of mistakes, Justin," she said. "We let our careers consume us."

"Just as you're doing," his father pointed out.

"That might be true, but I don't have a family."

"That's a high cost to pay for success in your job," his dad said. "Don't make the same mistakes we made, Justin. Put the people you love first."

He wanted to say he didn't love anyone, but then Lizzie's pretty face filled his head. He shoved her image aside. He was no longer angry with her about the blindside, but he was still leaving tomorrow. He still had a career to get back to. They'd had one incredible night. Maybe that was all they were ever meant to have.

He shoved back his chair and stood up. "I'll see you at the ceremony. Beyond that, we'll have to see how it goes." He'd like to believe things could change with his parents, but he'd been burned by that thought before, far too many times.

"It's almost time," Lizzie told Marie as she looked over her shoulder at their reflection in the mirror. After a day of pampering, massage, nails, and hair, she'd helped Marie get dressed in a white silk dress. In twenty minutes, they'd make their way down to the garden for the ceremony. "You look beautiful. Just like a bride should," she added.

"It's funny that I feel as nervous and excited as I did fifty-seven years ago. I was twenty years old when I walked down the aisle. I had no idea what my life would be like, but I couldn't wait to start it. Ben was twenty-two and in graduate school, getting a teaching degree. We had hardly any money. After our marriage, we lived in a tiny one-bedroom apartment that barely fit a double bed and a small sofa. The kitchen only fit one person and the countertop was barely big enough to hold a toaster."

She smiled at the look of wonder in Marie's eyes. "But you were in love, so it didn't matter."

"Exactly. We were in love from the first moment we met. We got engaged after six months and married two months later. It was a whirlwind of passion. We had Grant right before our first anniversary. We were so young. We made a lot of mistakes, and we've had our share of disagreements, but we always found a way to work through them."

"You were lucky."

"Not lucky, just determined. Deep down, no matter how angry we were about something, we both knew we weren't going to walk away. We were going to fight to stay together. That's what love is. That's what marriage is."

"Well, you two make it look easy."

"Never easy, but always worth it." Marie paused. "I want Justin to have that kind of love, but he doesn't like to open his heart. I was surprised and impressed that he told you about Sean, that he let you in that way. You two got close. I had a feeling you would like each other."

"That's why you set us up on the boat."

"I hope you don't hate me for that or for putting you in an awkward position with my secret."

"I don't hate you, Marie. I understand everything that you did. But I shouldn't have promised to keep your secret, not when I knew Justin would be hurt. I was actually going to talk to you about it last night, but then his parents showed up."

"I was going to tell him, too. Ben had just convinced me to come clean when Grant texted that they'd decided to come early."

"Well, it's done now."

"And I am hopeful that we may have turned an important corner," Marie said. "That's probably because of you."

"I don't think so."

"You told Grant and Katherine that they needed to fight for Justin, and that's why they stayed, why they all talked this morning."

"You're giving me too much credit, but I'm glad that they spoke." She'd been wondering all day what had happened, but she hadn't had a chance to ask Marie until now. Marie and Katherine had spent most of the day together, and she'd only popped in every now and then to let them know what was next. She hadn't really wanted to talk to Katherine at all, although she'd noticed Justin's mother giving her more than a few speculative looks.

Marie stood up. "I think I'm ready."

She smiled. "Good. Because we need to get you married to the man of your dreams—for the second time."

"There's nothing as wonderful as going through life with your best friend, your soul mate. I hope you find what I found, Lizzie, even if it's not with Justin. Although, I haven't given up hope there."

"You should give up hope. It's not going to happen."

"He'll get past his anger, if he hasn't already."

"It's not just that. We want different things."

"Not if you want each other."

She smiled. "You have love on the brain right now."

"Weddings tend to do that," Marie said, smiling back at her.

"Let's go. Your handsome groom is waiting."

CHAPTER TWENTY-ONE

THEY MADE their way into the garden where Lizzie had set up chairs for the two-dozen guests, all of which were filled. Justin's parents were seated in the front row. Justin sat on the aisle opposite his parents. They weren't together, but they were close. It was a start. She hoped they would one day find a way to forgive each other. She thought it would be good for all of them.

The violinist she had hired for the ceremony began to play, and Marie walked down the aisle to join Ben under an arch of beautiful white flowers, in front of a female minister. Everyone from the inn had come down for the ceremony. Noah and Alice were sitting together, holding hands, their reunion still going strong. Some of her friends were here as well.

Hannah and Keira both gave her small nods, as she looked in their direction. Chloe and Adam were seated in the row behind them, and she was struck again by how close they seemed to be. She hadn't had time to catch up with Chloe in the past few days. She wondered what had happened with the text she'd seen on Kevin's phone, or if Chloe had heard about Kevin spending so much time in the bar late at night.

Chloe looked pretty relaxed today. So did her brother. But

she had the feeling they were both playing with fire. She hoped no one got burned.

But there she went again, getting way too involved in everyone's business. She really needed to just pay attention to herself.

Drawing her gaze away from the crowd, she listened to the minister talk about the love Marie and Ben shared. She was a personal friend of the couple and had flown up from Los Angeles for the ceremony, so she was able to share amusing and beautiful stories about Marie and Ben that made the ceremony feel intimate and fun.

At the end, Marie and Ben sealed their promises with a kiss that almost made Lizzie blush. Clearly, they were not only best friends, but they were also passionate lovers. *Fifty-seven years and counting.* She felt a rush of envy and a painful ache as her gaze came to rest on Justin.

He turned his head and caught her eye and for a long minute they just looked at each other.

Then the crowd clapped as the minister pronounced Marie and Ben husband and wife—again—and they made their way down the aisle.

She moved to the nearby bar and grabbed the tray of champagne glasses. Victor helped her pass them out to the guests.

Once everyone had a glass, Justin asked for their attention.

"I'd like to make a toast," he said, looking at his grandparents. "The way you live your lives and the way you love each other has always been an inspiration to me. Your energy for life, your constant smiles, your endless support, and your generosity are unmatched. You are the best role models anyone could have, and I hope you will live every day feeling the same kind of happiness that you've shown each and every one of us. I wouldn't be the man I am without you. Thanks Grandma, Grandpa. Here's to another fifty-seven years!"

Lizzie's eyes filled with tears at Justin's words, and she slipped away, needing a minute to compose herself. Despite her best efforts to protect her heart, she'd fallen in love with Justin. And now he was going to break her heart. She was going to lose him, just as she'd feared.

As she entered the inn, she ran into Paula Wickmayer in the dining room.

"I'm sorry; I'm early. I didn't realize you were having a wedding here," Paula said. "I was just excited that you agreed to speak to me tonight. But I'll come back in an hour, when we said we were going to talk."

"It's fine. You're here now. We should do this. Let's go into my office." Before they could take a step, Keira called her name.

"Lizzie, are you—" Keira stopped talking, surprise filling her gaze. "Paula, I didn't know you were coming here."

"Lizzie and I are going to discuss my proposal."

Keira's surprised gaze sought hers. "Oh, okay. You're doing that now? There's a wedding reception going on."

"I've done all I needed to do for that," Lizzie said. "Go enjoy yourself, Keira. We'll talk later."

"Sure, of course."

Lizzie turned her back on Keira and led Paula into the office. She wasn't quite sure where the conversation would go. There was a good chance she wasn't just going to lose her heart today, but also her business. It was time to stop living in a dream world and face reality.

Justin smiled as his grandparents posed for yet another photo. They'd taken pictures with just about everyone in the crowd, including several with himself and with his parents. It was probably the first family photo they'd taken in twenty years. There was still awkward tension between them, but they had managed to get into the same shot. Maybe there was hope for more. And he was beginning to think he might want more.

His grandmother broke away from the group and joined him. "I want to thank you again for staying, Justin. It meant a lot to me. And the toast you made was beautiful."

"I meant every word."

"I love you so much, honey." Her eyes got teary.

"Hey, no crying."

"I always cry at weddings."

"Not at your own."

She shrugged. "I cried the first time with happiness, and this time I feel it even more deeply, because I know how precious love is. I want you to feel this, Justin. I hope you'll find a way to open your heart."

"The ice around my heart might be cracking just a little," he admitted.

"I'm so glad. I knew Whisper Lake would work its magic on you. Or was it Lizzie who did that?"

He smiled at the gleam in her eyes. "It might have been both. I've definitely changed since I got here."

"Change is good. It keeps life interesting." She let out a sigh. "I just love this inn. It feels like home."

"That's what Lizzie wants every guest to feel."

"Is that how you feel?"

"I know you're trying to get me to say something, Grandma."

She grinned. "Then say it already."

"I can't."

Her humor faded. "Well, I'm sorry to hear that."

"Not until—" he began, stopping abruptly when Keira knocked into him.

"Sorry, Justin," she said quickly. "I wasn't watching where I was going."

"It's fine. Are you all right?" She had an odd look on her face.

"I'm all right, but I don't know about Lizzie."

"What does that mean? Where is she?" he asked, suddenly realizing she was nowhere to be seen.

"She's in her office. She's having a meeting with my friend from Falcon Properties."

"What? Are you serious?"

"I think she's going to sell the inn, Justin."

"She can't do that," he said.

"She can't," his grandmother echoed. "She loves this place. Why would she sell it?"

He knew why. "Because she's struggling."

"This is my fault," Keira said. "I never should have introduced them."

"It's not your fault, it's mine," he said, remembering all the hard truths he'd shouted at Lizzie the night before. He'd taken his anger out on her, and she hadn't deserved that. "I made her doubt herself."

"Why would you do that?" Keira demanded.

"I'm going to stop this," he said, ignoring her question. "Lizzie is not going to lose her inn."

"Make sure she doesn't," his grandmother said, urging him on.

He rushed across the patio and jogged through the inn. He didn't even bother to knock on Lizzie's office door. He just threw it open and stormed in. "You can't sell," he said, as Lizzie jumped to her feet. "Not to her. Not to Falcon Properties. I won't let you."

"It's not your call," Lizzie said.

"I didn't mean what I said last night. You're not drowning; you're just treading water, but you're not going under. You're too strong for that. You're smarter than you think. And you're creative. You make everyone who stays here feel like they're part of your family, and that is an incredible gift."

"Justin—"

"No, don't argue. I was wrong when I said you couldn't do

this. You can, and you have to. This is your dream, babe. Don't give up on it. Tell her no." He looked at Paula. "I'm sorry. It's a good offer, a fair one, but this inn is Lizzie's heart and her soul."

"I know," Paula said. "But—"

"There's no buts," he interrupted. "She's not selling. If she needs money, I'll give it to her. But I'm not letting her give up this inn. She has worked too hard."

"Justin," Lizzie said again. "Paula already knows that."

"What?"

"I just told her I couldn't sell the inn."

"You did?"

"She did," Paula confirmed. "But I told her if she ever changes her mind, or if she ever wants to work for Falcon, we'd be more than happy to have her. Now, I'm going to let you two finish whatever this is..." She looked at Lizzie. "Thanks for hearing me out."

"I'm sorry if I wasted your time," Lizzie said.

"It's never a waste of time, and I understand your passion for this lovely inn. I wish you nothing but success."

"Thank you."

Justin moved aside, so Paula could leave. When the door closed behind her, he was suddenly at a loss for words.

Lizzie walked around her desk to face him. "Well, look who got in the middle of my business."

"When Keira said you were talking to Paula, I knew I had to stop you from selling. But I guess you weren't going to do that."

"Actually, I was seriously considering it," she admitted. "The things you said to me last night hurt, but they were true."

"No, they weren't. I was angry."

"You were angry, but your words were also true. I have been burying my head in the sand, avoiding my problems, pretending everything is okay. It's what I've always done. But I couldn't keep doing it with the inn, not if I wanted to succeed. So I went over Paula's offer again, and I asked her to meet me to discuss it.

But as we talked, I just got this feeling that I shouldn't sell, that I wasn't ready to give up yet. It might be a huge mistake. I could go under six months from now and have no offer to pay off my investors."

"You won't go under. I won't let you," he said.

"You won't let me," she echoed, doubt in her eyes. "Aren't you leaving tonight?"

"That's a good question," he conceded. "I don't know."

"What don't you know?" she challenged, a wary gleam in her beautiful green eyes.

"During the ceremony tonight, I was thinking about you —about us."

"Is there an us?"

"I want there to be. Do you?"

She let out a breath. "More than anything. But how can we possibly make it work?"

"I don't know," he admitted.

"It's complicated. You have your dream business; I have mine. But they're not in the same place. It's not like I can move the inn to San Francisco. And I can't ask you to move here. This is all moving too fast."

"I like fast," he said with a smile.

She smiled back at him. "This fast? For a guy who doesn't do relationships, it seems a little like you've lost your mind."

He laughed. "I think I have lost my mind. Or maybe I've finally found it. My grandparents knew instantly that they were meant to be together and they've lasted fifty-seven years."

"They didn't live in different states," she reminded him. "We both love our careers."

"I do love my job." He stepped forward and took her hands in his. "But I'm also falling in love with you. Honestly, Lizzie, I haven't been the same since I ran into that fence."

"Which was not my fault," she said lightly.

"Maybe not, but it was the beginning of something incredibly special. You have upended my life. You cracked open my heart. You've made me laugh and smile more than I have in a decade. You brought me into your fun, crazy group of friends and made me feel like I belonged. You made me relax, take a breath, and live in the moment. You encouraged me to unload the heavy secret I've been carrying around since I was fourteen. I am not the same man who arrived here five days ago."

"It wasn't one-sided, Justin. You brought me back into the world, too, a world that wasn't just the inn and my guests but was fun and romantic and sexy. You were also honest with me, and you made me look at my life and my business in a completely different way. You've pushed me to do better, and I need someone who encourages me to be my best self. More importantly, I need someone who believes in me."

"I do believe in you. I feel so bad about what I said last night."

"I know you were hurting."

"But I shouldn't have hurt you."

"I probably deserved it a little."

"You're too generous. But I'm thankful you're able to forgive me."

"If you can forgive me."

"I forgave you last night; I was just too stubborn to tell you. You're an amazing woman, Lizzie Cole. And you're building something here that is incredible and unique. I want to see how far you can go."

"That means a lot to me."

"And I want to be here to see it."

"What about your business? Your trips?"

"I'm not giving them up. I'm just going to change the way I do business. I might need to get some office space in town."

Her eyes glowed with happiness. "You'd do that for me? You'd work from here?"

"Yes." He took in a slow breath, thinking it would be difficult to say the words, but surprisingly, it wasn't. "I'm in love with you, Lizzie. I've never told a woman that before."

"Not ever?"

He shook his head. "No. I couldn't let myself be that exposed, that vulnerable."

"Your heart is safe with me, Justin," she said softly.

"I know. That's why I'm giving it to you, if you want it."

"I do." She laughed. "But we're not getting married. We're just going to see where this goes."

"I think it's going to go all the way."

She gave him a wide-eyed smile. "What now?"

"What do you think?" he asked, as he crushed his mouth against hers.

He kissed her with the wonder of a love he'd never thought he'd experience, but it was here. It was real. It was everything.

And then the door flew open.

"Well?" Keira demanded.

"Oh, my goodness, they're kissing," his grandmother said with delight.

"Let me see," Hannah interjected.

"Give 'em a break," Adam said.

"This is amazing," Chloe declared.

They broke apart as their friends and family crowded into the small office.

"You're not selling the inn, are you?" Keira asked.

"No," Lizzie said, dragging her mouth from his, but she kept her arms wrapped around his neck. "I'm keeping the inn, and Justin and I are keeping each other. We're going to see where this goes."

"I'm so happy," his grandmother said, clapping her hands with delight. "I knew this would work. I just knew it." She reached for his grandfather's hand. "Didn't I tell you, Ben? Didn't I tell you they'd be perfect for each other?"

"You did," Ben said with a laugh. "Why don't we give these two some privacy?"

"We'll be right out," Lizzie promised.

"Well, maybe not right out," he said, as he smiled into her eyes. "We might need a few more minutes."

As the door closed, leaving them alone once more, she said, "We've got more than minutes, Justin. We have a whole lifetime ahead of us. Maybe fifty-seven years."

"Or more. You know I always want more."

"Me, too. But right now, I just want you."

# # #

WHAT TO READ NEXT ...

Don't miss Just One Kiss, the next book in the Whisper Lake Series!

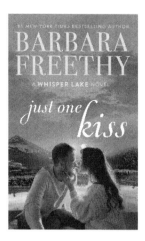

ABOUT THE AUTHOR

Barbara Freethy is a #1 New York Times Bestselling Author of 68 novels ranging from contemporary romance to romantic suspense and women's fiction. With over 12 million copies sold, twenty-three of Barbara's books have appeared on the New York Times and USA Today Bestseller Lists, including SUMMER SECRETS which hit #1 on the New York Times!

Known for her emotional and compelling stories of love, family, mystery and romance, Barbara enjoys writing about ordinary people caught up in extraordinary adventures. Library Journal says, "Freethy has a gift for creating unforgettable characters."

For additional information, please visit Barbara's website at www.barbarafreethy.com.

Made in the USA
Middletown, DE
07 May 2020